The BODY in BERKELEY SQUARE

Book 3 in the Mayfair 100 series

Lynn Brittney

IRIS BOOKS

IRIS BOOKS

First published by Iris Books, London in 2021

Iris Books is an imprint of Write Publications Ltd

© Lynn Brittney

The rights of Lynn Brittney to be identified as the author of this book
have been asserted, in accordance with the Copyright, Designs and Patents Act
1988. This publication is protected under the Copyright laws currently existing
in every country throughout the world.

ISBN 978-1-907147-79-1

Design by Kate Lowe

Printed in the United Kingdom

Dedicated to all the women
who damaged their health and wellbeing
working for the British munitions industry.

Contents

CHAPTER ONE

AUGUST 1915

Chief Inspector Peter Beech sat in a corner of the parlour nursing his teacup and surveying the room. The Mayfair 100 team was gathered at Lady Maud's house for one of their meetings, despite not having had a criminal case to investigate for several weeks. A lavish tea had been served and there was a low hum of conversation. Occasionally, Victoria Ellingham would glance over at Beech, hopefully, but he would just give her a rueful smile and refuse to be drawn into the general hubbub of social interaction. He knew that they were all wondering when he would come up with another case for them to solve and he sincerely wished that he had been able to bring a smile to the faces of all concerned, but nothing had presented itself.

"It's the long days of summer," he had explained upon arrival that afternoon. "The light nights make crime less easy. Besides, people are too preoccupied with the war and hoping for some warm weather, to be thinking about crime." It was a feeble excuse, he knew, but Detective Sargeant Tollman, recognising a man beset by females and in need of baling out, nodded sagely and added "Yes, Mr Beech. It's a well-known fact that crime rates go down in the summer."

So, talk turned to how they were all, individually, occupying themselves whilst waiting for another interesting case to be discovered and tossed their way.

Victoria and Lady Maud were discussing the June trial

of Sam Joseph Smith, the "Brides in the Bath Murderer". It had been the trial of the century and Beech had been able to arrange a courtroom pass for Victoria, who had attended every day, without fail.

"Even though he lost the case for his client," said Victoria, "Mr Edward Marshall Hall really is the most charismatic defence lawyer I have ever seen. I could sit and listen to him talk all day."

"When is Sam Smith due to be executed?" asked Beech, who hadn't been following current events, other than the war progress, of late.

"Ten days," said the ever-knowledgeable Tollman.

"The forensic evidence in that case was so amazing. Bernard Spilsbury is such a revolutionary pathologist." Dr Caroline Allardyce commented. "All those experiments with baths and female swimmers, just to prove how Smith could actually drown the women easily by pulling up their legs!"

PC Billy Rigsby was grinning from ear to ear. "Now that is the sort of job I'd like!" he said irreverently, "rounding up female swimmers for a pathologist!" Rigsby went into comic policeman mode as he said pompously, "'Scuse me Miss, that's a lovely bathing costume you're wearing. Would you accompany down to the Yard for some experiments?"

Everyone laughed. Billy's aunt, Sissy, and his mother, Elsie, laughed until the tears appeared in their eyes. "Billy Rigsby!" Elsie said between giggles, "I should wash your mouth out with soap and water!" Even Mabel Summersby, the usually serious pharmacist, managed a broad smile.

When the laughter had died down, Caroline announced

that she and Mabel were going to attend a lecture next week, by Bernard Spilsbury, at the London Medical School for Women.

"That sounds interesting, Doctor," said DS Tollman. "What topic is being covered?" Tollman was interested in everything, and it was all stored away in his constantly busy brain, for future use.

"Toxicology" was the answer.

"Ah," Tollman brightened and turned to Mabel, "that's your speciality Miss Summersby, isn't it?"

Mabel flushed slightly. "Well, I wouldn't say 'speciality' as such, Mr Tollman, but I am keenly interested in the subject."

"Oh Mabel, don't be so modest!" Caroline interjected, "You're brilliant at it! The lecture is really for my benefit, Mr Tollman. I need to know, as a doctor and a surgeon, how to spot the signs of various toxic substances, externally and internally, in a corpse, and I'm hoping that will be the thrust of the lecture. This is all in case...one day in the not too distant future, I hope...they allow women to be registered pathologists."

There was a pause and then Sissy piped up "Elsie and me are going to Blackfriars on Friday to watch this young lad fight that Billy's been training up!"

A murmur of appreciation went around the room and Beech smiled at Rigsby. "Is he any good, Rigsby? Your lad?"

Billy nodded and looked hopeful. "He's got a good right hand, Mr Beech, but he's young. He's not too clever at dodging the blows. I'm trying to get him to be a bit more nimble."

"Yes. No good having a strong punch if you don't learn to get out of the way of the other fellas' punches," commented

Tollman sagely. Billy nodded and grinned.

"I'm not sure I should have the stomach to watch two men beat the living daylights out of each other," said Caroline, pulling a face. "I would be wanting to jump in the ring and tend to the injuries."

"Queensbury Rules, doctor!" protested Billy. "They stop the fight if there's too much blood."

"Garn! Who are you kidding, Billy?" said Elsie with a grin and a wink.

Billy winked back. "Well, they're supposed to…" he answered lamely.

"Well, we're a right bunch of gory people, aren't we?" commented Victoria brightly. "We've talked about a murder trial, Caroline and Mabel are going to a pathology lecture and Billy and his ladies are off to a blood-spattered boxing match!"

"Count me out, Mrs E," said Tollman firmly. "I shall be in my garden, this weekend, planting out my geraniums."

Lady Maud feigned disapproval and said, "I was rather hoping that you would find time for some games of cribbage, Detective Sargeant Tollman!"

Tollman nodded and smiled. "As if I could refuse you anything, Your Ladyship."

"And what about you, Peter?" Caroline turned her attention to the unusually silent Beech, "Any activities planned for the coming weekend?"

Beech shook his head and gave a small smile of regret. "Sadly, no, Caroline. I shall be at Scotland Yard, catching up on paperwork. We have so few policemen at the moment. There's been another dash to the recruiting office. London lost another 270 policemen to the Army last week."

Everyone looked sombre. Beech in particular. He had realised, during the course of the afternoon's conversations, that he truly missed being part of a team that did actual detective work. His rank at Scotland Yard made him a virtual prisoner behind his desk and sometimes he felt that shuffling papers would drive him mad.

"Well then, the police should be more sensible about allowing women to do real police work, shouldn't they?" Caroline observed tartly.

"Sadly, Doctor," Tollman observed, "the powers-that-be in the Metropolitan Police would rather bring back retired policeman than employ women in a professional capacity. In fact, that's the job that Mr Beech and I are engaged on at the moment – going to see retired policemen to persuade them to come back into service."

Caroline looked at Beech in astonishment and he nodded in confirmation. "That's ridiculous!" she said with some irritation in her voice. "With all due respect, Mr Tollman, a young, healthy woman could beat you with ease, when it came to running after a suspect!"

Billy grinned and Tollman looked slightly uncomfortable. "Well, I grant you that as a man approaching sixty I am not as nimble as I once was…but with all due respect, Doctor, what would a young woman do if she ran after, and caught up with, a particularly nasty armed villain? Hit him with her handbag?"

"I think you've led a bit of a sheltered life, Mr Tollman," said Elsie Rigsby, with a laugh. "There's plenty of women in

London who know how to look after themselves…"

"A swift kick in the family jewels usually does the trick…" agreed Sissy, which prompted Beech to laugh out loud.

Tollman conceded defeat with a small smile and a nod. "It's true," he agreed. "I've seen plenty of suffragettes and women factory workers knock a man unconscious in my time. I take it back, ladies," he added graciously, "I'm sure the right women would make excellent police officers."

"Well they'll have to do something soon," Victoria added. "All sorts of professions are feeling the lack of men and, now, women are stepping up to be bus drivers…"

"Ambulance drivers…" volunteered Mabel.

"I hear that they're working in the fire brigade in Sussex!" Lady Maud added.

"Ooh! I almost forgot!" Mabel rummaged around in her handbag and produced a folded-up piece of newspaper, "Last month…5th of June…a tiny little piece in the Times…anyone would have missed it…women in Denmark got the vote! Full voting rights. All women in Denmark."

There was an explosion of surprise from all the women in the room as they crowded around Mabel Summersby to get a look at the newspaper. The men just looked at each other in astonishment.

"Well! They've kept quiet about that, haven't they?" said Victoria, with some irritation.

"Probably didn't want to give British women any ideas!" Caroline responded scornfully.

"I'm surprised that the Times was allowed to print it at all," Lady Maud added, with some feeling.

"Well, I guess it won't be long now, ladies!" Sissy said confidently. "This time next year, I reckon, it'll be our turn. What d'you think, Arthur?"

Tollman smiled and shook his head. "I shouldn't be surprised, Sissy...I shouldn't be at all surprised."

So, it was in a hopeful mood that the afternoon tea meeting broke up, and everyone left to their respective residences and places of work, leaving Lady Maud and Victoria alone.

"Do you think that Peter looked a bit down in the mouth this afternoon, Mother?" Victoria couldn't help feeling that there was something wrong. Beech had been unusually quiet.

"He's probably just pre-occupied with work, dear. And I expect he misses the regular company of the team – as does everyone."

"True. I think we all miss working together. I do wish Peter would find another case for us soon."

"Patience, Victoria," Lady Maud counselled. "You never know...a case may find *you*."

CHAPTER TWO

MEETING AN OLD FRIEND

Billy Rigsby loved everything about boxing. He stood in the corner of the empty hall and breathed deeply, taking in the smell of sweat, cigarette smoke, canvas, beer, rosin and liniment. His Aunt Sissy always said that boxing halls smelt 'like a soldier's armpit', which made Billy laugh, but he reflected that it was true. It was a very masculine smell. Boxing and the Army had always seemed interchangeable to him – as it had been with his father. The odour of it all, rank though it was, comforted him.

He looked down at his damaged hand and felt the usual stab of disappointment that he was prevented from being an active boxer…a champion boxer…as he once was. Living with the limitations had become slightly easier but the sadness was still there.

In his dark days, after he had been invalided out of the Grenadier Guards, he had almost lost the will to carry on, because he had been deprived of both pursuits that gave his life some meaning, and he sank into a depression. Thankfully, his mum and aunty had recognised that, in Sissy's words, he "needed chivvying up", and Elsie had added that "no son of mine is going to sit around feeling sorry for himself, when there is war work to be done."

That was when they brought in a retired bobby, Eric Mitchell. Eric was a local hero and legend, because, thirty years before, on the 24th January 1885, he had been the victim, along with another policeman and four civilians, of an Irish Nationalist bomb, which cost him his right leg. Eric then became deskbound at the local station in Hoxton, organising the rotas, training up young policemen and running community events. Everyone knew Eric but hardly anyone knew the physical and mental pain he had suffered as a result of his life-changing injury. So, for four hours, he sat and told Billy all about his personal and secret battle with depression. Then he arranged for Billy to join the police force and get his sense of purpose back.

"Sorry about the hand, mate," said a deep voice, that made Billy jump and he turned to see a familiar black face smiling at him.

"Sam! Sam Abbot, you old devil! Where have you been?" Billy instinctively hugged his former sparring partner, delighted to see an old friend.

"Joined up, for my sins," said Sam, shaking his head at his own stupidity.

"You never!" Billy was astounded. "What did you do that for, you chump?"

Sam shrugged. "Kept getting nagged by the women. Seemed like a good idea at the time."

Billy shook his head in despair. "So, what you doing here then, mate?"

Sam grinned. "I got sent home on extended leave, on account of having pneumonia. Said I wasn't to go back to France for six weeks."

"So how many weeks you got left?"

Sam grinned again, "Five! Bloody Army medics don't

know their arse from their elbow! I had a cold, that's all! Still, I'm grateful to breathe a bit of the old London smoke again. What about you? I heard you joined the police! That's a bit of a turn-up, ain't it?"

Billy was about to regale him with all the details of his new career, when the manager of the sports hall came in.

"Billy! I'm about to open the doors! You'd better tend to your lad. He's puking up in a bucket in the dressing room!"

"Oh, what?!" Billy made a face of disgust. "Bloody amateurs! I told him not to eat before the fight! Now he's gonna have gas in his belly. Here, Sam! Come and help me get this idiot ready for his fight, will ya?"

"With pleasure, my son." Sam patted Billy on the back, and for one glorious moment, Billy felt like he was back in the old days, when he and Sam would square up and knock seven bells out of each other.

The young lad Billy was training, Walter, was pale and contrite in the dressing room but there was no time for argument or reasoning. Billy and Sam took a hand each and started taping up. Sam kept up a constant barrage of funny stories about boxing, which made Walter laugh and soon, they were lacing on his gloves and giving him encouragement. Billy started shoving pellets of cotton wool around Walter's gums and Sam finished lacing up the lad's boots. Then Billy smeared Vaseline on the lad's face and winked at Sam.

"He sweats a bit this lad," he said with a grin," so, for some reason, the other blokes' punches just seem to slide right off his face." Sam nodded and laughed.

Walter, whose physical demeanour and broad ugly face

made him look a great deal tougher than Billy knew he was, stood up and took a few deep breaths. He wasn't quite as tall as Billy and Sam, but he was solid.

"Middleweight?" asked Sam.

Billy shook his head. "Too heavy. Had to be light heavyweight. Not happy about it, are we Walter?" The lad, unable to speak with a mouth full of cotton wool, shook his head and scowled. "Mainly because it means he has to fight his way through most of the Camden Town gang."

"Oh, bad luck, Walter," was Sam's sympathetic response. "But then I've always found that these so-called hard men are always a bit soft round the middle, if you get my drift. One good punch around here," and he pointed at his diaphragm, "knocks the wind out of them, and you can finish them off." Walter seemed to brighten and lifted up his gloved hands and tapped them together in approval.

Billy and Sam escorted the tense young lad to the doorway. The crowd was settled in the seats. Billy noted with a grin that Sissy and Elsie were on the end of a row about six from the front.

"I've always found that to be the best place to sit," Sissy had once advised everyone, "near enough to get a good view but far enough away so as to avoid being sprayed with blood or sweat." The two women were busy unpacking various items of food and drink from Sissy's capacious bag. The sight of men beating each other to a pulp was not something to put either of them off their food – not in the slightest. Billy nudged Sam and whispered, "Go and sit next to my womenfolk. You'll get some grub off them! They'll be over the moon to see you."

Sam smiled from ear to ear. "I didn't know Sissy and Elsie were coming tonight!"

"They wouldn't miss a decent fight for the world," and Billy motioned Sam to go now, as the referee had entered the ring. Then he watched as Sam snuck up on the two women, who burst into squeals of delight, hugged him, kissed him and had him seated between them with a sandwich in his hand before he knew what was happening.

***

The fight was good. Young Walter took Sam's advice and, in round two, he went for the solar plexus in his opponent, then he achieved a knockout. So, it was a dazed but happy young man who headed off to the pub with his young mates to celebrate his first win.

Billy, Sam, Elsie and Sissy gathered together, outside the venue and watched the lads singing and shouting, as they linked arms unsteadily to cross the road to the famous Ring pub. Some of Walter's friends had already been drinking throughout the evening and Billy nudged Sam, inclining his head towards a uniformed man, leaning casually against the wall of the pub.

"Aye, aye," said Sam softly. "What's the betting that's a recruiting sergeant on the prowl for fresh recruits."

Billy nodded grimly. "Half those lads are so pie-eyed, they'd agree to anything. Let's have a quiet word, shall we?" He turned to the ladies. "Mum, Aunty, wait here a minute, will you?"

"Billy, don't do nothing stupid," said Elsie anxiously.

Billy kissed her on the forehead reassuringly. "Just having a word. That's all. Just wait here."

Elsie clutched Sissy's arm for support and both women watched as Billy and Sam marched purposefully towards the soldier, who suddenly looked somewhat anxious at the sight of two very tall and powerful men bearing down on him. When they reached him, the women could see that Sam and Billy towered over him, and leaning on the wall either side of him, they began to talk. The soldier began to nod, as if agreeing with everything that was being said.

"He'll have a terrible stiff neck, looking up at the pair of them, if this goes on for much longer," muttered Sissy.

Then, to the women's relief, the soldier shook both men's hands and marched off, rather quickly, in the direction of Blackfriars Bridge. Billy and Sam returned, grinning.

"So, what happened then?" demanded Elsie.

"The pair of you are grinning like Cheshire cats, so it must be good," Sissy chimed in.

"Nah, it was easy, ladies," said Sam with a laugh. "Old Billy here pulls the 'I'm an ex-professional soldier – lately of His Majesty's Grenadier Guards'…"

Billy stamped his foot and saluted, shouting "Yes sir!" for effect and Sam continued,

"…so he says, 'I saw you eyeing up those young lads in there and here's a friendly word of advice – you don't want none of them.' So, I says, 'Straight up, mate, this lot in here are damaged goods. You won't get no pats on the back signing them up.' So, Billy says 'Too right. The big thick one with the black eye and two of his mates are up before the magistrate in two days' time, for aggravated burglary…two of the others have got a dose of the clap…and the last two are nancy boys… so I'd take yourself off up to the Black Friar pub over the bridge and see if you can't drum up some recruits that aren't a blight on your regiment."

Elsie and Sissy shrieked with laughter. "You pair of con artists!" Sissy declared, "So what did matey say?"

Billy put his arm round her shoulder and said, "Why he thanked us profusely, Aunty Sissy, shook our hands and buggered off up the road, like a sensible little sergeant. Walter and his mates are safe to drink themselves stupid – at least until closing time."

"Well, we'd best be on our way," said Elsie, briskly. "I've got mince and dumplings in the bread oven that will be dried to nothing if we don't get home sharpish." Then she looked at Sam with concern for a moment, remembering that he had no family to speak of. "Sam, where are you staying, love?"

Sam looked a bit sheepish and muttered something about 'dossing down on a mate's floor'.

Sissy raised her eyebrows at Elsie and, as was often the way with the sisters, they reached an unspoken agreement with one look.

"No, you're not," said Elsie firmly, hooking her arm through Sam's. "You're staying with us in our mansion in Belgravia."

"What?" Sam laughed, playing along with the joke.

"Straight up," said Billy seriously. "My family now live in a mansion in Belgravia. Let's go and catch the number 11 bus and we'll tell you the whole amazing story."

So, as they walked briskly, arm in arm, up the road to Fleet Street, Billy, his mum and his aunt told a baffled Sam about the murder that had taken place in the house in Belgravia; how a titled lady had confessed to it, but then was proved to be innocent; how she decided she didn't want to set foot in the house anymore but she didn't want to sell it; then how Elsie and Sissy had been bombed out of Hoxton and ended up as paid caretakers of the house.

"I'm breathless just listening to you!" said Sam, his eyes wide throughout the whole rambling story. "Are you sure I can stay there? Won't no one complain?"

"There's no one *to* complain," said Elsie. "We never see any neighbours. Most of them have packed up their posh houses in London and gone to the countryside. Scared of the Zeppelin raids, I expect. Anyway, you're going to be our temporary handyman...isn't that right, Sis?"

"On the button, Elsie. We've got a few little jobs that need doing and in return, Sam, you'll have a nice warm bed and all the food you can eat. Does that sound like a good deal?"

Sam nodded, unable to think of the right words of gratitude, so he just kissed both their hands.

"Daft 'aporth," said Sissy and Billy passed her his handkerchief, just in case a stray tear escaped from her eye.

When they all reached the warm basement kitchen of the Belgravia house, Elsie's Jack Russell dog, Timmy, came hurtling down the stairs from his chosen bed in the attic room and launched himself at the two men. Billy, of course, was his favourite man in the whole world but he remembered Sam, even though it had been a few years, and he had decided that Sam was his second favourite man.

The women began to bustle. Sissy put some water on to boil, so that she could fill a hot water bottle to put in Sam's bed.

"Do you mind sharing a room with Timmy, at the top of the house, Sam?" she asked, "Only, all the other bedrooms are locked up and Elsie and I have got the two bedrooms down here in the basement."

"Having a proper bed, anywhere, would be a real treat for me," said Sam happily and Elsie and Sissy exchanged looks again. "But where do *you* sleep, mate?" he asked Billy.

"Oh, I don't sleep here. I sleep in another mansion in Mayfair," answered Billy with a grin.

"You're having me on," Sam looked at the women, "Is he having me on?"

They both shook their heads. Elsie produced a casserole dish from the oven and said, "Sit down, Sam, we've got a lot more to tell you and we want to know what you've been up to as well."

So, over beef mince, carrots and dumplings, the four of them chatted for nearly two hours. Billy, because he trusted Sam, told him all about the secret Mayfair 100 team. Elsie and Sissy told him about the case they had both been involved in and Sam just sat, dumbstruck by it all.

Then it was his turn. He told them about joining up – sent to the Royal Engineers, no less. "I thought I would be fighting alongside other men, but no. I found myself, along with other black blokes, humping around ammunition, digging trenches and doing any hard labour that was around. Might as well of stayed working in the docks," he explained sardonically.

Billy shook his head and flushed slightly. He knew how the army felt about mixing races in the ranks.

Sam continued. "So, when I asked the sergeant when we were going to give us rifles and let us fight, he said 'We can't give rifles to darkies! They might turn them on their officers!', so I said "Blimey Sarge, don't give us ideas!" Sissy and Elsie giggled, and Billy grinned. "I got two days half rations for that bit of cheek," Sam said sheepishly.

"Sorry, mate," Billy said regretfully.

"Nah, you're alright. Used to it. Anyway, didn't stop me having a bit of a laugh. Some of these farm boys that enlisted ain't never seen a black bloke. This kid from Cornwall, couldn't have been more than sixteen, says to me 'You coming from the Dark Continent, like...you must be used to all the killing and such.'" Sissy raised her eyebrows and Sam continued, "So I motioned him over and whispers, 'where I come from, they would cut your throat for the clothes off your back,' and he says in a shocked voice 'Where's that then?' and I said 'London'. Me and my mates all fell about laughing and he goes bright red and swears at me."

The story was funny, but Elsie and Sissy found it difficult to raise a smile.

"Well, it sounds to me, like the last laugh is yours, Sam," Sissy pronounced. "If they think that boys with white skin deserve to get killed more than those with a black skin, then they've made their decision and you've come out of it better off." Sissy was flushed with righteousness.

"Hear, hear," said Elsie, with feeling.

Sissy continued. "This whole bloody war's a nonsense, if you ask me. Elsie and me are just grateful Billy's out of it, and if the colour of your skin keeps you out of harm's way then I, for one, won't complain about that."

Billy stood up and started to put his jacket on. "Well, I've got to walk back to Mayfair now and do my duty guarding the ladies." He held out his hand to Sam and they shook. "I'll come round tomorrow night after work and we can go for a pint, eh? That is if these two women haven't driven you mad with endless gossip or fed you so much food you can't move." He winked, Sam grinned, and the women tutted.

Billy left, Elsie made cocoa, Sissy produced biscuits and it was a good half an hour before Sam carried a snoring Timmy up the grand staircase to the attic bedroom. He placed Timmy down on his special blanket on one bed, undressed and climbed gratefully into the other bed, luxuriating in its softness and warmth. It had been a long time he'd had such pampering and he drifted off to sleep with a smile on his face, oblivious to the small yips of a dreaming Timmy.

CHAPTER THREE

THE PUZZLE OF THE UNKNOWN CORPSE

The lecture theatre at the Medical School for Women was packed. Caroline and Mabel had arrived especially early so that they could find seats in the front row and get a better view of Bernard Spilsbury's surgical work. Notebooks and pencils poised, they awaited the great man himself, as the hall filled up behind them. Looking around, Caroline noted a few young male medical students, who were huddled together in one corner of the hall, as if for protection. She nudged Mabel and nodded towards the men with a smile.

"Hmm," Mabel whispered, "They'll be off to the Front as soon as they qualify, Soon, the only doctors left in Britain will be women and old men."

"It's the same with nurses," Caroline whispered back, in irritation. "This week, our hospital has lost another three nurses to the field hospitals in France and Belgium. We can't afford to lose them. The medical problems in the civilian population are getting worse – malnutrition, industrial accidents – all sorts of things."

Mabel was about to respond when Spilsbury entered the arena, to a round of applause from the assembled audience. Then everyone settled down to hear the great man speak. With the aid of projected slides, and small grunts of approval from Mabel, who applauded the use of cameras whenever possible, Spilsbury outlined the signs of various poisons in the liver, kidneys, hair shaft, nails and so on. Mabel took frantic notes, but Caroline was disappointed that he seemed to be aiming his lecture at first year students and, so far, had not covered anything that she did not already know.

But then, two thirds of the way through the lecture, an assistant wheeled on a body, covered by a sheet and Caroline perked up, hopeful that she would now see a live autopsy. However, she was disappointed when, on removal of the sheet, it was obvious that the autopsy had already been performed.

"Ladies and gentlemen," Spilsbury said, "I would like to present you with a mystery and invite you to, perhaps, solve the mystery."

Caroline and Mabel looked at each other. Their interest was piqued.

Spilsbury continued. "This young woman's body was found in the bushes in Berkeley Square, on the twelfth of July at one in the morning. She had been stabbed through the heart with a long stiletto-like blade. In fact, it was so long that it went right through her and must have impaled her to a tree." There was a murmur of distaste went through the audience. Spilsbury continued. "Then the blade was withdrawn, which must have taken some strength. I found traces of tree bark in the exit wound. Death would have been instantaneous. The police made enquiries, but she was not known to any of the residents or their servants in Berkeley Square. She was wearing, so my wife tells me, a dress from a reasonably expensive couture label in London…" A small ripple of laughter emanated from the audience. "She was also wearing a dark wig…" Spilsbury removed the wig to show that the woman had strange-coloured hair. It was light brown but appeared, in the front, to have been dyed a bright orange colour. "Can anyone comment on the real hair?" He threw the question out to the audience. There was a momentary silence whilst a few hands were raised. Spilsbury pointed to a woman at the back and said "Yes?"

"Is it TNT poisoning?" the woman asked and Spilsbury smiled. "It is indeed," acknowledging the murmur of surprise that came from the audience. He continued. "She was also wearing a lot of make-up, which when removed, revealed a distinct yellow tinge to her skin…I'm afraid you can't see it under this harsh spotlight. This is again a feature of TNT poisoning but, on examination of her liver, which showed some minor damage but evidence of healing, it would suggest that the woman had worked, at some time in the recent past, with TNT, but was recovering from its effects. The whites of her eyes were a little jaundiced but, again, showed signs, in one eye, of an improving situation. However, this was not the end of this poor woman's misfortunes…" he paused and took a swig of water before continuing, then raised his hand to the projectionist to proceed to the next slide. "Examination of the deceased's throat…" The slide appeared on the screen, showing a dark discolouration at the back of the throat and some sepsis of the tonsils, "…showed that there was some destruction of the tissue of the mucous membranes. Now," he turned once more to the audience, "I confess that I was at a loss with this, until I called in a specialist doctor who has done some work in the munitions industry. He told me immediately what had caused the condition of the deceased's throat. Can anyone hazard a guess at what that might be?" Spilsbury threw it open to the students again. This time there were no hands raised.

"Black powder, I was reliably informed." He continued. "Black powder, used as an explosive in the munitions industry, is a composite of a nitrate, charcoal and sulphur." There was a murmur of interest from the audience again. "Sulphur dioxide is extremely destructive to tissue of the mucous membranes and upper respiratory tract, eyes and skin. Inhalation may result in spasm, inflammation and edema of the larynx and bronchi, chemical pneumonitis and pulmonary edema. Thus, exposure to sulfur dioxide can lead to a series of health problems and, in the case of extended exposure, death. Now, this woman's throat condition, again, as with the TNT exposure, appeared to be in the process of healing. Tissues taken from the back of her throat showed, under magnification, new cells were developing, which would suggest that she had once been in a position to inhale black powder but had removed herself from that situation."

Spilsbury covered over the body and came to the front of the arena. Caroline prepared herself to make detailed notes. "What we are seeing here, ladies and gentlemen," Spilsbury began, "is a relatively new phenomenon...illnesses, and possibly, in time...deaths...caused by working in the munitions industry. TNT is a relatively new explosive, I am given to understand, not yet in common use throughout the industry. We must familiarize ourselves with these manifestations of toxicity because, as this war progresses, more and more women are going to be working in munitions, if the new Ministry of Munitions has its way. This means that when you are qualified, you will be confronted by these women who need treatment. It is possible that women may be more susceptible to these chemicals, having, in the main, more delicate tissues." Caroline tutted at what she suspected was a sweeping generalisation. Spilsbury continued. "Obviously, what is needed is more protection for these workers, who are handling such dangerous substances and I shall be making my recommendations to the new Ministry, which has recently opened its doors. But, I suspect, that the safety of workers will be way down the list of priorities of both the government-run and privately-run munitions establishments, particularly in light of the recent national scandal over the shortage of shells for the Army. But, as frequently happens in the world of pathology, we will be called upon to prove negligence on behalf of the employers when these women start dying and their relatives start claiming compensation. You, as doctors in general practice or in hospitals, will be called upon to give your opinion when these women are disabled by their work environment and can no longer earn a living. So, we must both find out all we can about munitions injuries and diseases…and we must learn very quickly, ladies and gentlemen, because the problem is starting now." He paused and took another drink of water. "Now, are there any questions?" Many hands shot up, but Caroline was spotted by Spilsbury first and he extended his hand in acknowledgement.

"What will happen to the body of this woman now?" she asked in a clear voice.

"I have requested to keep the corpse in the mortuary at St Mary's Hospital, so that I may do further investigations and produce a paper for the Ministry of Munitions. This will probably take a couple of months. After that, if the police have not got any further with their enquiries, the body will be buried in an unmarked grave somewhere suitable."

As Spilsbury smiled and moved on to the next question, Caroline realized that, more than anything, she wanted to find out the identity of the murdered woman munitions worker, and she needed to speak to Beech as a matter of urgency.

She raised her hand again and, after a short wait, Spilsbury turned his attention to her once more. "Yes?" he asked her again.

"Sir...the expensive dress she was wearing...can you remember the name of the couturier?"

Spilsbury looked amused. "Why yes. It was Renee LaJeune." He looked quizzically at Caroline, as she wrote the name down with a satisfied look on her face, but then his attention was demanded elsewhere.

"Mabel," Caroline whispered. "I think we have found ourselves a case to work on. But we must speak to Peter first."

Mabel nodded and smiled. "A cup of tea before we go to Scotland Yard?" she ventured and was rewarded by an enthusiastic nod.

✳✳✳

Beech was a little exasperated that Caroline and Mabel had turned up at Scotland Yard. They were under strict orders, as was everyone in the team, to keep Mayfair 100's existence a secret. Turning up at the Yard was certainly not discreet. However, he was somewhat mollified that the ladies pretended not to know him, when they were ushered in by the sergeant on duty. Beech stood and motioned them to sit.

"Good day, Chief Inspector," Caroline said formally, shaking Beech's hand as the sergeant left the room.

"Good day, Doctor Allardyce," Beech responded in kind and he sat down himself.

The sergeant had gone so Beech said wearily, "Caroline, what are you playing at? You know that this visit is against the rules."

"Yes, I know. But we played the game and told the sergeant that we had come here, at your request, to give some statements. No-one suspects anything."

"So, what is this all about?

Caroline, with the help of some of Mabel's notes, explained the mystery of the dead woman munition worker, stabbed in Berkeley Square whilst wearing an expensive couture gown.

"We wanted to ask your permission to investigate a little and see if we can find out who this woman is, at least."

Mabel added her voice to the request, "But we need a photograph of her face and a photograph of the dress she was wearing, before we can proceed."

Beech looked thoughtful and tried to conceal his hopefulness that this might be a case for the team, at last.

"I will ask Tollman to see what there is in the files on this woman. It is very likely that it is a case that has been pushed to one side because of our shortage of manpower, at the moment, and it may very well be that only a woman can investigate effectively the business about the dress. But," he said with great emphasis, "and this is important Caroline and

Mabel…if, at any time…the police turn up some evidence or someone steps forward to claim this woman's body, then you must call a halt to everything. Do you understand?"

Mabel and Caroline both nodded in relief.

"We promise that we will be extremely discreet and will report back to you every time we make any progress."

Beech nodded. "Well make sure that you do. But do not do anything until Tollman has discovered what official investigations have been done, if any. Are you both available tomorrow?" They nodded. "Good. Then We will meet up after breakfast and share information. Tollman can tell us what he has found out and hopefully furnish you with the photographs you will need."

After the two women had left, Beech wondered if he had made the right decision. Caroline could be rather headstrong, and she might easily exceed her authority if not supervised. He decided to talk it over with Tollman.

He found Tollman in one of the interview rooms in a huddle with Sergeant Stenton, another returned, formerly retired, policeman. They were surrounded by piles of police files and looking harassed.

"How's it going, chaps?" Beech asked as he sat down.

"Slowly, sir," replied Stenton gloomily.

"I asked Horace here to help me weed out potential returnees," explained Tollman, "since he has worked on personnel and records since Noah's Flood."

Beech grinned. "Any joy, Tollman?"

"Not much, sir, I'm afraid," was the answer. "We found a potential batch of twenty-four men who retired in the last two years. Four have died…almost immediately upon retirement…"

"Mm. Often happens," commented Beech. "The old adrenaline stops kicking in and the heart stops. Sad."

The two older men looked at Beech with an expression of distaste. Beech realised he had been insensitive and mumbled an apology. "So, what of the other twenty men?" he asked awkwardly.

Sergeant Stenton took up the reins. "Six have been ruled out by us because their injuries on the job caused their early retirement on account of disability…"

Beech interrupted again. "Ah, but they may be disqualified on fitness grounds for active service, but can they deal with the paperwork and free up some of the other men?"

Tollman nodded. "Good point, sir. We'll have another look."

Stenton continued, "Two men, regretfully, are now in prison, because they put their insider knowledge of crime to use as a civilian…" Beech tutted loudly and then motioned Stenton to carry on, "Six of the men have completely left the Metropolitan area and retired to the South coast, or somewhere similar. So, we have identified twelve that could be approached about returning."

"Right," Beech sighed. "Well it's not as many as I'd hoped for, but beggars can't be choosers. Let's send the letter out to them then – inviting them to come in and have a chat. And," he reminded Stenton, "have another look at the disabled veterans and see if they can sit behind a desk and do paperwork. Tollman," he added, "If, when you are finished, you could come to my office, I would be grateful."

"Yes, sir. I'll be about fifteen minutes."

Beech nodded and left the two men to their paper shuffling. As he headed back up to his room, he felt a lightness wash over him. It was an expectation of working with the team once more…a feeling of looking forward to some excitement. He decided he would not approach the Commissioner about the case yet. Not until they had something more tangible.

CHAPTER FOUR

THE SEARCH BEGINS

There was a general meeting of some of the Mayfair 100 team after breakfast. Beech, Tollman and Rigsby were there, plus Victoria, Caroline and Lady Maud. Mabel Summersby was working an early morning shift at the hospital pharmacy but had given her extensive notes on the Spilsbury lecture to Caroline. Beech led the way by cautioning that investigation of this case had not, as yet, been sanctioned by the Commissioner, Sir Edward.

"I don't want to approach him at the moment," Beech explained, "until we have some more information on the victim and whether or not it is a pedestrian police matter."

"What do you mean by 'pedestrian'?" asked Caroline, a little miffed that her interesting case was being downplayed.

"If I might, Mr Beech?" Tollman, with the fine-tuned instincts of a father of three quarrelsome daughters, he sensed a 'difference of opinion' brewing and decided to step in. Beech nodded, gratefully.

"Whilst we are all agreed that, on the surface, this lady who works or worked in munitions and is stabbed through the heart in Mayfair whilst wearing a posh dress, looks intriguing…" Tollman began, being as conciliatory as possible, "it could turn out, for example, that she was simply engaged in a bit of part-time prostitution and, not having a pimp to protect her, she was murdered by a nasty piece of work who gets his kicks from violence. Or, we could find that she was a former servant of one of the large houses around that square, who came to revisit her old employment in a fancy dress , to show off her new wealth – I hear munitions workers can earn six times more than servants – and someone killed her in a fit of jealousy." Tollman paused for effect and, encouraged by the fact that Caroline had not jumped in to defend her position, he continued. "So, this is what Mr Beech is describing as a 'pedestrian police affair' – a case that can easily be solved by CID and does not require the special talents of this group."

Caroline nodded her understanding and Beech flashed Tollman a smile of gratitude. "Would you like to like to continue, Tollman, and tell us what you discovered about this case so far?"

Tollman looked at his notes. "Yes, sir. As Dr Allardyce and Miss Summersby have reported, she was found in the bushes in Berkeley Square, stabbed through the heart, at about one in the morning, but estimate of actual death is put at about an hour earlier. She was found by the night beat constable out of Division D, District 2 – Marylebone," he added, for the benefit on the ladies. Then he turned back to his notes. "The pathologist discovered physical evidence that this woman worked or had recently worked in munitions. She was wearing an expensive dress bearing the label Renee LaJeune..." he held up a photograph of the dress, "she was also wearing plain heeled court shoes and the stamp on the arch of the sole designates that they were manufactured by a firm called Simons in Leicester." Tollman held up a photograph of the shoes, then continued. "Now there is also this item. Something a little surprising. A few feet away from her was a bag, a small silver mesh bag with clasp and chain. Actually, real sterling silver and hallmarked Birmingham 1912." He held up another photograph.

There was a murmur of surprise from the ladies and Victoria asked to have a closer look at the photograph of the bag. As Lady Maud and Caroline leant over the image, Caroline commented, "Well, unless she was a prostitute, earning good money, or she stole the bag, this would appear to me an item that would only be in possession of a woman of means." There were murmurs of agreement from the other two.

"Was anything found in the bag?" asked Beech.

"It was open, and the lining was pulled out, as though the contents had been removed," Tollman replied, "but whoever did that, failed to spot a door key that was caught in the lining."

"I don't suppose there is anyway we can get hold of that key, is there?" asked Beech hopefully.

"Actually, sir, I took it upon myself to have a copy made and then returned the original to the evidence box." Tollman looked a bit sheepish.

Billy grinned and Beech simply said, "Good man."

"So, the key could be to her front door?" asked Victoria.

"Possibly," agreed Tollman, "but until we know who 'she' is, we have no way of finding her address."
"Right!" Beech's tone was brisk. "I suggest we proceed as follows…Tollman, I'm afraid you are going to have to do a tour of the munitions factories with a picture of the deceased to see if anyone has ever employed her or are missing her as a current employee. I imagine that's going to take you a few

days, as I would think that there are a considerable number of establishments that qualify as munitions factories nowadays."

"Yes sir. Munitions factories are springing up all over the place, at the moment. I think Billy and I may need to split the job between us. I took the liberty of also having several pictures of the deceased printed off at the Yard, so we can all have one."

"Yes, good." Beech agreed. "So, Caroline, Victoria and Maud – would you like to track down the dress and accessories by going to the necessary shops and seeing if you can pinpoint the name of a purchaser?"

Lady Maud looked delighted to be included but Caroline looked disappointed. "I'd much rather go round munitions factories with Mr Tollman."

Tollman shook his head firmly. "Sorry, Doctor, I know that women are beginning to be employed in these factories but I'm afraid you need a security clearance to visit such establishments, which policemen automatically have, by virtue of signing the Official Secrets Act. Also, in the main, they are rough and dangerous places and we might have to get tough with some of these employers in order to get answers. I would rather you left this one to Billy and I."

Caroline sighed and accepted defeat. "Shopping it must be, then," she said in resignation and everyone gathered up photographs and went to retrieve their coats and hats.

"And, please, everybody," Beech said in a firm voice, "Absolute discretion. I don't want it getting back to Sir Edward that we have embarked upon a case without consulting him first, and receiving the necessary permission."

***

"So, where do we start, Mr Tollman?" asked Billy eagerly as they stepped out of the front door of Lady Maud's house and into the pleasant July sunshine.

"I think we'd better go to the new Ministry of Munitions in Whitehall Gardens," was Tollman's decision. "We need a list of all the munitions facilities in and around London and I suspect we might need some sort of authorisation from them to conduct our investigation." And he set off briskly in the direction of the bus stop, with Billy eagerly matching his steps.

The new Ministry was in chaos. It took several attempts by Tollman and Billy to find the right entrance, office, and person to be able to answer any requests. Boxes were piled up everywhere. Furniture was being carried up flights of stairs and telephones were being installed. There was a continuous sound of drilling, hammering and shouting. Creating a new branch of the Civil Service was, obviously, the closest to Purgatory on earth that could be devised.

Eventually, they found themselves on the third floor of the second building, trying to find the room that contained a 'Mr Eversham'. They had been assured that he was the oracle who would be able to tell them what they wanted to know. Eversham was standing in a sea of cardboard boxes, calmly and carefully decanting their contents into metal filing cabinets.

"Mr Eversham?" enquired Tollman, displaying his warrant card.

"Yes – that is me," Eversham said with a small nod. "How can I help you?"

Tollman explained that they were investigating the murder of an unknown woman who had been a worker in a munitions' facility, and they needed to show her picture around the factories in order to try and discover her identity.

Eversham smiled, nodded, said, "Just one moment..." and stepped over some boxes to rummage in another filing cabinet. "Here you are," he said and flourished a three-page document at Tollman. "This is the latest list of all factories and workshops doing munitions work." He stepped back over the boxes and handed the list over. "It's quite comprehensive and the column on the right-hand side of each sheet gives you a description of the function of the factory...for example, it could be manufacturing tents, making chemicals or filling shells. This new department is bringing a lot more industrial functions under the umbrella of munitions." Eversham dropped his voice down to a confidential level, "Basically, we're taking a whole load of procurement control away from the Army and the navy, because they couldn't cope, and the system had become unwieldy. Fresh broom and all that. By the way, that list is top secret. I hope I can trust you to ensure that it doesn't fall into the wrong hands."

Tollman gave him firm assurances and Eversham turned back to his filing, but then had another thought and turned back to Tollman and Rigsby. "Actually, I know that one of our Dilution Officers is going to the Arsenal at Woolwich this morning – by automobile – and I'm sure he would be happy to give you a lift. You might as well start at the biggest munitions company in London."

"And where would we find this D..D.."

"Dilution Officer. His name is Captain Wallace and you will find him in the Ordnance Section of the War Office. Walk through to Whitehall and it's the building on the corner as you go through to Horse Guards. I think he's on the second floor. We are moving various army and navy personnel into this department but only when we have all the communications sorted out. Wallace will be only too glad to help you, I'm sure."

Tollman thanked Mr Eversham, Rigsby nodded, and they left him to his filing cabinets as they proceeded to pick their way out of the chaotic buildings and out into the street.

"Gawd, what a mess!" observed Billy as he brushed some wood dust off his sleeve, which had landed there, courtesy of someone drilling through the skirting boards above them on the staircase.

"Government departments," replied Tollman with a certain amount of bitterness. "If there's one thing you can rely on them to do, is to expand and create more work for themselves. Pretty soon we'll have more civil servants in Whitehall than we will have soldiers at the front. Right," he began to walk briskly away from the river, "Let's find this Captain Wallace and see if we can scrounge a lift to Woolwich."

Once found, the amiable Wallace proved to be extremely co-operative and rather pleased to have company on his journey. Tollman judged him to be in his late fifties and was relieved to find that, despite his rank, he was not upper class, but a down-to-earth engineer, who, before the war, had worked in a factory that manufactured railway carriages.

"They only made me an officer because I have to deal

with the owners of the factories all the time," he explained as they strode out towards an army automobile, parked amongst many on Horse Guards Parade. "Gives me a bit of clout and extra respect I suppose, especially when I have to get tough with them."

"So, what is a Dilution officer, Captain? If you don't mind me asking?" enquired Billy, as he squeezed himself into the back seat of the Vauxhall staff car. There wasn't much leg room, so he was forced to sit at a sideways slant. Fortunately, the canvas top was down, so he didn't have to remove his helmet.

"Ah yes," replied Wallace as he climbed over the spare wheel on the driver's door and sank into position. "It's a new title – for me, anyway. I used to be a Procurement Officer, dealing with the contracts for ordnance between the Army and the manufacturers. But, since the disgrace of the Shell Crisis, all Army and Navy personnel have been absorbed into the new Ministry of Munitions or they have been sent elsewhere. Can't be trusted anymore to grab the ball and run with it, so to speak!" He winked at Tollman and Billy and grinned. He lowered his voice and leaned in towards his passengers, "Quite right too, if you ask me," he said confidentially. "The Army wallahs were taking too damn long to process the contracts. The boys on the ground, like me, were agreeing quantities and production schedules, getting the contracts signed by the manufacturers and then the bloody Army sat on them for ages. I can't speak for the navy, but I suspect it was the same. Pull your hat on hard, Sergeant Tollman!" he advised, as he turned the engine on and they moved out into the slow-moving traffic of buses, taxi cabs and horse carts in Whitehall.

Wallace raised the volume of his voice to overcome the engine noise and continued, "So, a Dilution Officer is someone who goes around to the factories and persuades them to 'dilute' their workforce with female employees."

"Oh dear," said Tollman, without thinking, and then was instantly grateful that no ladies were present in the car.

"Oh dear, indeed, Sergeant Tollman!" said Wallace breezily. "There are actually quite a few women already working in munitions – as you will see when we get to the Arsenal – and the factory owners are quite impressed with women workers for certain jobs..."

"Like what?" asked Billy, always curious.

"Filling cartridges and small shells, sewing tents and backpacks, mixing explosives, that sort of stuff. Anything that requires small nimble fingers. They actually outperform the men in those sorts of tasks. Of course, men are still needed for skilled engineering and heavy manual labour. But anyway, as I say, the owners are open to dilution of the workforce – the biggest barriers are put up by the unions. The Amalgamated Society of Engineers has already got the Government to sign an agreement that all women undertaking work that pertains to their members, will be sacked the moment the war ends. Very militant they were. And most of the unions have had the right hump about the suggestion that women should be paid the same as men, so they have insisted, in a lot of factories, that the jobs are very slightly changed, so that the women are paid a lot less."

Tollman tutted and Billy muttered, "That doesn't seem

fair – if they're taking the same risks as men, with all this gunpowder and chemical stuff."

Wallace nodded agreement and concentrated on getting past a stationary horse and cart outside Lambeth Palace.

"That's a manure cart!" observed Tollman, as Billy wrinkled his nose in disgust.

"Ah yes, Sergeant Tollman," agreed Wallace, "We're all being encouraged to grow our own food now...even the Archbishop. Do you garden, Tollman?"

Billy recognised that a serious discussion of Tollman's favourite subject was about to take place, so he mentally switched off, settled back in his seat and watched the world go by.

It was just past eleven o'clock when the car drew in through the large gateway of the Woolwich Arsenal. Captain Wallace was obviously a regular visitor, judging by the banter exchanged between him, the armed soldier and the uniformed policeman in the gatehouse. Wallace introduced Tollman and Rigsby, warrant cards were inspected, and the car allowed to pass through into the walled city known as the Royal Arsenal.

✳✳✳

Lady Maud stood in The Royal Arcade and pursed her lips in irritation.

"I could have sworn that Renee LaJeune's shop was here, the last time I came through."

"When was that, Mother?" asked Victoria, suspecting that was probable quite a while ago..

"Well...I suppose it must have been a few years ago now. I used to come and collect your father's shirts from Bretell's, before meeting friends at Fortnum's for tea."

"Mother," Victoria tried to be as gentle as possible. "Father died four years ago. A lot can happen in four years."

"Well, obviously!" Maud was exasperated – more with herself than anything else. She pointed her parasol at the notice on the door of the shop in front of them, which said, simply, The establishment of Renee LaJeune has relocated to number 74 Barrett Street (behind Selfridges in Oxford Street). "And now we shall have to go to the odious Oxford Street to find it!"

Caroline and Victoria both knew that Maud loathed Oxford Street. She had once described it as "a mile long highway of pimps, prostitutes and unpleasant shops" and it had taken Victoria a great deal of persuasion to get her mother to visit the new department store, Selfridges, when it opened in 1909.

"Look on the bright side, Maud," said Caroline cheerfully, "We have to pass the Coburg Hotel on our way and..." she lowered her voice conspiratorially, "I hear they are still serving good coffee and biscuits."

Lady Maud visibly brightened. "Just the thing to fortify ourselves for the assault on the retail industry! Come along!" She marched determinedly ahead, and Caroline winked at Victoria, as they followed the revived Maud out of the Arcade.

The coffee at the Coburg was indeed good and it provided a pleasant oasis of calm before the ladies attempted to cross the traffic nightmare of Oxford Street. As usual, it was clogged with horses and carts, omnibuses and automobiles. A lone policeman stood in front of Selfridges directing traffic and, occasionally halting the flow so that shoppers could cross the street.

Caroline took it upon herself to steer everyone around the piles of horse manure that were deposited on the road.

"We need those boys back at work on the streets...you know...in Dicken's books...what are they called?"

"Crossing sweepers," said Victoria loudly, over the noise of idling motor vehicles and horse's hooves, as the traffic continued on its way.

"Yes, the ones that sweep away the horse manure so that you don't get it on your shoes and hemlines," Caroline said as she lifted up her feet to make sure there were no deposits on her soles.

The ladies continued slowly down the side of Selfridges department store, often coming to a complete stop as they gazed at the beautifully dressed windows.

"There is no doubt that Mr Selfridge knows how to sell to people," observed Maud as they stood, with many other ladies, gazing at a particularly beautiful bridal display. The dress was exquisite and the long lace veil, although not hand-made lace, was impressive. Everything in the window was marked with a price and to Maud's eye, everything seemed extremely cheap. "It's a wonder that such things can be made for such a low price," she murmured.

"Factory made, I assume," answered Victoria.

"I would imagine some girl working in an office or shop would be very pleased to wear such a garment on her wedding day, wouldn't you?" Caroline added.

With the wonderment of 'ready-to-wear' clothing in their heads, it then came as no surprise when they found Renee LaJeune's establishment had copied the ethos of Selfridges and was displaying ready-made frocks in the window.

"It would seem, Mother, as though the fashion industry is all headed in the same direction," Victoria muttered, as the three of them entered the once-exclusive establishment.

There was a young girl seated on a chair in the corner, who sprang up ready to assist, as soon as they entered the shop. Her enthusiasm quickly waned when they asked to see the proprietor "on a confidential matter" and she went through a curtain to a back room to find Madame Renee.

It had been agreed with Beech that the ladies would present themselves as a lady's welfare organisation trying to investigate the disappearance of a female factory worker – and that they were assisting the hard-pressed police by making some initial enquiries.

Madame Renee appeared – a careworn but elegant woman – and, after introductions, she invited them through to her office. It was cramped but there was just about enough room for everyone to be seated. They explained their mission and Madame said she would help in any way she could. Then she looked at the photograph Victoria held out and recoiled. "Good God! Is that blood?" she asked pointing at the stain on the dress.

"I'm afraid we don't know, Madame." Victoria lied.

"Well, I can tell you that the dress is definitely our design and manufacture and not some cheap copy. But that's all I can tell you, I'm afraid," she said regretfully.

"Do you not keep records of your customers?" asked Lady Maud.

Victoria fancied that she saw a slight flush creep across Madame Renee's face as she replied, "Once upon a time we would, Lady Maud, of course, have the name and address of any customer who bought an exclusive dress from us. A couture dress that was handmade to the customer's specifications. We do still have a handful of customers who have accounts with us...but they are fast disappearing. This dress..." she pointed at the photograph, "was part of a range that we made last year – for the 1914 summer season. We made twelve in various sizes and in two colours – eau de nil and oyster. It was very successful, as we sold eleven of them and remade the unsold dress into another design."

Perhaps Madame Renee saw Lady Maud's eyes widen and she became defensive. "Times have changed in the fashion industry, ladies. Once upon a time I had a proper couture establishment and clients, with accounts, that ordered a full bespoke range of gowns and tailored wear for each season. The War put paid to all that. The landed gentry have moved out of London for the duration. The Season doesn't happen anymore. No more Ascot, Henley Regatta, parties and soirees. No need for new clothes. However, we now have a rising female professional and middle class. Female civil servants, who can't afford haute couture, but they can afford high-class ready-made garments, like the type offered by the department stores. I have chosen to cater to that clientele now. They pay cash and therefore I don't keep details of their addresses. I'm so sorry that I can't help you."

"If we showed you a photograph of the young woman in question, might you recognise her?" Victoria was hesitant, because to show Madame Renee the photograph of what was obviously a corpse would give the game away, but Madame firmly shook her head.

"No, I don't recognise customers anymore," she said with a resigned air. "When we were an exclusive business – everything made to order, and customers had to come in for regular fittings – then, obviously, I got to know ladies, and their families. But now, a customer comes in, tries on a gown, pays and leaves. I take no notice of their faces I'm afraid."

Caroline proffered the photographs of the shoes and the bag. "Is it possible that you could give us some advice about these items?"

Madame Renee softened, and the sight of the bag even raised a small smile. "Very nice accessories," she murmured. Then she became brisk once more, "The shoes, I would suggest, are from a department store. If they don't have one of the recognisable London or Paris names on the sole, then they will have been commissioned and bought in, in bulk, by one of the stores. The bag is, of course, exquisite and looks as though it is silver…is it?" she enquired. Caroline nodded. "Then you must go to the Assay Office and get them to check the hallmark. They will tell you the manufacturer and the company will keep records of sales. Now, ladies, if you will excuse me, I have another appointment."

Everyone rose from their seats and Victoria thanked Madame Renee for her time. Lady Maud, always concerned for the welfare of others, expressed a wish that the proprietor's business would improve in time.

Renee smiled and replied, "Thank you for your concern, Lady Maud, but I am one of the fortunate ones in this industry. I started as a skilled seamstress and cutter, so I am able, now, to supplement my income by teaching in the new Barrett Street Trade School that has been set up along this road. That's why I moved here. I can run the shop and teach young girls tailoring and dressmaking in the afternoons." With that, she gave a few instructions to her assistant, before ushering the visitors out through the front door and bidding them goodbye.

"Resourceful," commented Caroline with admiration, as they watched Madame Renee bustling up the street.

"Oh dear, things are changing at an alarming rate," bemoaned Maud, to no one in particular. "And I don't suppose they will change back, once the war is over," she added.

"No, Mother," said Victoria firmly. "You had better get used to the fact that the old life we used to lead has gone forever."

CHAPTER FIVE

THE BUSINESS OF DEATH

Tollman and Rigsby were introduced to the General Manager of the Royal Arsenal, Alfred Taylor – a harassed individual who was about to go into lengthy 'discussions' with various union representatives, armed only with some Government regulations and the ever-cheerful Captain Wallace.

"Dear me…a female munitions worker murdered? Dear me," he seemed to add it to his list of worries, as though it was something that might crop up in his pending negotiations. "We don't have many female workers at the moment, do we, Captain Wallace?" This afterthought seemed to make Mr Taylor brighten up a little. "So, she may not be one of ours. But you'll have to ask the supervisors. I'll get my secretary to give you a letter of authority…Miss Moffatt!" he bawled, and an unsmiling middle-aged woman entered with a pad and pencil.

"Miss Moffatt, these policemen need letters of authorisation to go and investigate a murder." The unflappable Miss Moffatt's reaction to the word murder was a brief raise of the eyebrows as she made some notes on her pad. Taylor rapidly dictated a letter and then said, "I shall be here for another half an hour discussing matters with Captain Wallace, so bring the letter in for signature."

"If it wouldn't be too great an inconvenience, might we have two letters, Mr Taylor?" asked Tollman, "Only this is a very big place and it would be better if Constable Rigsby and I split up…"

"Oh, you don't need to do that, Sergeant! We only, at the moment, employ women in three areas in the Composition Establishment – that's a group of buildings here…" Taylor jabbed at a large map on the wall. "That's where we assemble cartridges and fuzes and so on. I mean we have women employed in the canteens and we have our own hospital, dispensary and mortuary…nurses and orderlies and the like… but you said you were looking for a woman who worked with explosives…is that correct?" Tollman nodded and Taylor continued, "Well then Composition is where to go, and you won't need to split up. So, if you would like to go with Miss Moffatt, she will do the necessary letter."

Tollman and Rigsby duly followed the secretary into the outer office and she motioned them to sit, while she rattled off a letter on her typewriter. Captain Wallace came out and said apologetically, "It looks as though I'm going to be stuck in a meeting all day, so I can't offer you a lift back to London, but the station is just up the road and that will take you straight to Charing Cross."

"No problem, Captain, thank you."

"Any time. I'm moving into the new Ministry in a few days, so if you need anything else, come and see me there and I'll help if I can." Then he ducked back into Mr Taylor's office, just as the efficient Miss Moffatt came out with the signed letter.

"Here you are, Sergeant." She said, handing over the letter. "Now, you will need to take the transport…"

"Oh, I'm sure we can find it on foot," interrupted Tollman genially.

"Sergeant Tollman" replied Miss Moffatt with a disdainful look, "the Composition sheds are nearly two miles away, in the eastern part of the site, and between here and there are a complete warren of buildings, railway lines, docks, storage huts and extremely dangerous facilities. I think you had better come with me."

Tollman and Rigsby meekly followed the formidable woman.

"That told you, didn't it?" whispered Rigsby cheekily and Tollman rewarded him with a glare.

Miss Moffatt led them out of the building and across to what appeared to be a goods yard, where wooden boxes marked with mysterious stencilled numbers were being loaded from a small train onto a much larger train.

"Cartridges," said Billy, knowledgeably, "I've opened many a crate of those in my time!"

Miss Moffatt spoke to the driver of the small train who nodded and motioned the two policemen to jump on board the footplate. It was a squeeze, especially for Billy, but they held on to whatever was to hand as the train jerked into life and began moving slowly along the tracks.

"Been here before?" shouted the driver, over the sound of the engine, and the noise of a standard gauge train passing them on a separate parallel track.

"No," said Tollman loudly. "I understand it's very big."

The driver smiled and nodded. "Nearly 100,000 people work for the Royal Arsenal."

Billy whistled and shook his head in disbelief.

They were passing a large number of factory buildings. "Those are the Gun and Carriage factories," explained the driver. "They make all the big guns there and all the wheels and stuff. After they've been to the proving ranges and tested, they get loaded straight onto ships at the docks, which are over the back there."

Through an open door, Tollman and Billy could see men, stripped to the waist, sweaty and blackened, pushing things into a furnace.

"Smelting works," said the driver and then pointed to a larger building behind. "They make the shell and cartridge casings in this part of the site but then they go up to the Composition Sheds to be filled. That's our own power station for the site and beyond that is the train sheds for the railway system, coal sheds, boiler houses, timber shops... coming up on the right is the fire station and police station..."

"What? You've got your own?" Billy was impressed.

"Oh, it's like a city of its own here, lad," answered the driver. "A very dangerous city. For example, the railway system doesn't go near the Composition Sheds, the Chemical Research Laboratories or the Lyddite Factory because train wheels on metal rails cause sparks, not to mention the fire in the engines, and a stray spark could cause all of those buildings to detonate. I can drop you off about 100 yards away, but you'll have to walk the rest. Oh, by the way, have you got metal studs on the soles of your boots?"

Billy and Tollman nodded.

"Then you'll have to go in the gate house, near where I

drop you off, and get some slipovers for your feet. Otherwise, you might cause sparks."

He slowed up the engine and the train drew to a halt. "Another bit of advice," he added, pointing into the distance, "they're testing all sorts of guns today on the proving ranges. See that red flag?"

Billy and Tollman peered at the expanse of marshland and could make out a red flag fluttering on a small hill.

"Don't go anywhere beyond the Combination sheds while that red flag is flying or you could get blown to bits."

"How do we get back to the main gate when we've finished?" asked Tollman, ever-mindful of his prone-to-aching feet.

"Come back to this spot. There's a narrow gauge train runs by every ten minutes or so. Just flag it down." He fired up the engine again, after they had climbed down on to the concrete and gently pulled away.

Tollman and Billy made their way over to the gate house and once inside, letter of authorisation and warrant cards produced, they were issued with overshoes made entirely of rubber.

"You'll have to leave your helmet here, son," Billy was advised, "And the contents of your pockets – coins, lighters, note clips – anything metal," he added, including Tollman as well.

"What about my jacket?" asked Billy, indicating the buttons.

"Nah. They're made of brass. Brass doesn't produce sparks. You're fine." He gave a small nod of encouragement.

So, off they went, towards the group of brick buildings that had curious elevated wooden walkways between them. They passed an open shed where two men were shovelling empty brass cartridges into boxes, from a large mountain of cartridges behind them. A young lad came out from one of the buildings and came over and collected two boxes of cartridges from the stack and took them back to the building, arriving at the same time as Billy, who opened the door for him.

Inside the building it was fairly quiet, although there was a strange background noise, like the clattering of typewriters, as the workers scooped cartridges out of the boxes in front of them, filled them with the necessary contents to make them into lethal bullets and placed them in individual holes in trays in front of them. There were about thirty workers in the hut – a mixture of women and young lads aged about 12 to 15. Billy supposed that it was because the lads had smallish hands, like the women and could do the fiddly work of filling the cartridges more easily than grown men.

A man was walking around, casually inspecting the silent work. Now and then he would remove a filled cartridge from its stand and reject it by dropping it into a bin under the workbench, presumably because his trained eye could see some defect in its assembly. As Tollman and Billy entered, preceded by the boy carrying two boxes of empty cartridges, the supervisor looked up and registered surprise at the police presence. He motioned Tollman and Billy to a small office, created from some partitioning in the corner of the hut. Once they had all stepped inside and the door had been shut, the man said "Right, so which one of the little beggars is in trouble this time?" The man's look of exasperation made Billy grin.

Tollman explained that they were not after any of his existing workers but hoping to track down a possible past member of the workforce. Then he produced the photograph.

The man looked at it long and hard and finally said, "I feel as though I know her but there's something about the picture that's not right."

"Well she is dead," said Tollman, with a degree of sarcasm.

The man smiled slightly and said, "No that's not it. Maybe it's the hair. Any women round here have to wear their hair covered up with these caps. It sort of makes them all look the same."

"Well, she's actually wearing a wig in this picture. Apparently the front of her hair had turned orange from exposure to TNT…" Tollman began helpfully, but the man interrupted him.

"TNT?" he said sharply. "Well she wasn't one of my girls, then. We don't use TNT…and if I have anything to do with it, we never will. We use Lyddite – make our own on site. It's dangerous mind – we had a big explosion about twelve years ago, but it doesn't turn you yellow like the TNT stuff."

Tollman was disgruntled. "Right, well it seems as though we have wasted our time coming down to Woolwich," and he prepared to go.

"Hang on though," said the man, "let me have a look at that photograph again." Tollman handed it back and the man made a face as if trying to remember. "I definitely think I've seen her," he said, "and the only place she could have been exposed to TNT is in the Chemical Research Laboratory. It's about fifty yards away. Go out of here and turn right and it's straight ahead. They're a funny lot in there and they don't like visitors. I'll get one of the lads to take you over." He opened the door and bawled "Ernest!" A young lad appeared, looking flustered, obviously thinking the police had come to arrest him. "Take these policemen over to the Research building and tell them that I sent them over."

Tollman and Billy dutifully followed their chaperone who took them over to a building that was surrounded by a high wall of sandbags, propped up against a wooden support wall and guarded by a soldier. This made Tollman feel uneasy.

Whilst the soldier was looking over their paperwork, the ground suddenly shook and there was a delayed sound of an explosion. Tollman looked concerned but Billy put his hand on his shoulder and tried to be reassuring, "They're just firing an eighteen-pounder", he said, but he could hear his voice echoing in his head. The sound of the blast, so familiar to him from the trenches in France, had made his mouth turn suddenly dry.

The soldier, recognising that Billy was an ex-comrade in arms, smiled, and said "They'll be firing a few more in the next hour and then, after lunch, they'll be firing some of new Stokes Mortars. They've got three-inch shells and they can fire about three of them in a minute. The Major can get you a pass to watch if you want."

By now, Billy was beginning to feel some of that familiar anxiety he had begun to feel in the trenches – waiting for the next earth-shaking explosion of the big gun before the shell screamed over his head. He could feel himself struggling to breathe properly and Tollman, with his famous ability to 'read' people, realised that Billy was in trouble. He grasped Billy's arm firmly and said briskly to the soldier, "That's very kind of you lad, but we have urgent police business that will take up most of the day," and he pushed Billy into the relative quiet of the building.

They stopped in the hallway and Tollman scanned Billy's face anxiously. "Just breathe, Billy," he said quietly, "In…and out…in…and out." He gripped both Billy's arms and looked at him squarely. "Are you feeling dizzy? Do you want us to go back to the train?"

Billy shook his head. His tongue seemed to be stuck to the roof of his mouth. "I'll be alright in a minute. It…just stirred up a few memories…that's all."

Tollman noticed a chair in the hallway and he brought it over. "You sit here and wait. I'll deal with this enquiry. I'll be back in a minute." Billy started to protest but Tollman was adamant. "You stay here. I don't want you passing out in there. You just sit here and get yourself together, lad." Then he entered the door at the end of the hallway. Billy slammed his good fist into his bad hand in frustration and then concentrated on bringing down his anxiety levels by closing his eyes and breathing slowly in through his nose and out through his mouth.

Tollman found himself confronted by men in white coats and masks, wielding tongs and pouring molten material into casts suspended over Bunsen burners.

"Close the door gently, man!" barked one of the men in the masks, "otherwise you will cause a draft!" Tollman stood perfectly still and closed the door behind him with exaggerated gentleness. "Right!" the same voice barked at one of the other men, "monitor that while I deal with this interruption!" With that, a tall, thin man turned, pulled his mask off and glared at Tollman.

"Who are you and what do you want?" he said impatiently, without the slightest attempt to be civil.

Tollman explained about his task and produced the photograph. The man looked at the photo and said, very quietly, "Oh my God, that is Agnes Whitlock."

CHAPTER SIX

THE GIRL WHO MOVED AROUND A LOT

Agnes, it seemed, was a girl who had had a few jobs in the munitions industry since war, and its preparations, started almost a year ago.

The man who had recognised her, Professor McCabe, said that she had worked in the laboratory section of the Royal Arsenal for a few months.

"She was just an assistant, really," he recalled. "It was obvious that she had been working with TNT and need a rest from it. So, we put her on to jobs that were mostly cleaning equipment, fetching and carrying, nothing too onerous. But then, about a month ago, she suddenly upped and left, just like that."

"Do you know where she went, Professor?" Tollman was prepared for a negative answer but, much to his surprise, the Professor said "Yes. She went to a private company called H, Mason & Co near Wanstead Flats. Not quite sure why she wanted to go there. As far as I am aware, they don't pay as well as here."

"Is there anything special about this establishment in Wanstead, Professor?"

"Not as far as I am aware," he answered, shaking his head. "They are only guncotton and cordite manufacturers – both are components created for use as propellants in guns of all calibres. What they make would then be sent to the larger factories that are filling small arms ammunition and shells. It's dangerous work," he added, "especially the production of cordite, which uses guncotton and nitro glycerine, both very explosive."

"And might you know, Professor, where Miss Whitlock had worked before she came to work here?"

"Um," McCabe screwed up his face, trying to remember, "Yes, it was TNT production, which then became a National Factory in December last year. I can't remember the name of it but it's in Worcestershire. Agnes said it was her first job and she worked there for four months but got sick, so she came here and worked for us for about four months too, then she moved on again. Restless sort of creature. Very bright though," he added, "middle class and you could have a good conversation with her. Good education I suspect but she never said. Bit of a secretive air about her."

"Do you think it possible that she was interested in your work here. I mean by that, sir, do you think she could have been a spy?" Tollman's sixth sense was beginning to vibrate about this case and he wanted to know more about this mysterious, well-educated Miss Whitlock.

Professor McCabe seemed to give it some thought but then dismissed it. He lowered his voice and said "Frankly, most of stuff we are working on now, or modifying should I say, was invented or discovered by the Germans before the war anyway. There isn't much they would learn from us, at the moment. In fact, we are playing 'catch-up', as it were, with the chemical gases being used at the front. I shouldn't say it but the Germans are damned good at this sort of thing. I don't think they would be bothered to spy on us."

"Do you have an address for Miss Whitlock, Professor?" Tollman asked hopefully.

"We do, but I doubt if she was still living there. As far as I can remember, it was an address in Woolwich and going from there to Wanstead every day, would not have been feasible, I fancy."

Tollman agreed, thanked the Professor and made his way back out to Billy, who was, by now, sitting quietly, but looking a little pale. Tollman realised that, in the hallway, he could hear the low thud of more shells being fired but had not really been aware of them in the laboratory. Probably specially insulated, he thought to himself.

"Come on, lad," he said cheerfully to Billy. "I've found out who our dead lady is,"

"Oh?" Billy gave a watery grin. "That's a result then."

"It certainly is," Tollman hauled Billy to his feet and said, "So, let's get out of this city of horrors and find ourselves the nearest pub. I could do with a pint and you, my lad, definitely need a brandy, before we get on the train for home."

***

Lady Maud sank into her favourite chair with a small sigh of relief. "I seem to have completely lost the ability to intensively shop," she said, her voice holding both surprise and weariness.

Caroline snorted. "I don't believe that I have ever had the stamina for shopping…although I don't remember it being as gruelling as our experience today."

"Well it wasn't…in the past," said Victoria. "From our privileged position in society, we were able to visit discreet establishments to get dresses and suits made. There was none of this jostling with the crowds to grab a piece of ready to wear clothing. Oh dear! "she added with dismay, "I've just realised that I sound like the most dreadful snob!"

"You do rather," smirked Caroline, "but we forgive you."

"But Victoria is absolutely right," Lady Maud, "Shopping used to be an amiable activity. Not rushed. I would potter along Bond Street, buying some perfume here, a hat there, some soap in another shop – and they would all be delivered! No-one would expect me to carry around parcels, no matter how small. Every shop had a few chairs, so that you could sit and be shown various items by a polite shop assistant. I mean, our experience in Marshall and Snelgrove today, was positively…" she grasped for the correct words and then said, triumphantly, "like shopping in a street market."

"It's the first time I have ever felt intimidated by a shop assistant," commented Caroline. "When you showed the woman in the shoe department the photograph of those shoes, she looked positively disdainful. What was it she said?"

"Those shoes are from last summer's season, madam. No-one is wearing pumps now that skirts are shorter." Victoria smiled as she recalled her mother's face as the shop assistant had turned away from them to deal with another customer.

"Cheeky little minx!" said Maud with feeling, "After she had made us all feel unfashionable, she then proceeded to ignore us! It made me feel like an ancient relic!" Maud's indignation threatened to overcome her, and Caroline leapt up, rang the bell for the kitchen and said, "Tea and cake is the order of the day, don't you think?" and everyone heartily agreed.

"So, we haven't really got anywhere today, have we?" Victoria felt rather frustrated. "I was so hoping that we would be able to crack this case and show Mr Tollman what good detectives we are."

"I am only too aware of what good detectives you are, ladies," said Mr Tollman, entering at that very moment, with a still-pale Billy trailing behind him.

"I gather you had no luck then?"

"No." said Lady Maud emphatically, but brightening up as the maid, Annie, wheeled in a trolley with tea, sandwiches and cake.

"It was a desperately tedious haul around lots of very overcrowded shops, Mr Tollman," added Caroline with feeling, whilst also eyeing an unusually quiet Billy. "I bet you had great fun, wherever you went."

"I wouldn't exactly say that," answered Tollman, grateful accepting a cup of tea from Annie. "We went to the Royal Arsenal at Woolwich," and he explained the wonders of the walled city where they made every conceivable type of gun and explosive shells and cartridges.

Caroline listened with great interest, but her gaze kept flickering over to Billy, who was quietly sipping his tea and showing no interest in the food. Her doctor's instinct was telling her that he had a problem but, also, that it was not something to be aired in public. She decided to bide her time.

When Tollman got to the part about the laboratory and discovering the name of the murdered woman, the ladies burst into envious cries of "Oh well done!", "Good job Mr Tollman!" and similar.

"Anyway, ladies," said Tollman briskly, "I shall leave you to your afternoon tea and I shall go and report to Mr Beech before I make my way home. Billy!" he looked over to the constable, "I'll pick you up tomorrow morning and we will make our way over to Wanstead. Alright?" Billy nodded. "Get some rest, lad."

It was too much for Caroline to bear, so when Tollman went into the hallway to get his coat and hat, she followed him.

"Mr Tollman, is Billy unwell?" she asked quietly.

Tollman lowered his voice and said, "Look doctor, I wouldn't tell anyone but you, but he had a funny turn at the Arsenal. They were testing these big guns on the proving range and he went pale and started breathing rapidly. It was just panic, I think. He said that it reminded him of the trenches. I sat him down for a while and he seemed to recover. I think it shocked him a bit. Don't say anything to him. I think he was a bit embarrassed by it all."

Caroline nodded and said that she understood. Then she added, "Mr Tollman, Mabel and I have a day off tomorrow. Could we come with you to this place in Wanstead?"

Tollman frowned and said, "Oh, I don't know about that, doctor. These munitions factories have lots of restrictions about who they let through their gates nowadays."

Caroline persisted, "Well, then obviously we can't come into the factory, but, if you get an address for this woman, Mabel and I really should be the ones to search her accommodation. You know how good Mabel is at finding the tiniest piece of forensic evidence."

Tollman considered her statement for a moment and then said, "Yes, I suppose you're right, doctor. You can come with us, but we'll have to find somewhere for you to wait until we've got the information we need. Mind..." he warned, "I shall have to get Mr Beech's permission for this."

Caroline nodded, content that she had put her case and Tollman had thought it reasonable. Peter Beech was always guided by Tollman's advice.

Tollman left and Caroline went back to the parlour. She was relieved to find that Billy seemed to have perked up a little and was engaging in some limited conversation and beginning to smile. *I suspect he was embarrassed because he felt he had shown weakness to Tollman*, she thought to herself, knowing that Billy held Sergeant Tollman in high regard. In any event, she had resolved to keep a close eye on Billy from now on.

✳✳✳

Beech had been struggling with composing a report on the latest statistics regarding night burglaries in Central London and so he welcomed Tollman's visit, which gave him a break from the endless paperwork.

Tollman recounted the day's work at the Royal Arsenal and Beech felt a surge of excitement that the case had achieved a breakthrough so quickly.

"Dr Allardyce and Miss Summersby have asked if they could come with Billy and I tomorrow, sir,"

"Well, they won't be able to go into the munitions

factory with you. That will be authorised personnel only, I would have thought," Beech responded.

"Yes, I've told them that, sir, and Dr Allardyce accepts that…but she did point out that Miss Summersby is very skilled at finding forensic evidence if they were allowed to search the deceased's accommodation."

Beech mulled this over for a moment and then nodded his head. "I suppose that will be helpful," he said grudgingly, realising that he felt quite jealous of Caroline being able to get involved intimately in the case.

"There is another thing, sir," Tollman said hesitantly and Beech waited for him to continue. "Young Rigsby had a funny turn today…"

"What d'you mean, Tollman?"

"Well, we were at the Arsenal and they were testing some big guns over on the marshes. When the sounds of the guns started, Billy went pale, couldn't breathe and started sweating a bit. He gradually recovered but it left him a bit subdued, to my mind."

Beech took a deep breath and cursed his own imagination, which was now reproducing the sound of those guns in his head. "Billy and I were in the battle of Mons, as you know…deemed a victory for the Allies, of sorts…but it was total bloody carnage…" he broke off from his explanation to ask Tollman, "Were they 18 pound guns being fired at the Arsenal?" Tollman nodded and Beech resumed, "Yes, they have a certain sound, the 18 pounders." He paused and took a mouthful of cold tea from his cup on the desk. "We were massively outnumbered by the Germans, and they also had some really heavy guns, but we had three field artillery brigades with, between them, fifty four 18 pound guns. There was also a heavy artillery battery with four 60 pound guns and a field howitzer brigade with about twenty 4.5 inch howitzers." Beech took another deep breath and another mouthful of tea. "There are lots of terrible things I remember about that battle, Tollman, but, most of all, I remember the constant barrage of the 18 pound guns. It was relentless. The sort of sound that would drive sane men mad – and it did. It was the first time that men came out of battle with what they call shell-shock, of which Billy Rigsby was one. I was lucky," he added, "I was unconscious with my leg wound for two days and then, after the operation, I was heavily sedated, so I didn't develop shell-shock. Apparently, the sound of the shells firing and exploding, stays with you for days after the event. It really sounds like the explosions are continuing in your head, apparently – or so one of my sergeants described to me, when he recovered."

Tollman had no words to describe the sense of horror he was feeling, so he decided to keep quiet and just nodded.

"So," said Beech, trying to be positive, "I can understand why the sound of those guns at Woolwich, started up memories of extreme fear, that Rigsby found hard to control. Will he be exposed to guns firing at this place you are going to tomorrow?" asked Beech as an afterthought.

Tollman shook his head. "No, Mr Beech. The place just manufactures cordite and gun cotton. Barring any accidental explosions, we should be fine."

Beech nodded. "If Rigsby has another episode, let me know. We may need to give him a rest for a couple of weeks."

Beech turned back to his paperwork but added, "Oh and Tollman, you have my permission to be very firm with Dr Allardyce if she oversteps the mark at any point."

"Yes, sir," Tollman grinned and left the Chief Inspector to his tedious task.

CHAPTER SEVEN

EVENTS TAKE AN UNUSUAL TURN

Caroline was thrilled to be working today with Mabel on doing some real forensic work. Victoria was a little envious, but she had promised her mother that she would accompany her to an event at Londonderry House.

"Lady Londonderry is setting up the Women's Legion today," then Victoria added, "We don't know what that is, but it sounds interesting."

"Knowing Edith, as I do," Lady Maud was on first name terms with the Marchioness of Londonderry, "It will be something militaristic. She was made Colonel in Chief of the Women's Volunteer Reserve when war broke out. It probably won't be my cup of tea, but one must go along and support the endeavour."

Billy Rigsby appeared, in uniform, having eaten a late large breakfast in the kitchen and feeling much more like himself than he did yesterday. Caroline noted his familiar enthusiasm was back and smiled. "You look raring to go, today, Billy," she said breezily, and Billy grinned. In truth, he had a 'bit of a head' from drinking in the pub the previous night with Sam Abbott, who had regaled him with stories about Elsie and Sissy overfeeding him.

"Straight up," Sam had begun, "I swear your womenfolk are trying to kill me with kindness. When I got up, they put a breakfast in front of me that was enough for three men, and I had to share some of it with the dog when they weren't looking…then they says to me 'Sam, could you do a bit of weeding in the garden' and I thought, lovely, that'll work off some of the breakfast. I'd only been out there an hour when Sissy comes out with a mug of tea and a big slab of cake! Then, when I came in at lunchtime, your mum has half a loaf of bread, a great big hunk of cheese and loads of pots of pickles on the table! I did me best but then Sissy appears with some treacle pudding for afters! So, after that they gets me moving furniture in the upstairs rooms, so they can clean and I'm thinking 'Thank Gawd, I'm working off a bit of the lunch and then they ambush me with afternoon tea! Sandwiches, cakes, the lot!" Billy by then was laughing so hard, the tears were rolling down his cheeks, but Sam wasn't finished. "So then, about six 'o'clock, Sissy shouts up the stairs 'Dinner's ready!' and my heart sinks. I come down to the kitchen and there's a big plate of steak and chips, with apple pie for afters. Honest to God, Billy, your women are cooking me into an early grave!"

A good laugh had been just what Billy had needed and he had reflected, as Sam had carried on with more funny tales, that he didn't need doctors or medications, he just need a pint with a mate and a few laughs and the world would right itself again.

Towards the end of the evening, as the landlord had rung the bell, and Billy and Sam had left the pub in a mellow mood, Sam had said seriously, "I hope you don't think I've been cheeky about Elsie and Sissy. Honest to God, I love them both and they are being so kind to me. More than I could have expected, mate. Never thought I'd spend my leave in a Belgravia mansion, with a proper soft bed and two women waiting on me hand and foot. It's like a dream."

Billy had put his arm round Sam's shoulder and said "Don't be daft mate. I love my mum and aunty to bits but why d'you think I don't live with them? When I was invalided out of the army, they pulled the same tactics on me. I put on two stone while I was convalescing! Look at it this way. You let them feed you up, so that when you get back to the Front you can manage on them poxy army rations!"

It had been a good night and Billy was now ready to face another day with his usual cheerfulness.

Caroline, Billy, Victoria and Lady Maud stepped outside on to the pavement in the watery sunshine of the morning.

"It's not nearly as warm as last summer, you know," Maud grumbled, as she and Victoria said their goodbyes and set out for a gentle stroll towards Londonderry House in Park Lane. They met Sergeant Tollman coming around the corner and stopped to exchange a few pleasantries.

A taxicab drew up and disgorged Mabel, in her usual state of disarray, with several bags of items she deemed necessary for a proper forensic study. There were sample bottles; cotton wool; labels; pens; scissors, string, waxed paper and more. Billy and Caroline moved the bags and baskets away from the kerb whilst Tollman settled with the cabbie and got a receipt. Then Caroline unbuttoned and rebuttoned Mabel's jacket, as she had obviously dressed in a hurry and was one button out down the length of the garment.

Just as they were organised, a police automobile drew up, driven by Beech.

"Run out of police drivers, have they, sir?" enquired

Tollman affably. Beech grinned sheepishly.

"I just thought I would get out of the office for a little while and bring the vehicle over myself," explained Beech. "Is it alright for you to be the driver today, Rigsby?"

Billy was delighted and removed his helmet so that he could more easily sit behind the wheel. He hadn't driven much since his army days and it was something he enjoyed.

Caroline said, "Oh Peter, you've just missed Victoria," automatically assuming that he always came to the house to see Victoria, the woman he had carried a torch for since adolescence, rather than anyone else.

"No, it's you I came to see," he said, and Caroline smiled. "Look, I...er...just wanted to say that...please bear in mind...today...that this investigation is only sanctioned by me...Sir Edward doesn't know anything about it yet. So... please...um...curb your enthusiasm today, Caro. Defer to Sergeant Tollman in all things."

The smile disappeared from Caroline's face and she said icily, "Well I am terribly sorry if you think I am too enthusiastic for this work, Peter!" she glared at him and he felt his stomach shrivel as he realised that, yet again, he had bungled everything when it came to speaking to a woman.

"Look, I'm sorry...I didn't mean to imply...it's just that, sometimes you can be a bit headstrong," he trailed off, unable to find the right words.

Caroline lowered her voice to a malevolent hiss. "I assure you that I shall act with perfect decorum today. What did you think I was going to do? Tear off my stockings and run amok in Wanstead Flats?" with a final glare, she flounced into the car and stared stonily ahead, her cheeks flushed with anger.

Tollman, who was a veteran of female grievances, looked at Beech with despair. Now, the occupants of the vehicle were facing a journey where the atmosphere was going to be several degrees colder than the Russian front in winter.

The car pulled away, leaving a dismayed Beech standing on the pavement. He had known Caroline all his life and he knew how long she could bear grudges. For all his good intentions, the day had not started well.

Fortunately, Billy was buoyed up by the thrill of being behind a steering wheel again and, by the time the vehicle had reached Piccadilly Circus, he was relaying his friend Sam's tales from the night before. Pretty soon, even Caroline thawed, everyone started chuckling and Tollman sent up a silent prayer for Billy Rigsby and his engaging personality.

***

It took a good two hours to get to Wanstead, even with Tollman's encyclopaedic knowledge of London roads and shortcuts. One of the problems was that traffic seemed to have increased of late with army vehicles and large commercial lorries. The government had added to the omnibus fleet as well and the trams in East London, although all-electric now, were especially slow. Horses and carts still wove in and out of the motorised transport because many traders found a horse more reliable than a motor vehicle, especially as many parts required for repair were German and, therefore, unobtainable. So, London seemed exceptionally busy. War had made it so.

Once they passed Stratford, though, and the rows of back to back houses that had sprung up in the Victorian era to follow the expansion of the train system, the urban surroundings gave way to bleak countryside – heathland, with gorse and heather – a sign of the reclaimed acid marshland beneath the grass. Eventually, thanks to Tollman's piece of paper and roughly drawn map, they came upon a series of buildings, in the middle of nowhere, bearing a sign that said H.MASON & CO. CHEMICAL WORKS.

Over in an area, at least 100 yards from the buildings, was a collection of men, who were huddled together having a smoke. Tollman assumed that they were only allowed to light up a cigarette or pipe some distance away from the factory, due to the explosives. He turned to Caroline and Mabel.

"Now ladies, I'm afraid I am going to have to ask you to stay in the car – and I have to be strict about this. You cannot enter the factory without the necessary security clearance, which Constable Rigsby and I have. I do not want you wandering about on this heathland because it is very remote, and we won't know where you are, if you get into trouble." He sensed that Caroline was about to protest, so he also added, for good effect, "There are adders on these lands. One bite from them can be fatal, as I'm sure you know, doctor." Billy smirked. He knew that Tollman was deliberately frightening the two ladies into being obedient. Caroline obviously thought better of speaking and nodded. Mabel looked a little concerned.

Tollman reached under his seat and produced a pack of cards, which he held out towards the women.

"Police vehicle," he explained. "Always carry playing

cards to while away the long hours of waiting for a suspect or waiting to pick up a high-ranking officer from his long luncheon. So," Tollman continued, "I would be grateful if you two ladies could have a little game of cards whilst we are in the factory. I doubt that we will be long. We just want a quick look around and an address for the deceased." He handed over the cards before exiting the car with Billy.

At the intimidating sight of Billy Rigsby, in police uniform, towering over the motor car, all the smokers in the huddle hastily stubbed out their cigarettes, emptied their pipes and hurried back to towards the buildings. The two policemen walked resolutely behind them.

Caroline held up the cards and said to Mabel, "Beggar-my-Neighbour or Rummy?"

***

Tollman and Rigsby entered, what seemed to be, the main shed of H.Mason & Co. As soon as they stepped over the threshold the smell of several chemicals hit their nostrils. Billy instinctively put his hand over his mouth and nose and his eyes began to water. Tollman began clearing his throat and produced a handkerchief to cover his mouth. Several of the workers looked across at them and grinned. They were obviously used to the pungent odours. The heat in this part of the building was tremendous – particularly from the left side, where a large industrial oven appeared to be operating.

Tollman stopped a man, who appeared to be rolling a large bale of cotton along the floor, asked where they could find the General Manager and was directed to the office that was at the back of the shed. Rigsby noted that large wooden doors led off the main shed, either side, and they were kept firmly shut.

The large bales of cotton were being shredded by a group of men and a few women and tossed into trays, which were being loaded into another industrial oven on the right hand side. This oven appeared to be cold at the moment, It wasn't a noisy factory, Rigsby noted, and he realised that it was because there was no sound of conversation, laughter or banter, like there had been in the cartridge filling sheds at Woolwich. The heat in this building may have been suffocating, but the atmosphere was cold, very cold, and he saw very few smiles from the workers.

Tollman knocked on the door of the office and hearing the command "Enter", stepped in, with Rigsby behind him.

"Mr Mason?" he enquired of a short, bald man with glasses, who looked distinctly nervous at the sight of a police uniform.

"There is no Mr Mason," said the man, glancing at Tollman's warrant card. "The factory was bought by a consortium just before the war, from the Mason family. They just kept the name. My name is Arnold Bradshaw, General Manager. What can I do for you?"

Tollman held up the picture of the deceased woman and Bradshaw looked aghast. "Agnes Whitlock!" There was no doubt that he recognised her, and he stared in disbelief at the picture. "What happened?"

"She was found dead, about a week ago, in Mayfair."

"Mayfair?" Bradshaw looked shocked. "What was she

doing in Mayfair?" He seemed genuinely puzzled and... something else. Tollman fancied he was flushing a little and a fine mist of sweat had appeared on his face.

"Are you alright, sir?" Tollman asked with a note of concern in his voice.

"What?" Bradshaw seemed transfixed by the picture of Agnes. "Yes, yes. It's just the shock and the heat from the drying ovens. The other oven will be starting up soon. Shall we step outside... er...detective...?"

"Detective Sergeant Tollman, sir. Yes by all means..."

Bradshaw opened a back door, which appeared to lead from his office into a courtyard at the back of the factory, and he motioned the policemen to follow him to a modest sized building at some distance from the rest. "Our very rudimentary canteen," he said by way of explanation. "We're so remote here that we have to offer something in the way of refreshment during shift breaks. I feel in need of a restorative cup of tea, Sergeant Tollman, and I'm sure you and the constable would like one too."

"I never say no to a brew," said Tollman affably, as he stepped through the door of what was a glorified shed, with about six tables, thirty chairs and some benches. There was a smell of frying in the air.

"Chips," said Rigsby appreciatively.

"Phyllis!" bawled Bradshaw and a harassed older woman in an apron appeared from a back room.

"Yess, sir?" she asked, without any enthusiasm.

"Three mugs of tea, as fast as possible, and bring the sugar out. I've had a shock." He slumped down into a chair, whilst Phyllis' open mouth, as she gazed at Billy in his uniform, betrayed her surprise.

"Yes, sir" she said feebly before turning back into her kitchen.

Tollman and Rigsby sat opposite Bradshaw and both started taking notes.

"So, Mr Bradshaw, how long had Miss Whitlock been working for the company?" Tollman started his line of questioning.

"About two months."

Phyllis appeared with a tray of mugs, steaming with hot tea and sugar, which she put down on the table, "I've already put the milk in" she said, and produced spoons from her apron pocket.

"Where are the biscuits, Phyllis?" said Bradshaw testily.

"You didn't ask for biscuits!" Phyllis glared at him.

"Well I'm asking now!"

Phyllis tutted and went off again. Rigsby supressed a grin.

"Women!" muttered Bradshaw with feeling. "Such difficult creatures! And the Government wants us to employ more!"

Phyllis returned with a plate of biscuits and put them down on the table with obvious lack of grace. It was plain that she did not find Mr Bradshaw a congenial person at all.

Tollman watched the sullen Phyllis disappear and said, "Was Miss Whitlock a difficult employee?"

Bradshaw ladled five teaspoons of sugar into his mug and stirred his tea fretfully. "If truth be known, she...could be difficult," his voice took on a confidential tone. "She caused a deal of trouble in the cordite room…that's where she was employed…cutting up the finished product - and that's where most of our women work. She was trying to get them interested in joining some union. And that didn't make her popular with the shop stewards of the men's union. And she was always snooping around. I caught her once in my office. I came back early from my lunchbreak and she was in there, where she had no right to be. Some of the men said she was always asking questions and she would often ignore the company rules."

"In what way?" Tollman interrupted.

"Well, she would go into places where the women have been told not to go. Like the nitro-glycerine shed. Very dangerous place. You have to be specially trained to handle that stuff. And sometimes she would go to the loading bays, where the cotton bales and drums of acids are unloaded, and the finished gun cotton and cordite are loaded for the filling factories. The women are told not to go there. It's not a fit place for women. Men are sometimes stripped to the waist, the language can get a bit ripe and we also employ a few black men in there."

Rigsby raised an eyebrow and wanted to speak but Tollman gave one of his small shakes of the head which meant "Leave it."

"I see. And when did Miss Whitlock last report for work, Mr Bradshaw?" Tollman asked smoothly.

"About a week ago. I'd have to look at the punch cards. I was a bit annoyed when she didn't turn up but, frankly, she was no great loss," he said without a trace of guilt.

"Did she have any friends in the cordite room?"

Bradshaw sniggered. "Not her. Most of the women found her a bit preachy. Always going on about worker's rights and so on. She got on their nerves."

"I take it you have an address for Miss Whitlock, Mr Bradshaw?"

Bradshaw nodded. "In the office. She lived over Stratford way. Alone. Most of our women share accommodation – we have an arrangement with various local landladies – but she wanted to sort out her own accommodation. How did she die?" he asked, suddenly nervous again, "I mean it can't have been anything to do with the work here. We have stringent safety standards, you know."

"She was stabbed."

"Oh. Terrible," was Bradshaw's response, trying to look regretful, yet managing only to look relieved.

✳✳✳

Mabel had won three games of Rummy in the time Tollman and Rigsby had been in the factory and Caroline silently vowed never to play cards with her again, unless she was partnering her for Bridge. So, when Tollman startled them by getting into the car, both women felt a sense of relief that, now, they might be called upon to do some work.

Billy took his helmet off and folded himself into the driving seat once more, whilst Tollman explained that Agnes Whitlock had, indeed, worked at H.Mason & Co., he had an address for her and, according to the General Manager, she was not particularly well-liked and wouldn't be missed.

"Which probably gives us a large pool of suspects to work through," Tollman finished, with a degree of irritation. "Anyway, first things first, ladies, you must do your examination of Miss Whitlock's room."

So, Billy turned the car around and off they went to Stratford New Town. As they left behind the bleakness of Wanstead Flats, they began to slow down to negotiate the narrow streets with their back to back houses, interspersed with large factories. It was a busy and thriving area. Women were scrubbing their doorsteps, small children were playing in the streets. Caroline smiled as she watched three small girls squabbling over who should push a precious pram and then, later in the street, grubby little boys were playing 'jacks' on the pavement. Billy came slowly to a halt by a row of terraced houses that were larger than most – three stories, rather than two – and built of a different brick from the others.

"Church housing," said Tollman by way of information. "Specifically designed to be inhabited by workers at the various factories."

Everyone got out of the car and unloaded all Mabel's bags and baskets, whilst a group of women stopped their chatter and stared in curiosity. Children stopped their play and Caroline could see that they were pointing at Billy. When he stamped his foot and gave them a salute, all the women and children started laughing, Confident that the police were not here to arrest anyone, the business of the street resumed.

The front door was open, so the four of them ascended the stairs until they came to Room 6, which was Agnes

Whitlock's poky attic room. Tollman produced the key and they all held their breath, hoping that it would fit the lock. It did.

Mabel asserted herself. "It's going to be very small in there and the less people we have disturbing the room the better, So I suggest, Sergeant Tollman, that you and Constable Rigsby, wait for us in the car."

Tollman gave her an old-fashioned look as he handed over the key to Room 6. "As you say, Miss Summersby. You're the expert." Mabel flushed but Caroline could tell that she was secretly pleased that she was being deferred to by Tollman.

"We'll leave you to it then, ladies," Tollman said cheerfully, as he descended the stairs, with Billy following. "Let us know if you need any help."

When they got outside to the car, Billy was about to open the door when Tollman said, "As we parked up, I noticed a pub on the corner, with a perfect view of this front door. As it's such a nice day, I say we take ourselves over there, sit outside, and have a pint. What do you say?" Billy agreed that it would be a splendid idea and Tollman replied, "Good, 'cos you're buying," and they set off towards the Bakers Arms at a pace.

***

Agnes' Whitlock's room was spartan, to say the least. There was a single bed, a chest of drawers and a row of pegs on the wall, upon which hung some basic clothing. Caroline looked puzzled.

"This does not look like the room of someone who could afford Rene LaJeune fashion and possessed a hallmarked silver evening bag that must have cost a pretty penny."

Mabel, who knew very little about fashion said she would bow to Caroline's superior knowledge on the matter. They both donned their gloves and Mabel set about looking through the clothes hanging on the pegs, to see if there was anything in the pockets. Caroline decided to tackle the chest of drawers. She found some expensive silk and lace underwear and held them up to show Mabel.

"Look!" she said excitedly, "Silk! Now why would a factory girl be wearing silk underwear."

"Sergeant Tollman did say that Miss Whitlock was middle-class, according to her previous employers in Woolwich." Mabel reminded her. "It's not so unusual for middle class women to work in factories now and there is no reason for her not to wear her preferred underwear, which she may have bought before the war." The answer was so sensible, that it deflated Caroline's sense of excitement. So, they both continued searching.

Mabel found a wrapped boiled sweet in one pocket and a piece of paper in another pocket, which had a drawing on.

"Look at this," she showed the paper to Caroline, "What do you think that is?"

Caroline peered at the drawing. "Looks like a sort of triangle, with some words in the centre...Belvedere S.C.?"

"Mm. I shall keep it and investigate," said Mabel, tucking it away in her own pocket.

Caroline turned back to ferreting amongst a drawer full of stockings and she found a printed card.

It bore a name and address:

**"Universel Import Co.
Kronprinsensgate 42
Kristiansand"**

She showed it to Mabel who ventured, "Kristiansand, Norway? Yes, Norway, I think. Interesting. We should definitely keep that," and Mabel tucked it away in her skirt pocket with the piece of paper.

Suddenly, the door opened wide and they were astonished to be confronted by a tall man in naval uniform, flanked by two naval police carrying rifles. Both women gasped.

"May I ask what you are doing here, ladies?" the man said abruptly.

Caroline flushed and replied, "We might ask you the same question!"

The corner of the man's mouth lifted in a grudging smile.

"I am Commander Todd from the Admiralty Trade Division and I am here on a matter of national security. Do you know where Agnes Whitlock is?"

"I am sorry to tell you, Commander, that Agnes Whitlock is dead. She was stabbed in Mayfair a week ago," Caroline said, matter-of-factly.

The Commander's face clouded over, and he replied curtly, "Then, ladies, I am afraid I must insist that you accompany me to Whitehall. I am formally placing you under arrest."

CHAPTER EIGHT

THE BIG GUNS AT THE ADMIRALTY

Billy had just walked out of the pub with two full pint glasses when Tollman shouted "Oi! Police! Stop right there!" and began to run across the road.

Billy dumped the glasses on the pavement and ran after Tollman when he realised what was happening. Dr Allardyce and Miss Summersby were being escorted out of the front door of the house and towards an automobile on the other side of the road. A man was following with all of Mabel Summersby's bags and baskets and all the men were wearing naval uniform.

The man carrying Mabel's stuff appeared to be in charge and said loudly "This is nothing to do with you!" as they continued to walk to the automobile and load the ladies into the back.

Tollman waved his warrant card as he arrived, out of breath from his sprint, and said belligerently, "It bloody well does have something to do with me! Detective Sergeant Tollman. These ladies are under my protection!"

The Commander stopped and look at the two policemen. "Are they?" he said with a note of interest in his voice. "Are they indeed? Well, gentlemen, they are now in the custody of the Admiralty Trade Division."

"You can't do that!" Billy protested.

"I'm afraid I can, constable. Powers of war and all that. This is a matter of national security and I am not at liberty to discuss the matter with you." His voice brooked no argument.

Caroline had rolled down the window of the car and called out "Mr Tollman! Call Peter!"

"Yes, I will, doctor!" he turned to the Commander, "Where are you taking them?"

"Our offices in the Admiralty buildings in Whitehall," was the answer, and then the Commander asked, "Who is Peter?"

"Chief Inspector Peter Beech, Scotland Yard. These ladies are here at his request."

The Commander looked amused. "Are they, by God! Right, well you'd better get your Chief Inspector to come around to my office – the name is Commander Todd. I will refrain from questioning the ladies until your Chief Inspector is there. I'm prepared to observe the niceties. We shall give them a cup of tea and keep them comfortable until he arrives. Tell him to call round in about an hour and a half. We should be back in Whitehall by then."

With that, he turned on his heel, passed all the bags and baskets to one of his men, to be loaded in the boot, and got in the car. Caroline waved forlornly as the car pulled away.

"Billy! Get the car going! There's a police station two streets across. I need to telephone Mr Beech immediately."

As they pulled away from the kerb, they noticed that two of the women who had been gossiping in the street had discovered their abandoned pints of beer and were helping themselves. As the car passed them, they gave the policemen a 'thumbs-up' and a two large grins.

**

Beech felt something akin to panic when Tollman had telephoned. It was possible that all the work of the Mayfair 100 team would now be open knowledge in Whitehall and the Commissioner, Sir Edward Henry, would be furious at such carelessness. And yet, he was curious as to why the navy was involved. As he strode out along Millbank towards the Houses of Parliament, he reflected on the struggle that was going on amongst the armed services to control various administrative aspects of the war. The creation of the new Ministry of Munitions had been a huge slap in the face for both the army and the navy because it had highlighted not only their incompetence at dealing with procurement from the munitions industry but also their counter-productive competitiveness with each other.

The navy had always regarded themselves as 'the Senior Service' and resented the army trying to compete to organise the war – which was ridiculous because the navy had very little experience of managing land warfare. But the one area in which the navy had always been superior was that of intelligence. Military intelligence had tended to confine itself to matters of the strength of the enemy, deployment of troops, type of armaments and location of military bases. The navy, on the other hand, over the centuries, had widened its scope to cover all matters domestic and foreign that might impact on Britain's supremacy at sea. This, of course, included merchant traffic and, presumably was why this Trade Division, described by Tollman, was poking its nose into the munitions industry.

When Beech arrived at the address in Whitehall he had been given, his feeling of panic had abated, and he resolved to immediately question why the Admiralty was treading on the toes of the Metropolitan Police in a murder enquiry. It wouldn't do to be intimidated by some shady department of the navy, he thought to himself. This is a police matter.

Caroline and Mabel were sitting, defiantly, in a waiting room, around a table with empty cups of tea in front of them. They both looked relieved when Beech appeared on the other side of the glass partition, but then dismayed when the armed guard at the door of their room refused Beech entry.

Commander Todd strode out of his office and shook hands with Beech.

"The Commander is quite dashing," observed Mabel, "and every bit as tall as Mr Beech."

Caroline looked in Mabel in astonishment, never having heard her comment on the looks of any man before. "I suppose he is," she said, after consideration. "But rather too sure of himself for my liking." Nevertheless, she found herself comparing Peter against the Commander and feeling that Beech could benefit from some of the confidence that Todd displayed.

The two men then went into Todd's office and shut the door. Caroline felt immediately cross.

"I think it's extremely impolite of them to be discussing us without us being present."

✳✳✳

Tollman fretted all the way back to the centre of London. He blamed himself for not spotting the other automobile that had been parked further down the street in Stratford. And not spotting the occupants, in navy uniform.

"How did I miss them?" he asked Rigsby, not really expecting an answer. "I'm losing my sharpness, that's the problem. This team lark is making me into a soft copper."

Rigsby felt he had to say something. "It was out of the blue, Mr Tollman. You can't be blamed. I mean who would have ever expected that the bloody navy would have an interest in a woman who worked in a factory."

"Ah," Tollman responded with an air of conspiracy, "to me that is proof positive that Agnes Whitlock was engaged in spying. We'll probably find out that, in reality, she had a German name, and she was reporting back to the Kaiser all along."

"So, wouldn't that make her someone who should have been arrested by the coppers in Special Branch?" Billy countered.

Tollman's face took on an expression of distaste. "Special Branch?!" There was no mistaking his opinion of that section of the police force. "When we humble police were running about like lunatics trying to combat every single devious and criminal stunt cooked up by the suffragettes, we argued that Special Branch should be covering them. They were terrorists, we argued, and we need proper intelligence on their movements." Tollman's tone got more strident. "But, oh no! They didn't have time. 'We have our hands full dealing with the Irish Republican Brotherhood' they said, and they're still obsessed with them. They recruited a load of Irish coppers to do undercover work and they're sticking with that. They should be recruiting German speaking detectives, shouldn't they? They should be getting information from the people living here who came from Austria, Hungary and Germany."

"Well they might be," replied Billy. "You don't know. No-one knows what Special Branch gets up to. It's all hush hush."

Tollman grunted and the rest of the journey passed in silence, as Tollman nursed his grievance with Special Branch, the navy and the rest of the world but, really, he was most aggrieved with himself.

***

The first thing that Commander Todd said, when Beech sat down in his office was, "Your ladies have refused to co-operate with us. You have trained them well."

Beech pretended to be puzzled. "I'm sorry...I don't understand..."

Todd leant forward and said confidentially, "Look, Beech, cards on the table. The women who work for you were investigating the woman who worked for us." Beech felt a tremendous sense of relief as Todd continued. "I understand, I do. The police won't countenance women officers, and neither will the navy – but, sometimes, a woman investigator can achieve far more than a man, which is why we used Agnes Whitlock. We had permission to do so, as long as we kept it confidential from the rest of the service."

Beech nodded. "Yes. The same for us. But what was this woman investigating for you?"

Todd produced a bottle of whisky from his desk drawer

and two glasses. He poured, handed a glass to Beech and began his story.

"The navy is running a blockade in the North Atlantic – stopping any merchant vessels that they suspect may have illegal cargoes destined for Germany. It's a dangerous job. The seas around that part of the coast are treacherous and the German U boats are always on patrol. Last October we lost 525 sailors from one U boat strike. Anyway, we were able to supply some intelligence to the officers manning the vessels on the blockade about certain ships that we felt were carrying cargo meant to aid the enemy. The navy ships are supposed to stop the suspect vessel, escort it to the Orkney Islands and impound the cargo. I won't go into the whole confiscation procedure just suffice to say that the officers on the navy ships running the blockade, started to complain to us that their actions were being countermanded."

Beech looked puzzled. "I'm sorry, I'm not with you."

Todd said quietly, "They were receiving instructions via the Foreign Office to return the cargoes to certain merchant ships and let them proceed. Now, we have a suspicion that there is some sort of cartel, involving very prominent people in government, that is, at the moment, making a lot of money out of selling stuff to the Germans which directly aid their war effort – and by that we mean materials used in munitions. The biggest problem is that highly placed people in the government refuse to remove cotton, oil and rubber from the free-to-trade category, which is a nonsense. They are all products used in the manufacture of munitions."

"Good Lord!" Beech exclaimed. "You really believe that

men in the government are making money at the expense of our troops?!"

"Oh, I'm sure of it," answered Todd grimly. "We just need absolute proof of this, in order to put a stop to it, and put pressure on the government to change the trade agreements with neutral countries. We think that Agnes was about to uncover that proof but then we lost communication with her. And now, we discover that she was murdered. Probably, because she was getting very close to the truth."

**

Beech took a deep breath before he entered Sir Edward Henry's office. Explaining the situation that had cropped up was going to be hard and he had decided to tell it in reverse order so that the 'grave danger to national security' element was foremost in in the Commissioner's mind when Beech explained the Mayfair 100 team's involvement.

Fortunately, Sir Edward was not a man given to interruption and, aside from the occasional raised eyebrow and look of astonishment, he allowed Beech to fully conclude his explanation.

There was a silence when Beech finished and he was aware that the back of his neck was damp with nervous sweat.

"Good Lord," was Sir Edward's understated reaction. "It would seem that Dr Allardyce and Miss Summersby have uncovered a nest of vipers. Extraordinary."

Beech felt his body relax and his breathing become less shallow. Sir Edward seemed to be thinking.

"So, what is the plan, Beech?" Sir Edward continued casually. "What do the Admiralty Trade Division want of us?"

"They want to use our ladies to investigate further the death of their agent, Agnes Whitlock, and our men, including me to help investigate this pro-German cartel."

Sir Edward nodded and seemed amenable, which rather surprised Beech. He had expected more resistance.

"I have a great deal of experience of trade, as you know," observed Sir Edward, referring to his past career in India. "I know how corrupt people in high places can be…and also how ruthless. I suspect that it is not a pro-German attitude that is the cause of all this, but purely a love of profit. It is astonishing the lengths that some men will go to in order to make money… and being a member of the aristocracy does not preclude them from such avarice."

Sir Edward looked at Beech intently and Beech realised, in that instant, that the Commissioner knew, or had suspicions, as to who might be involved in this cartel.

"Are there any particular individuals in government that might warrant our special investigation?" Beech asked tentatively.

Sir Edward shook his head. "I cannot be specific at this moment. I have heard rumours – but nothing more than that. I do not feel that I should point you in any direction until the evidence you uncover marks the way, so to speak."

Beech felt frustrated at Sir Edward's caution. *Dammit! If he knows something, why doesn't he just say?*

Sir Edward continued. "I should like to be involved in the meeting that determines your team's next course of action and I believe that Captain Webb, the Director of the Admiralty Trade Division, should be present as well. So, Beech, I want you to gather your whole team, including your redoubtable ladies in Belgravia, for tomorrow morning, and I shall personally telephone Lady Maud to ask if she can host all of us. I think we must move quickly on this one."

CHAPTER NINE

SEA AND CITY UNITE

All the Mayfair 100 team looked nervously at each other. Not a word had been spoken since they had exchanged small pleasantries upon arrival. Caroline and Mabel had been unable to tell them anything, other than they had been arrested, taken to the Admiralty, Beech had arrived, spoken to Commander Todd, Beech left, and then they were released.

Tollman and Rigsby had related the trauma of seeing Caroline and Mabel marched off by the navy and Lady Maud had told everyone the news, when she telephoned them the night before, that the Director of the Admiralty Trade Division and the Commissioner of the Metropolitan Police were going to be present for that morning's meeting, which had sent Elsie and Sissy into a flap.

"Else, we're summoned to a meeting in Mayfair and it's a best frock job," Sissy had said when she had put the phone down from speaking to Lady Maud. So, they were there, corsets tightened, in their best outfits and a little flushed, waiting for the great men to turn up.

When the doorbell rang, several of the women were involuntarily startled, and Billy was sent to answer the door. He returned, accompanied by Beech, Commander Todd, Sir Edward Henry and Captain Webb, the surprisingly young Director of the Admiralty Trade Division.

"Are all naval men so dashing?" Mabel murmured to Caroline, with a note of appreciation in her voice.

Caroline gave her yet another surprised look. "Really, Mabel," she whispered back, "I had no idea you admired sailors so much," causing Mabel to blush.

Sir Edward came forward, took Lady Maud's hand and bowed slightly in deference. "Lady Maud, thank you so much for agreeing to host this meeting. May I present Captain Webb, the Director of the Admiralty Trade Division…" Captain Webb inclined his head as he shook Maud's hand, "and Commander Todd, from the same Division." Commander Todd gave a dazzling smile and bowed to Lady Maud. Beech noted that all six women in the room smiled as well.

"Right, well please do be seated gentlemen. Refreshments will be with us in a twinkling of an eye," Maud pulled the bell cord which signalled to the kitchen that tea should be brought up. Billy stationed himself by the door to assist the maid, Mary.

Meanwhile, there were murmurings of conversation, as everyone introduced themselves and negotiated seats for the forthcoming meeting. Beech and Todd chose to stand, but not before the Commander had come across and enquired after the health of Caroline and Mabel and apologised for their arrest. He seemed particularly interested in Caroline, lingering a little longer with her than with Mabel. Victoria was intrigued and sought out Beech.

"The handsome Commander seems very friendly with Caroline," she observed.

Beech feigned disinterest. "Mmm? Does he? Well I suppose anyone bold enough to arrest Caro is probably a good match for her," and he smiled at the thought.

Tea and biscuits arrived and there was much hubbub as Mary and Billy sought to serve everyone present. Sissy was about to get up and help but Billy shook his head. "You're not a servant, Aunty," he said quietly, "You are a valuable member of the team, so sit down."

"You're an even more valuable member of this team," retorted Sissy.

"Yes, and I'm guarding the biscuits," he replied with a wink. "Making sure the greedy buggers from the navy don't make off with the lot.".

Once Mary departed and everyone was catered for, the meeting began.

Beech kicked the first ball. "For the benefit of those who have not been involved in this investigation from the start, I will recap what has happened so far..." He then explained, mostly for the Commissioner and the Director, how Caroline and Mabel's interest in the body of an unknown woman had led to a tentative investigation by Tollman, Rigsby, Caroline, Mabel, Victoria and Lady Maud – culminating in their appearance at the home of Agnes Whitlock and the arrest by Commander Todd.

The Commander then took over and explained, for the benefit of everyone in the room, the serious situation regarding possible war profiteering and treason in high places plus Agnes Whitlock's involvement, as an operative of the Trade Division.

The Mayfair team were shocked – even outraged. Billy seemed stunned that anyone involved with the government could be involved in such a crime and said so. There were several expressions of anger and a general feeling of disgust.

Beech stepped forward once more and raised his hands for calm. "Fortunately, we, collectively, in this room, are in a position to help solve these crimes and, it has been proposed, by both Sir Edward Henry and Captain Webb, that we join forces, as it were, to bring all the people involved in both crimes, to justice."

"Hear, hear," responded Tollman with feeling.

Todd picked up the ball once more. "The reason we put Agnes into various munitions factories was because women are increasingly becoming part of the workforce and, being new on the scene, gives them ample opportunity to ask questions, perhaps without raising suspicion."

Caroline raised her hand to ask a question and everyone noted that this caused the Commander's eyes to light up.

"Yes, Doctor Allardyce?"

"Do you think that Agnes was murdered because she was investigating the profiteering crime or because of something else?"

"Well, that is a good point," was the response from Todd. "Agnes was, shall we say, a fiercely intelligent woman, but a bit prone to rubbing people up the wrong way. She had a bee in her bonnet about working conditions in the munitions industry and had become involved in union activity. In other words, she got distracted from the job she was given, and it is possible that she was murdered for any number of reasons. We also suspect that she might have been involved with some man who worked for Mason's and that she had a scrap with some female employee about it. She was also locked into some permanent conflict with the shop steward of the Amalgamated

Society of Engineers over union issues. Apparently, his union is deeply against women being employed."

"Ah," commented Tollman, "all the usual motives, then, - money, jealousy, revenge…"

Beech chipped in. "Yes, so this makes our job doubly difficult. We need to investigate Agnes Whitlock's murder and also investigate, on behalf of the Admiralty, this business of aiding the enemy."

"And, may I say," Captain Webb suddenly spoke and everyone turned to look at him, "your team has been an absolute gift to our Division because it would have taken us quite a while to replace Agnes, and now we can proceed with all speed, as it is absolutely vital that we stop this traffic of munitions material to the Germans. Every day lost means more of our soldiers and seamen are killed."

"So, what is the plan, sir?" Tollman was anxious to receive some definite instruction.

"Well, we need to get as many of you as we can into the company at Wanstead Flats…" Beech began, "Except for you, Tollman, and Constable Rigsby. You are already known to the general manager there."

"Unless," offered Tollman, "We were to scare him and say that we suspected that several munitions companies were being targeted by German spies and we were posting police officers at every company until the spies are apprehended. That would be a way of getting Billy in there during the day."

"That's not a bad idea, Tollman" Beech seemed heartened by this, "It would provide some protection for the ladies, once we get them in there."

Victoria piped up "Are we all to be munitions workers then?" She seemed quite delighted at the thought.

"No," Todd was quite firm. "We have been down that route before and we don't intend to allow another woman to become ill through munitions work. Agnes suffered continual health problems and I wanted her to stop completely – but she was insistent." He turned to Beech in acknowledgement, "Chief Inspector Beech suggests that there are two areas in which the Mayfair 100 team can be of service. One is – Doctor Allardyce…" he flashed Caroline one of his smiles, which made her feel a little flustered, "a medical team. We will get a factory inspector to go in and insist that the government requires a female medical team to examine all of the female staff, in order to make recommendations for the health and welfare of the workers."

"Good idea! I shall take a week's leave." Caroline was in favour. "Can I have Mabel and Victoria as part of the team? Mabel can process any samples and Victoria can be a nurse. Then we can make a proper job of it."

Everyone agreed. Sissy put her hand up and said nervously, "Do you have a job for us?"

Beech pulled a regretful face, which made Elsie and Sissy look dismayed, when Lady Maud exclaimed loudly, "Lady Londonderry!"

Victoria said "Of course!" and everyone else looked puzzled.

Lady Maud continued, "Didn't you say that this place had a canteen, Mr Tollman?"

Tollman curled his lip, "Of sorts…" he said scornfully.

"One miserable woman and a teapot."

"Well that's it!" Maud looked triumphant. "Victoria and I attended the launch of Lady Londonderry's Women's Legion. The first batch of them are going to be cooks to replace the men in the army and to cook for hospitals. Why don't we fabricate a reason for a couple of Women's Legion cooks – in other words, Sissy and Elsie – to go into the canteen and improve it? I could ask Lady Londonderry for a couple of the uniforms. I'll tell her I plan to promote her little venture at various soirees. What do you think?"

Elsie and Sissy were beaming hopefully and when the men from the Admiralty nodded in agreement, they clapped their hands happily.

"Right up our street, that is Lady Maud! We'll have that canteen running like a Piccadilly restaurant inside a couple of days!" Elsie was delighted and Maud looked pleased with herself for having thought of the idea.

Tollman, however, had mulled over the situation and felt moved to add some more to the picture.

"It strikes me, Mr Beech, that we could do with a certain Ministry of Munitions Dilution Officer, of our acquaintance, to go in and tell the manager of Mason's that the government requires him to do all these things, otherwise he will never agree to it. We know just the man for it, a Captain Wallace. He was very helpful to us when we were pursuing our enquiries over the death of Agnes Whitlock. I think he'd be only too happy to assist us again." Tollman looked at Billy for support, who nodded in agreement.

Once again, the Admiralty men looked suitably

impressed and indicated their pleasure that the Mayfair Team were willing to be as supportive as possible.

Mabel now asked a question. "But, Commander Todd, you haven't actually explained what it is we are looking for, or are supposed to find out?"

There was a small silence as everyone realised that they had been so caught up in the excitement of having a case to work on, that they had not asked the most important question. What exactly were they supposed to find out?

"Well done, Mabel," said Caroline quietly, in appreciation of her friend's total clarity, at all times.

"Yes, yes, of course!" Todd seemed amused by the fact that he had overlooked the most important elements of the case. "There are three elements. Agnes was trying to find out the chain of supply. We suspect that large cargoes of raw cotton are being bought by Mason's from America– which, as you know is a neutral country, so far, in this war. We think that they are coming into the Port of London, unloaded, some of the cotton is going to Mason's but the rest of it is being re-labelled and shipped, ostensibly to Scandinavia – also neutral countries. Finally, it is re-labelled again, then loaded onto trains and sent across the border into Germany, where it is processed into gun cotton for munitions..."

"I think you might need these..." Mabel stood up and retrieved the piece of paper and the card from her skirt pocket and handed them over to Todd.

He looked at them and seemed astonished. "Where did you get these, Miss Summersby?"

"Our search of Agnes Whitlock's room."

Todd gave them to his superior and Captain Webb looked at him in surprise. Then Webb spoke to Mabel with admiration in his voice. "Miss Summersby, you have just given us some very valuable information. This symbol here…" he displayed the piece of paper with the triangle shape and the words 'Belvedere S.C.' "…is the Belvedere Cotton Plantation and Mills in South Carolina. And this card here, is the business card of an import company in Norway, which could very well be the unknown company linked to Mason's, which is processing the cotton on to Germany." Webb looked like a man who had just received a birthday present. "Thank you, Miss Summersby. You may have saved us a great deal of work."

"So, to return to your question," Todd continued, "Firstly, we want you to find out all you can from the women who worked with Agnes Whitlock, as to whether there was any other reason or cause why she was murdered. We need to know, and so do the police, of course, whether it was by the people behind this act of treason or whether it was for another reason altogether. Secondly, we need to know anything you can find out about the business – in particular – who are the real bosses? Who does the manager report to? Who makes the decisions? We know very little."

"I'm not sure that the ladies will be able to do that on their own," observed Tollman. "It strikes me that you need a man in there as well. Billy won't be able to pick up much in his role as watching policeman and I'm known by the manager. Besides, I'm too old to be a labourer. Strikes me you need a big strong bloke in there, working in the thick of it…"

"What about Sam?" Billy volunteered, Sissy and Elsie

loudly agreeing that Sam would be a perfect choice. Billy then explained about Sam Abbott, former docker, his sparring partner and someone who would, probably, be only too glad to help.

For the first time in the meeting, Sir Edward Henry spoke. Fortunately, it was with some amusement. "This team of yours, Beech, seems to grow and grow. Take care that you continue to keep its operation confidential…or we shall all be in hot water otherwise. However," he continued, "this present work is of utmost importance and speed is of the essence. We need as many hands as we can to press into this endeavour."

More tea was summoned, and everyone relaxed into socialising a little more – except for Sir Edward and Captain Webb – who were needed back at their respective helms. They made their apologies and left.

"Well," said Lady Maud to Arthur Tollman, as everyone milled around excitedly, filled with enthusiasm for the job ahead, "It appears that we are surplus to requirements, Mr Tollman." Her voice had a wistful tone.

Just then, an anxious Sissy and Elsie appeared in front of Lady Maud. "Your Ladyship, we have a bit of a problem and we wondered if you could help…"

Maud brightened up. "Anything, ladies, I assure you."

"Well…" Elsie looked hopeful, "It's our little dog, Timmy. If we're going to be working all day, we can't leave him on his own. We wondered if you could possibly look after him for us? He wouldn't be any bother. He's such a good, well-behaved dog…" Elsie was crossing her fingers behind her back, hoping that Timmy really *would* be on his best behaviour.

"Of course!" Lady Maud said magnanimously. "Bring him round here. I shall enjoy the company! And Mr Tollman will take him for walks – won't you Mr Tollman?"

Tollman could see that Sissy was giving him an old-fashioned look which said *If you want to continue to walk out with me on Sundays, you'd better take damn good care of Timmy,* so he smiled with as much enthusiasm he could muster and said "It will be a pleasure, ladies."

"Oh, that's a relief!" Elsie was deeply grateful, and Sissy winked at Tollman warmly.

After the two ladies had left, Lady Maud turned to Tollman and said "So, it seems that you and I are to be foster parents to a small terrier for the duration of this investigation?"

"Yes, Lady Maud, it does," and he gave her a half-hearted smile. Privately he wondered just how long it would take Timmy to wrap both of them round his front paws. *That dog is probably smarter than everyone in this room,* he reflected, with a sense of resignation.

CHAPTER TEN

THE TEAM DESCENDS ON MASON'S

Arnold Bradshaw was not happy. He had had two days of being pushed this way and that by, first, an officious Captain Wallace, who told him that he must employ more women, he must set up a proper canteen and he must allow a medical team to inspect his workers, Then he had spent a day being threatened by Malcolm Sinclair, the shop steward of the Amalgamated Society of Engineers.

"You put any bloody women in any of my member's jobs and I'll bring the lot out on strike," Sinclair had growled.

"Don't make pointless threats, Sinclair," Bradshaw had sneered, in response, "You know that industrial action is outlawed for the duration of the war, so don't try it on."

Sinclair's eyes had glittered, and he had given a mirthless smile. "You know that I can always find a way around that," had been his response. "Let me see…sudden spate of illness might be going around the men…or we might spot an infestation in one of the sheds and the factory will have to close for fumigation…do you want me to go on?"

Bradshaw had swallowed the bitter pill of Sinclair's threats in the past. He knew how easily the union could bring the company to its knees. He was stuck between a rock and a hard place.

So, when the medical team, consisting of three women, turned up in his office, he was not in a good mood.

"Doctor Caroline Allardyce," Caroline was brisk and

efficient, "and this is Miss Summersby, my assistant and Mrs Ellingham, my nurse. We are here at the request of the Factories Inspectorate to do a routine assessment of the health of your female employees." She flourished an official-looking document which had been obtained from the actual Inspectorate after a little pressure from Scotland Yard. "We shall require a room – a private room – in which to conduct our medical examinations. I trust that you have somewhere suitable?"

Bradshaw grunted and led Caroline and the others to a small storeroom. It was barely adequate, having one small window and being rather cramped for the equipment they had brought with them, but Caroline pronounced that "it would have to do." So, they set about instructing the men who had brought them to the factory in an army lorry, to unload a folding screen, an examination table, a desk and three chairs and various smaller pieces of medical equipment. The room quickly filled up.

Victoria noted, however, that the room had the advantage of having a view of the back door that led out of Mr Bradshaw's office into the rear yard, so they would know if he was absent for any period. Commander Todd had expressed the hope that the ladies might be able to search the General Manager's office at some point. Some distraction would have to be arranged, when the team was fully in position.

Whilst the 'medical team' busied themselves arranging the equipment in the storeroom, the workers in the factory were astonished further by a strange procession of people that marched through the factory floor to the manager's office.

Many of them recognised the tall young policeman from a couple of days earlier, as some of the women had been on the receiving end of one of his smiles, and he was accompanied by the shorter plain clothes policeman in the bowler hat, which they also recognised. But behind them was an obviously upper class lady, with an extravagant hat, and behind her were two other women in strange uniforms – long khaki dresses and snood caps with badges. They were carrying bags that seemed to contain kitchen equipment – rolling pins, bowls, pots and pans. As they entered Arnold Bradshaw's office, the factory workers heard an anguished cry of "What now?!!" from the besieged general manager, which made them all snigger.

Tollman took the lead and commiserated with Bradshaw on invading his factory yet again, then he introduced Lady Maud, causing the general manager to look flustered and bow deeply.

"Mr Bradshaw," said Lady Maud, in her best and loudest charity committee voice. "I am here on behalf of the Women's Legion, which has been organised by my dear friend Lady Londonderry. These two ladies – Mrs Potts and Miss Vickers – are from the Cookery Section of the Legion and are here to create a properly functioning staff canteen for your workforce." It had, of course, been necessary to give Elsie Rigsby a false name, for the duration of the investigation.

"Ah, most kind your Ladyship," Bradshaw mumbled, his personal love of food and the possibility of getting a decent lunch for once, outweighing his resentment at having the factory invaded by all these new people.

"However," added Tollman, "Constable Rigsby and I are

here on quite different business, which we may only speak about in the strictest confidence. So, if you would like to escort Lady Maud and the other ladies to show them your present canteen facilities, we will wait here until you return."

Bradshaw nodded and edged his way through the group, indicating that the ladies should follow him, which they duly did.

As they left, Tollman swiftly closed the office door and said "Billy, keep an eye out for matey coming back! Can't waste this opportunity." Billy watched through the window whilst Tollman deftly went through the papers on Bradshaw's desk and made some notes.

In what passed for a staff canteen, Elsie, Sissy and Lady Maud surveyed the kitchen with dismay. When they had entered, Sissy had been unable to refrain from blurting out "Oh my Gawd!" at the sight before her eyes.

"Yes, well I can see that our services are desperately needed, Mr Bradshaw," said Lady Maud in a disapproving tone, which caused Bradshaw to become red-faced and apologetic. The much put-upon Phyllis, meanwhile, stood open-mouthed at the sight of a grand lady and her two khaki-clad attendants.

"What's this all about, Mr Bradshaw?" she asked in confusion.

"Mind your manners, please, Phyllis!" said Bradshaw sharply. "This is Lady Maud Winterbourne, representing the Cookery Section of the Women's Legion. She and her ladies have come to set up a proper canteen. Government orders."

Phyllis' face lit up as she thought she recognised

'liberation' from a hated responsibility. "So, you won't need me no more then, Mr Bradshaw?" she asked hopefully.

"Oh no! Far from it!" Lady Maud was quite firm. "Our ladies are here to help you set up and run a proper canteen. The Women's Legion does not run canteens on a permanent basis – at least, not at the moment."

Phyllis' face fell as she realised that she was not being offered an escape and she resumed her usual taciturn manner. "Fine," she said dismissively.

Lady Maud assumed a fixed smile and said, "Might I have a word with my ladies in private a moment, Mr Bradshaw? Then I can leave them to their work, and you can escort me back to your office."

"Of course," he said deferentially. "Phyllis! Come with me!" Bradshaw grabbed a reluctant Phyllis by the arm and propelled her outside into the yard.

"Blimey, I bet he's giving her a right earful out there," observed Elsie as the door to the canteen slammed behind the manager.

"I'm afraid you seem to have drawn the short straw here, ladies," said Lady Maud, looking around at the grease-encrusted kitchen that barely paid lip service to cleanliness.

Sissy laughed. "Don't you worry, Lady Maud! Elsie and I have cleaned much worse places in our time!"

"Yes!" Elsie agreed. "We'll have this place looking like the kitchens at the Savoy in no time…with food to match!"

Maud smiled. "I have no doubt. I think your biggest challenge is going to be getting friendly with the unhappy Phyllis and seeing what you can find out from her in the way of gossip. That may not be an easy task."

"We'll win her round, don't worry, your Ladyship." Sissy saw no obstacle that couldn't be overcome. "Ooh, would you mind getting Billy to bring in the box of food from the automobile, please? We need to get a nice shepherd's pie going for their lunch."

Lady Maud took her leave, promising that she would faithfully follow the list of their dog's requirements and she stepped out into the yard as Phyllis said in a loud and threatening voice "And don't bleedin' think I won't!" to the harassed Mr Bradshaw who was, by now, puce with fury. Seeing the grand lady, Phyllis gave Bradshaw a last menacing glare, bobbed a quick curtsey to Lady Maud and went back into the canteen shed.

Lady Maud raised an eyebrow at Bradshaw and said "I'm sure that some of these women are quite a trial for you. The working class can be so vocal at times," in her best tone of commiseration and he nodded gratefully. *Really, I should have been an actress,* she thought with some measure of satisfaction as Mr Bradshaw escorted her back to his office.

"On his way back," warned Billy as he observed the progress of Lady Maud and the manager.

"Drat!" was Tollman's response as he closed the drawer he had been about to inspect. His hurried search of the desk had yielded limited information.

Bradshaw stuck his head round the door of his office and said that Lady Winterbourne wanted the young constable to fetch some things from the car. Billy left with Lady Maud and Bradshaw sat down to deal with Tollman.

"What a morning!" Bradshaw complained, "And now I suppose you are going to add to my problems. What is all this 'confidential' matter about?" He was irritable and Tollman had to restrain a smile at the fact that he was about to make the manager a great deal more irritable.

"I'm sorry to say, Mr Bradshaw, that we have had intelligence from Special Branch that a group of German sympathisers are planning attacks on munition facilities."

"What!" Bradshaw's face was a picture of alarm and horror. "Are you sure?"

"I'm afraid so, sir," was Tollman's solemn answer.

"Well why haven't Special Branch just rounded these people up?"

"Ah, it's not as simple as that, sir..."

"No, it never is, is it?"

Tollman leaned forward and spoke confidentially. "The thing is that they want to draw them out into the open, so that they can capture the whole ring of them. Get all of these traitors at once."

"So, what am I supposed to do? Just sit here and let them attack this factory?"

"No, sir," Tollman tried to sound reassuring. "We are proposing to put a policeman on guard at each factory, just to keep an eye on things. They can report back to the Yard if there is any suspicious activity. So, we are proposing to leave Constable Rigsby with you..." Tollman pointed towards the window and Bradshaw turned, to witness Billy effortlessly carrying a very large load of boxes.

"Perhaps he can help out in the loading bay, while he's

here," murmured an impressed Bradshaw.

"I'm sure he'll be only too happy to do so," Tollman replied enthusiastically.

Bradshaw looked unsure but his equilibrium had been assaulted from all sides today and he was on the verge of admitting defeat. At least that was Tollman's assessment of the situation and one that he would happily report to Chief Inspector Beech once he got back to Scotland Yard.

***

Sam Abbott had nervously delivered Elsie and Sissy's dog, Timmy, to Lady Maud's house in Mayfair. He had been almost relieved when the cook, Mrs Beddowes, said everyone was out but she knew all about Timmy coming to stay for a while. Sam was invited in for a cup of tea in the kitchen, which he duly accepted. Timmy had been unusually quiet all morning, being unsure, probably, of what was happening. Although Sam had been taking him out for walks during the past few days, he sensed that something was different today and his usually exuberant personality was subdued.

"Quiet little thing, isn't he?" observed Mrs Beddowes, giving Timmy a pat.

"Not usually, Mrs Beddowes," replied Sam, stirring sugar into his tea. "He can be a right little monkey at times. I think he's just confused today."

"Oh, bless him. Well perhaps this'll cheer him up," she said, going into the cold room and returning with a bone on a metal plate. "The butcher dropped off my order this morning and this nice fresh bone is full of marrow. There we are sweetheart." She put it on the floor, in the corner, and Sam was amused to see Timmy, after a moment's hesitation, crawl across the floor on his stomach and sniff the bone, then attack it with gusto, licking out the marrow as fast as he could.

"Nice cup of tea, Mrs Beddowes, thank you," said Sam, draining his cup. "So, I'll be off back to Belgravia then. I'm expecting a visit from Mr Tollman later."

"Oh, nice man Mr Tollman," Mrs Beddowes said with a smile. If truth be told, she would have been very happy to get much closer to Arthur Tollman but Sissy had caught his eye and Mrs Beddowes had made a strategic withdrawal. Still, she lived in hope. "Give him my best!" she added pleasantly.

"I will," Sam bent down and patted Timmy, "See you later, little fellow." Timmy swivelled his eyes towards Sam, gave a half-hearted wag of his tail but continued his relentless pursuit of bone marrow. "I see you've perked up then!" Sam laughed. "Mind you don't let him run rings around you, Mrs Beddowes!" he said, as he left.

Mrs Beddowes turned to Timmy and laughed. "Oh, it isn't me that's looking after you, Master Timmy. I made it quite clear to her Ladyship that I can't do my work and look after a dog. No, you, young Timmy, are going to be the sole responsibility of Lady Maud."

Then she chuckled again and gave Timmy another pat before she busied herself shelling peas for tonight's dinner.

***

Tollman did not enjoy driving automobiles but, nevertheless, he had no choice when it came to ferrying himself and Lady Maud back to the centre of London from Wanstead Flats. So, the combination of the intense concentration required to navigate the dockland traffic in East London and listening, and responding, to Lady Maud's comments and questions, Tollman found he had a splitting headache when he finally dropped her Ladyship off in Mayfair and continued on his way to Scotland Yard.

Sergeant Stenton was on the main desk when Tollman arrived. "Have you got any of those headache powders handy?" asked Tollman wearily.

Stenton smiled and produced a rectangular piece of folded waxed paper marked "Asprin". "You want a cup of tea and a handful of biscuits to go with that, Arthur. You going in to see Inspector Beech?" Tollman nodded.

"I'll get a constable to fetch some refreshments in right away."

"Thank you, Albert. Now I suppose I'll have to let you win at dominoes."

Stenton laughed. "Well, you're used to losing Arthur."

Tollman grinned and made his way up the stairs to Beech's room to report on this morning's proceedings.

When Tollman knocked and entered, Beech was pacing the floor, which he knew was always a sign that the Chief Inspector was wrestling with a problem. Beech motioned him to sit down and then, finally, sat down himself, to hear about the successful introduction of the team into the munitions factory. Tollman reported that all had gone remarkably well.

The General Manager, Mr Bradshaw had been well-primed by Tollman's friend, the Dilutions Officer, Captain Wallace.

"Bradshaw was bad-tempered about all the government interference but he accepted that he didn't have a choice," Tollman, then he proceeded to make Beech smile – laugh even – when he described Lady Maud's conversation on the way back to London about her involvement in the set up. "Her Ladyship was a real pro, apparently," Tollman said. "She went into that factory with her best hat on and her loudest voice and intimidated Bradshaw right from the off. He was grovelling around her all the time she was there. His nose was practically touching the ground all the time!"

They were both laughing when there was a knock at the door and, surprisingly, Detective Carter, the bent copper that Tollman loathed more than anyone in Scotland Yard, entered with a tray of tea and biscuits.

"Doing tea deliveries now, Carter?" Tollman couldn't resist a jab.

Carter gave a sarcastic smile. "I was coming to ask the Chief Inspector something and I passed a constable carrying your tea, so I offered to take it off him."

"Very good of you, Detective Carter," murmured Beech as Carter put the tray on his desk. "Did you want to see me privately or is it something that can wait?"

Carter looked at Tollman and said "No, it's nothing private, sir. In fact it's probably fortunate that DS Tollman is here because he always knows everything that is going on." Tollman's pursed his lips and decided not to respond to the barb. Carter continued, "It's just that me and the lads in CID have heard a rumour that Special Branch are concerned about a possible attack on munitions factories by German sympathisers. I wondered if you knew anything about it, sir?" Carter turned his face towards Beech.

Tollman's blood ran cold. It had taken precisely three hours for the confidential conversation with the General Manager of Mason's to reach the ears of Detective Carter. But, at the same time, Tollman felt a surge of exhilaration. This was proof that they were on the right track. Mason's was obviously linked to some very powerful and corrupt people. Exactly the sort of people that Detective Carter had cultivated in his career at Scotland Yard.

Beech feigned disinterest, as he fiddled with the tea things, and he responded to Carter by saying, "No, I'm afraid I know nothing about any such problem, Detective Carter. I'm flattered that you think that I am privy to Special Branch operations – however, I can assure that I am not. They keep their cards very close to their chest at all times. Was there anything else?"

"No sir. Thank you, sir," Carter gave Tollman a searching look, as if hoping to find some element of guilt in his face but obviously found nothing and he left.

Beech was about to speak, when Tollman put a warning finger to his lips and sprang up to listen at the door. After about a minute, he heard Carter's footsteps going down the corridor and he opened it a crack to satisfy himself that Carter was indeed disappearing out of sight.

"Crafty bleeder was listening at the door," he said quietly as he resumed his seat. He opened the packet of powdered aspirin, emptied it into his mouth, took a large swig of tea to wash it down and then shuddered. "Gaah, that tastes horrible!" he said, eating a biscuit to get rid of the taste. His head was pounding more than ever.

"It seems we have a problem, Tollman," said Beech.

Tollman nodded and swallowed the last of his biscuit. "Yes, sir, it does. However, it proves that Agnes Whitlock was right. Mason and Co. is involved in some shady business. Bradshaw must have phoned his anonymous masters after I left and told them that the police were going to be around for a while, and Carter must have been contacted by these people to find out what he knows."

"Supposing he goes straight to Special Branch?" Beech was a little anxious.

Tollman smiled grimly. "He won't, because they hate him more than we do. But, I might have a little word with my contact there and intimate that if Carter does come sniffing around that we are actually running an operation to entrap some crooked cops – namely Carter – and ask them if they could tell him nothing but, at the same time suggest that there is something going on. The only problem is that the real villains may decide to lay low for a while and we won't be able to stop this treason."

"They won't," said Beech firmly, which caused Tollman to raise an eyebrow. "Because Commander Todd told me this morning that they have investigated the line of supply, based on the information Miss Summersby found, and they now know that a large cargo of cotton waste is on route from America, for Mason & Co, expected to arrive at Victoria Docks in two days' time and unload shortly after that."

"So, they will have to see it through," was Tollman's gleeful response. He could already taste a successful conclusion to the case in hand.

"Yes," Beech agreed, "and this is something that I wanted to talk to you about, Tollman…" he hesitated, looked uncomfortable and Tollman wondered if this was the reason that his boss had been pacing the floor when he came in. "Do you think that you could assume full responsibility for this operation?" Beech took a deep breath, "because I would like to go to Norway with Commander Todd, so that I can confirm, on behalf of the Metropolitan Police, that this cargo is being sent onwards to Germany."

CHAPTER ELEVEN

NO-ONE LIKED AGNES

Word had definitely gone around Mason's factory that Agnes Whitlock had been murdered. Elsie and Sissy discovered that from Phyllis as they casually chatted whilst cleaning the kitchen and preparing the lunch.

At first, Phylllis had been surly and unco-operative but, eventually, she was overcome by the relentless cheer of the two women who had come to set up a 'proper canteen.' By the time the three of them had scrubbed every trace of grease from the walls, tables, oven and floors – and burst into a quick rendition of, "Oh Mr Porter"…whilst cutting up onions and potatoes – the three women were firm friends.

"So, what's the story about this woman being murdered?" asked Sissy casually as she was frying up the mince for the shepherd's pie.

"Oh, you've heard about Agnes, have you?" Phyllis seemed surprised.

"That policeman told us when we got here, confidential like, that someone had been murdered and we should watch our backs," said Elsie conspiratorially. "Fair put the wind up us, it did. I think he was only trying to be helpful…but still… it gave me the collywobbles", she tried to give the impression that she was worried about it.

"Nah, nothing to worry about," Phyllis replied dismissively. "I'm sorry to say it but that Agnes Whitlock was her own worst enemy. She rubbed so many people up the wrong way, I'm surprised it didn't happen sooner. Anyway, she wasn't murdered here. Somewhere up West, Mr Bradshaw said."

"Oh?" Sissy transferred the tons of browned mince to several large metal baking pans. "Well, Phyllis, after I've made the gravy and we've put them onions and tatties on this mince, and it's all in the oven, we'll have to have a sit down with a cup of tea and you can tell us all about this unfortunate girl that got murdered."

Phyllis smiled at her two new friends and nodded.

This is going to be easy, thought Elsie, with some satisfaction, as she winked at Sissy.

∗∗∗

Victoria, dressed smartly in her nurses' uniform, was picking her way through the factory, to the cordite shed. Unfortunately, she had to endure endless sniggers, winks and comments from the men working on the cotton ovens and generally labouring in the main factory.

"Nurse! Nurse! Would you come and have a look at my bad back?" called out one young man, showing off for his workmates, who all laughed. Victoria ignored them – and the wolf whistles that came from various quarters. What she did notice, however, was the amount of rotten or missing teeth on display, and also evidence of bowed legs, from childhood rickets. The men were strong, able to carry heavy loads and work in the tremendous heat of the main shed, but they were thin and malnourished. Some of them, she suspected, looked older than their years. In between the wolf whistles and cheeky comments, she had noted several chesty coughs. This work is possibly not good for the lungs, she thought as she tried, in vain, to brush clinging cotton fibres from her skirt.

Although her brief was to summon the women in the cordite shed first, she took mental note of the women in the main shed, sitting around a giant bale of cotton and picking it apart for the oven trays. She would tell Caroline that these women must be examined too. She knew that Caroline wanted to do a proper job of inspecting the female staff at the factory, even though they were there under false pretences.

Finally, she arrived at the cordite shed and, as she opened the door and stepped into the room, she noticed that the hum of conversation amongst the women stopped and she found herself being scrutinised by forty pairs of eyes.

The only woman on her feet came forward with a wary look on her face.

"I'm the supervisor, Mrs Hawkesworth, how can I help you?"

Victoria extended her hand and said "Mrs Ellingham, how do you do?"

There was a collective, sarcastic, "Ooh!" mocking, Victoria supposed, her upper class accent. Nevertheless, she continued, "I'm here with a female medical team. We're set up by the manager's office and we are ready to examine your ladies as soon as you care to send them along."

"And supposing we don't want to be examined?" a loud, surly voice came from the end of the room. Without even looking, Mrs Hawkesworth said in an equally loud voice, "Shut up, Myrtle Dimmock, and you'll do as you're told!" Victoria guessed that Myrtle was, as her father, the General, would have said, 'the resident barrack-room lawyer and all-round troublemaker.'

Victoria raised her voice too and announced, "I'm afraid it is compulsory for you to have a medical examination," she lied in her best stern manner. "The government has decided that women in munitions factories must be examined, for their own protection. It will help them make laws to ensure that your health is protected in these factories."

"Well I've not heard anything about this!" A very pretty but aggressive girl stood up at the end of the long working table.

Mrs Hawkesworth lost her patience and bawled, "That's because you can't bloody read, Myrtle! Now sit down and get on with your work!" A few of the women laughed and Myrtle turned pink with embarrassment before sitting down once more. Mrs Hawkesworth turned back to Victoria and asked perfunctorily, "How many do you want at a time?"

"If you could send us a group of four and then when we send them back, send another four? If we work it like that, would that be convenient?"

Mrs Hawkesworth nodded and selected four women at the end of the room. "You four, go with the nurse! Wash your hands before you leave this room." The women dutifully obeyed and Victoria noted the brown staining of their hands and the colour of the water as they scrubbed it off with soap and a small brush.

They followed her through the factory – the men, once

again, cat-calling and making the women from the cordite room laugh, until Bradshaw opened his door in a fury and told the men, in no uncertain terms, that if he heard another comment pass anyone's lips they would be sacked on the spot. The main shed fell silent and Bradshaw went back into his office. Victoria motioned three of the women to sit on the chairs they had provided outside the door of the medical room and she took the first woman inside.

***

Tollman knocked on the front door of the modest terraced house in Battersea and noted, with approval, the pots of plants in bud, ranked on the windowsill and held in place by cast iron protectors. The door was opened by a man in his sixties, who broke into a large grin and held out his hand in greeting.

"Arthur Tollman! As I live and breathe!"

"Hello Eustace. How ya doing, mate?"

"Come in, come in! Got time for a brew, Arthur?

"Always got time for a brew, Eustace! You know me."

Tollman stepped inside the neat hallway and took off his hat. It was just as he remembered it.

Eustace King was, of course, a retired policeman and, now, a private investigator, employed by the legal profession to do 'searches', in other words, dig out any criminal past on their clients or those who were being called as witnesses. He, like Tollman, was a man possessed of great knowledge, picked up and filed away in his very active brain for many years.

Tollman had come, armed with money from Inspector Beech, to ask Eustace to do some work for them.

"It's a follow job, I'm afraid," said Tollman, savouring his freshly brewed cup of tea. "Follow" meant that Tollman wanted Eustace to tail someone and find out where he went and what he was up to.

Eustace nodded. "As long as he's not a sprinter, I think I'm up to that. Who is it?"

"It's a bent copper."

Eustace tutted and shook his head. "I won't be able to do it if it's someone I know."

"You don't know him, Eustace, don't worry about that. He transferred to Scotland Yard after you retired. He's a CID bloke called Carter." Tollman passed over a copy of Carter's official staff photograph.

Eustace looked at the photo long and hard. Then he picked up the teapot and stood up. "I'm going to make a fresh brew and then you can tell me all about what Mr Carter has done and what I'm supposed to find out."

Tollman sank back into his armchair and gave a small smile of contentment. Beech had put him in charge, and he was working with Eustace again, a copper he trusted above all others. Things were just how he liked them.

✳✳✳

Caroline had examined the first four women so far and found that they all had fast heart rates and suffered from regular bouts of dizziness and headaches.

"But only on Mondays, doctor," said one cheerful girl called Emily. "It's what we all call the Monday sickness. Must be the heat and suchlike in this place. It goes away during the day. I always start Mondays with a splitting headache, but it goes."

Mabel, who was busy swabbing Liza's hands with damp cotton wool and putting the samples in glass jars, suddenly asked, "Cordite is made with nitro-glycerine, isn't it?"

Emily was impressed. "Fancy you knowing that, doctor!" With her free hand, she pointed out of the window, into the courtyard. "That's the nitro shed over there." They all looked at the building that was at the far end of the courtyard. "But we're not allowed there. We got told off about it only last month. But that was 'cos Agnes Whitlock was found in there." Emily looked irritated. "She was always sticking her nose in where it wasn't wanted and getting us into trouble."

"Right, that's you finished here, Emily," Caroline said, "You can do up your blouse now. Nurse will take you all back to your workplace. If you just wait outside, please, I would like to have a word with Nurse first."

When Emily had gone, the three women began a discussion about their findings so far.

"It's pretty obvious to me that these women are suffering from the effects of nitro-glycerine. The headaches, dizziness and tachycardia are all obvious when they come in on a Monday morning, after their day off on Sunday, then it adjusts through the week." Caroline was concerned. "I regularly prescribe nitro-glycerine drops to be put under the tongue for patients with heart failure."

"They are absorbing it through the skin on their hands," Mabel held up four labelled jars of cotton swabs, all with distinct brown traces on the cotton. "God knows what dosage they are absorbing during the week. They should be wearing gloves but possibly that would hamper them from doing their job."

Victoria explained that she had watched the girls washing their hands before they came for their medicals and the water had definitely turned brown. "If you don't mind, I'd quite like to make some notes about the cordite process when I go back for the next batch of women."

Caroline agreed but then added, "We don't seem to be getting anywhere with our investigation into Agnes, though."

"Well, Emily told us she was nosy," said Mabel, "but we knew that already."

"I'll see if I can get some information out of the supervisor in the cordite shed," Victoria offered. "She might be willing to gossip a bit."

Just then, Sissy entered with a welcome tray of tea. "Refreshment for the workers!" she said breezily. Then, when she had closed the door she said confidentially, "How's it all going then?"

"Not much so far, I'm afraid," said Caroline, gulping down a cup of tea as though her life depended upon it. "We're finding out quite a lot about the health problems these women have but nothing much about Agnes, so far."

Sissy smiled. "Don't you worry, ladies. Elsie and I have been having a right chin wag with our new best friend, Phyllis, and she's told us plenty about this place and about Agnes. But we'll have to tell you tonight, because we don't have the time now. We're serving up lunch in about an hour and it's all hands to the pump!"

***

Billy Rigsby had decided to station himself in the loading bay of the factory. It was cooler than anywhere else, as it was perpetually open for the deliveries and collections by vans and carts.

He was greeted with suspicion by the men, at first, but his naturally congenial personality quickly won them round.

"So, what are you doing here then?" asked a fairly aggressive Scotsman, who introduced himself as Malcolm Sinclair, shop steward of the Amalgamated Society of Engineers.

"On the look-out for German spies, apparently," replied Billy with a grin. "Only trouble is, mate, I would know a German spy if I fell over one!" and he laughed, to reinforce his chosen image as a clueless beat copper.

Sinclair gave, what Billy imagined was a rare smile. "If you want to know anything about this place, ask me," he said confidently. "No point in asking any of this lot," he waved his hand around the shed, "they're as thick as two short planks and Bradshaw, the manager, is an idiot." Billy caught the look of contempt that one labourer flashed to another. *Strikes me that Mr Sinclair is the idiot,* thought Billy, whilst keeping a fixed grin on his face and nodding amiably. *Too full of his own importance to see what's going on under his nose.* Sinclair continued, "You can usually find me in the main shed, keeping an eye on the ovens. If not there, then I'll be in the nitro-glycerine shed at the end of the yard."

"Thanks, I'll remember that," replied Billy, shaking Sinclair's hand and watching him disappear into the main building. Then Billy turned to the men in the shed and said loudly, "Right! That's me told what's what! So, who really knows what's going on here?" Several of the men laughed and nodded.

One of them said, "My missus knows more about what's going on in this place than Malcolm Sinclair!" and Billy joined in the laughter as he took off his helmet. He saw that several men reacted to the big scar down his face and, quick as a flash, Billy said, "You should have seen the other bloke…bloody great German…took him out with one shot though and my Ma sent the Kaiser a letter thanking him for invaliding me out of the war." The men smiled and nodded and a couple of them came up and patted him on the back. Billy relaxed and took off his jacket. If there was anything to be found out in the loading bay, he would have no trouble talking to the men now.

✳✳✳

Eustace King had been fully briefed by Tollman, and would be shadowing Detective Carter tomorrow, for the day and, possibly, the evening. Tollman badly needed to know Carter's contacts and who, exactly, had telephoned him so quickly about the operation at Mason's.

Tollman's next visit was to Sam Abbott, at the house

in Belgravia. Sam answered the kitchen door and looked hesitant, until Tollman smiled and held out his hand. "Arthur Tollman. You must be Billy's friend Sam. We need to talk."

Over yet more tea, Tollman outlined to Sam the case that they were investigating and explained in detail how Sam could help by being part of the undercover team at Mason's. Sam was agreeable but wondered if he would be able to get a job at Mason's easily.

"Not everyone wants to employ a black bloke, Mr Tollman," he said simply.

"Well, you're in luck there, son," answered Tollman with a grin, as he fished a folded up paper out of his coat pocket. "They already employ some black blokes and I found this."

Sam opened up the piece of paper and it was a notice that Tollman had taken away from a small pile of them on Mr Bradshaw's desk that very morning. "There was a list of pubs that he had ticked off. I checked a couple of them on the way back to the Yard. Bradshaw had circulated these notices around all the pubs within a couple of miles radius of Wanstead Flats."

STRONG, FIT LABOURERS WANTED
AT H. MASON & CO. LTD CHEMICAL WORKS
ON WANSTEAD FLATS

ALL SUBJECTS OF THE EMPIRE ACCEPTED
NO MATTER WHAT SKIN COLOUR

NO TIMEWASTERS
Come to the factory and see Mr Bradshaw

Sam smiled and said, "When do I start, then?"

Tollman nodded with satisfaction and said, "Tomorrow, lad. Here's an Army travel warrant, I've arranged through a friend of mine. A very nice Captain in the Ministry of Munitions – but keep it to yourself. I suggest you get the 6 am train from Liverpool Street to Forest Gate, then it's about a mile hike from there. Here's a map showing where Mason's is in relation to the station. When you get there and he gives you a job, just remember – you don't know Billy, Sissy or Elsie. You've never clapped eyes on them before. Understand?"

"I understand."

Tollman rose and put his hat back on. "Now, if you'll excuse me, I have to go to Lady Maud's and walk that little rascal Timmy." Sam grinned and Tollman shook his hand again. "Welcome to the team, son. Even if it is only temporary."

CHAPTER TWELVE

BEECH SAYS GOODBYE...FOR NOW

At the end of the working day at Mason's, 6 p.m., the regular omnibus appeared at the factory gates to take the workers to Stratford, where they would all disperse to their rented accommodation, or to trains, trams and buses. Billy Rigsby joined the men on the omnibus and endured unwanted attention from some of the women workers. A few of the comments from the younger girls would have made him blush, in other circumstances. They were eventually silenced by a couple of older women. One told them, in no uncertain terms, "that they were behaving like trollops and should go home and wash their mouths out with soap and water!"

Billy nodded and smiled. A couple of the labourers winked at him and grinned. The noise of the girls chattering had subsided, but then it gradually grew again as, released from their daily drudge of almost silent working, the excited but tired female workforce exploded into much-needed verbal communication. The men were mostly quiet, weary and sore from heavy lifting or the heat and the tension of working in the dangerous environment of the explosives shed. Bradshaw was still on the premises and a night security man had arrived at about 5 'o'clock. A burly ex-soldier called Winkler. This he would report to the team when he got back.

The army truck, arranged by Tollman, had arrived at 5, to take the medical team, and Sissy and Elsie, back to London. The normally truculent Phyllis had, by then, formed a close bond with the two women who had transformed her kitchen and she was anxious that they might not come back the next day. Sissy assured her they would. They would be back at 7 a.m. the next morning, ready to dispense tea, dripping on toast and good cheer to the workforce.

*****

A weary group of workers gathered in Lady Maud's parlour and devoured the cold cuts and pickles Mrs Beddowes and Annie had laid out for them. Billy had not yet arrived, as he had left an hour later and was coming back by train.

Elsie noticed that Timmy, whilst he gave them an enthusiastic welcome when they arrived, very quickly went back to Lady Maud's lap. Elsie nudged her sister, "Look at his lordship," she whispered, "He's made himself right at home. He won't want to come back to us."

Sissy raised an eyebrow and whispered back, "Look at him now! Little monkey!" Lady Maud was feeding him small pieces of cold beef and when she stopped, Timmy snuggled further into her lap and decided to have a nap. "Getting ideas above his station, that dog is," muttered Sissy.

Elsie shrugged and replied "Oh well, not much we can do about it. Might as well let him enjoy his little holiday. We'll all be back to normal in a week or so."

Beech arrived, and, to Victoria's astonishment, he was wearing old, baggy trousers and a thick crew neck jumper.

"Peter, you look like an old sailor or something!" she said in surprise. She had never seen him in scruffy clothes before.

"Er…that's rather the idea…" he said sheepishly and then asked if he could have a quiet word with her in private. She followed him out into the hallway, and she noted that there was a rucksack laying in the corner.

"Are you going somewhere?" she asked anxiously, then listened patiently whilst Beech explained that he was going up to Scotland, then on to Norway with Commander Todd, to follow the trail of the cargo.

Victoria was concerned that his health would suffer, and she said so, which seemed to make Beech a little irritable.

"For God's sake, Victoria, I'm not an invalid!" he said sharply, then immediately regretted it. He kissed her gently on the cheek. "I will be careful. I won't take any unnecessary risks. But I must do this."

The doorbell rang and Victoria answered. It was Tollman. He had come from Scotland Yard with some paperwork for Beech to sign. She left them to it.

"You've had a busy day I see, Tollman," said Beech as he signed various papers.

"Yes, sir. I felt I should make provisions in case something happened during your absence. I want to be able to get warrants issued quickly if I need to go into any premises and it seemed advisable to get your signature on as many bits of paper as possible, to avoid hold-ups."

"Good thinking, man."

"Is Billy here yet, Mr Beech?"

"No. But I need to start the meeting now because I have to catch the night sleeper to Scotland."

The two men went into the parlour and the meeting

began. First there was the astonishing news that Beech was leaving them all under the management of Tollman, while he went off to Norway with Commander Todd. There was a short, stunned silence whilst everyone digested this piece of information, then Tollman stepped up and outlined what had been achieved so far.

"So, at Mason's, the medical team is in place, the canteen staff is in place, Constable Rigsby is also in place. Tomorrow, Sam Abbott will be turning up to ask for a job in the loading bay..." At that moment the doorbell rang, Caroline jumped up to answer it and returned with Billy. Tollman nodded at Billy and continued, "As I said, tomorrow Sam Abbott will be turning up to ask for a job as a labourer. Some of you haven't met him but those of you who have..." he nodded at Elsie and Sissy, "must, on no account, give away that you know him. This is very important. We don't want Sam to raise any suspicions." The two sisters nodded in agreement. Tollman looked at Beech, as if asking for permission to continue, and, satisfied that it had been given, he then took a deep breath and tried to inject a strong note of warning into his voice.

"Mr Beech and I discovered, very recently, that there is a breach in our security – namely that the manager of Mason's rang whomever is behind this criminal act – and that person, we believe, then contacted a person in Scotland Yard to query our cover story for Billy..."

"Carter?" asked Billy, with a venomous look.

Tollman nodded and continued. "However, today I employed a skilled investigator – former copper – to follow

Detective Sergeant Carter, in order to find out who he contacts. This, we hope, will lead us to the person who is the real owner of Mason's and organising the criminal activity. However, I need to stress to all of you, that this work has now become a little more dangerous than before and you must all be very, very careful. If you have any worries at all, you must tell Billy, and he will contact me by telephone. I have arranged for the local police at Stratford to be on standby. They can be at Mason's in ten minutes, if there is a problem."

Everyone, in turn, was asked to report on what they had found out during the day. The medical team had uncovered very little to do with the investigation but much about the health problems of the women workers, which was not relevant at this time. Billy relayed his information, which was only that Mason's had a night watchman and Bradshaw had stayed behind after everyone had left.

By far the richest source of information about Agnes Whitlock was from Sissy and Elsie. Constant gossip with Phyllis throughout the day had revealed that Agnes was universally regarded as an irritation because she 'poked her nose in where it wasn't wanted' and she kept trying to get the women to sign up to the National Federation of Women Workers. She particularly ran foul of the militant shop steward, Malcolm Sinclair, who regarded her as a rival. But it appeared that a couple of the girls in the cordite shed were friends with Agnes and, it was said, that she had a 'sweetheart', Peter, who was one of the men in the loading bay. This, apparently, had caused some friction between Agnes and another girl, renowned for her temper, one Myrtle Dimmock.

"Oh, I came across her!" Victoria commented. "She was loudly complaining about everyone having to have medical examinations. By the way the supervisor reacted, I suspect she is a constant troublemaker."

Everyone was tired and Beech had to make a move in order to catch his train, so the meeting, by mutual agreement, broke up.

Caroline noted that Beech gave Victoria a perfunctory peck on the cheek and a brief wave to others, before departing. *He's anxious to start his adventure*, she thought enviously.

Elsie thanked Lady Maud for taking care of Timmy. It had been decided not to take him back to Belgravia every night, as they could be working late, and it was best not to unsettle him. She gave Timmy a pat and he wagged his tail a little but barely opened his eyes in acknowledgement.

"That dog is rapidly turning into a right little lordship," whispered Sissy to Tollman, who smiled in agreement. "I hope you're giving him some good long walks, Arthur, because the way Lady Maud is spoiling him, he's going to be as fat as a pig in a week's time."

***

Todd flopped down in the train seat opposite Beech and laughed. "I'm guessing that you are not too comfortable in old clothes," he said with an amused look.

Beech flushed slightly and agreed that he was more at home in a suit and tie or a uniform. He envied Todd's vitality and confidence. The man was obviously at ease in any company, tall, rangy, well-muscled and intelligent – a handsome face, he supposed. He had caught Caroline smiling when Todd spoke during the meeting two nights ago. He had sensed her grudging admiration of the man who had arrested her. There weren't many men that Caroline deferred to. Beech had known her all his life and she had always made him feel that she tolerated him because he was a childhood friend. But then Beech was only too willing to admit that he was hopeless at dealing with women. Even with Victoria, the woman he adored, he could never quite get past the fact that she had once rejected his marriage proposal and, in his eyes, that made him a failure. He shook himself out of his momentary self-pity and concentrated on Todd's conversation. Beech learned that Alexander Todd was from a long line of naval men – going back to the battle of Trafalgar – but he had only ever served in Naval Intelligence.

"I suppose I'm a bit of a rebel," he said, in his good natured way. "I like dealing in the unconventional, I like the detective work and the chase. I like being my own man. I'd go mad confined on a ship in the rigid naval hierarchy."

Beech reflected that Todd was the perfect representation of how Beech wished to be. Peter Beech had never expected to be promoted into basically what was a deskbound job, managing the day to day logistics of the Metropolitan Police. It was, he suspected, the reason he had argued so eloquently for the creation of the Mayfair 100 team. It was his little bit of rebellion against the system. It was some excitement in an otherwise dull existence.

Other people came into the carriage and the two men

were forced to stop talking about confidential matters. A guard came through the corridor announcing the second sitting of dinner and Beech realised that he was rather hungry.

"Shall we?" he asked Todd.

"Absolutely!" was the reply. "I could do with a stiff drink too."

The two men made their way to the dining car. It was a sign of the times that the waiter did not bat an eyelid at the way they were dressed. An elderly woman, sporting a fox fur tippet and a lorgnette, looked at them distastefully, but they ignored her and sat down. They shared some level of amusement as they scanned the menu. Beech hadn't felt so liberated in a long time.

Over chicken pie and a couple of generous scotches, they talked generally about the war in low voices.

"I hear that you were invalided out early on, Beech?" Todd asked quietly.

"Mm. Mons…" Beech answered. "Terrible battle. Huge loss of life. I was lucky to escape, I suppose."

"I keep feeling as though I ought to volunteer," said Todd, reluctantly.

Beech shook his head. "You are much more valuable to the effort by being in…the work that you are doing now…" he stopped himself from saying Naval Intelligence, which could have been overheard. Then he added, "Anyone can carry a rifle and end up dead in No Mans Land or at the bottom of the sea. It doesn't bring the conflict to an end. But those who work behind the scenes…like you…I suppose, even like me, to a much lesser degree…we can make a significant difference to the outcome. Especially in the current…er…case."

Todd nodded and then raised his glass. "To success," he said softly and then said even more quietly, "Let's put the bastards in front of a firing squad."

***

There were those who could not sleep that night. Not Elsie and Sissy, weary from scrubbing a kitchen from top to bottom and feeding a small army of workers, and not Arthur Tollman, who had run around London like a headless chicken all day, putting processes and people in place, so that the team's activities would play out smoothly during the week. And not Mabel, who had been pleased with her day's work, written up her notes, and tested her samples, late at night at the Women's Hospital. When she finally got home, she slept the sleep of the righteous, after setting her alarm clock for five in the morning.

No, those who lay awake, were busy playing the day's events over and over in their heads, wondering if there was something they had missed, or could change, or improve or they were fearful of what lay ahead.

Victoria kept thinking about the working conditions in the factory and how she would word a report asking the Ministry of Munitions to make improvements. She was also worried about Peter and whether his wounded leg would cope with this rugged adventure he was undertaking.

Caroline lay awake wondering how she could prevent or treat the 'Monday Sickness' of the women exposed to nitro-glycerine but she was occasionally irritated by the fact that she kept thinking about Commander Todd. Eventually she took a sleeping draught to close her thoughts down altogether.

Billy Rigsby lay awake for a while, fretting about being, effectively, in charge of the whole operation in the factory. He was used to being Tollman's sidekick and he was now uncertain that he was up to the job of decision-making in an emergency.

Sam Abbott was just plain nervous about presenting himself for work at the factory tomorrow. His adult life as a docker – waiting every morning on the dockside to be selected for work by the foreman – had given him a lifetime of experience in rejection. Only a favoured few dockers were full time employees. The rest, like Sam, were lifelong 'casuals' with no guarantee of employment. Fortunately, he had been able to get extra work as a sparring partner and cornerman in the boxing world. He had always been able to earn money, just by his strength and muscles. His greatest fear was what would happen when he got older. He eventually fell asleep after exhausting all his worries.

And, finally, Lady Maud had made the grave mistake of allowing herself to be manipulated by the pleading eyes of young Timmy and she had, unwisely, allowed him to sleep on her bed. She was very fond of stroking his little warm body and reasoned that it would be more or less the same as having a hot water bottle to hand. Anyone who knew Timmy could have told her that he snored terribly and, as she lay awake, counting the seconds between the snores, she determined that tomorrow, she would be firmer with the wretched animal.

CHAPTER THIRTEEN

SCOTLAND AND STRATFORD

It was seven in the morning when Beech and Todd arrived in Glasgow and gathered themselves together to change to the train for Inverness. Sleeping upright in the carriage had made Beech's leg throb and he was limping somewhat. Todd expressed concern but was brushed off with "It's always bad first thing in the morning. Just stiff. Not a problem." Privately Beech cursed and became anxious again about whether he would be able to keep up with his strong and agile companion.

As they left the platform and made their way to the next train, they found themselves surrounded by sailors, all headed in the same direction.

"All headed for the North Atlantic blockade ships," shouted Todd over the noise of the crowd. "It must be time for a crew change!" Beech nodded, concentrating grimly on minimising his limp. Much as he disliked taking medication, he felt that he may have to resort to some pain relief once they boarded the next train. He had visited an army medic the day before and had been given a large tin of the new aspirin tablets. So, when the two men boarded the train to Inverness, Beech heaved a sigh of relief when they were able to sit in the dining car and order some breakfast. When Todd left briefly, to find a toilet, Beech was able to put two tablets into his mouth and take a large swig of hot tea to wash them down. The tablets had stuck slightly at the back of his throat and they tasted vile, so he was grateful for being able to immediately eat some eggs.

By the time Todd returned, Beech was happily eating a cooked breakfast and able to dismiss the ache in his leg, which was gradually receding.

***

It was a nervous Sam Abbott who stepped off the train at Forest Gate station and began a brisk walk to the munition's factory. He needn't have worried. When Sam arrived, cap in hand, asking for a job, Bradshaw took one look at the size of the man and the muscles and hired him immediately.

"I hope you're as strong as you look," said Bradshaw curtly. "Where have you worked before?"

"On the docks, all my life, sir" replied Sam.

Bradshaw raised an eyebrow. "Why did you leave? There's plenty of work on the docks at the moment."

"Nah. Not for casuals. I wanted a regular job with regular wages, sir," Sam lied.

"Right. Twenty two shillings a week, until I decide to keep you on, and I think you are worth more. If you're happy with that, put your name and address on the top there and sign at the bottom. Can you read and write?" he added, as an afterthought.

Sam replied that he could and duly filled in the form, giving a friend's address in Poplar, as he obviously couldn't say that he lived in Belgravia.

Bradshaw then took him through to the loading bay and introduced him to the crowd of men that were loading bales of cotton on to trolleys to take into the processing room. Sam could see the uniformed Billy loitering in the background but avoided any eye contact.

"This is Sam Abbott," Bradshaw said perfunctorily, "Ex-docker, plenty of muscles. Put him to good use, Tom," he said to an older man, who seemed to be in charge. Then Bradshaw left.

Sam felt slightly relieved, as he could see two other black men in the loading bay and was even more relieved when Tom shook his hand, bid him welcome and told him where to put his coat and hat. As he rolled up his shirt sleeves, he thought about his work in the trenches, back-breaking work loading heavy shells on to carts to be transported to the front, digging trenches and carrying men on stretchers. Moving a few cotton bales around for twenty two shillings a week was going to be a walk in the park.

***

Eustace King was waiting patiently, reading a newspaper on a bench by the river, opposite Scotland Yard. He had seen Detective Carter enter, about fifteen minutes ago. Eustace knew the drill in CID. They would arrive. The Duty Sergeant and leading detective would then be reviewing all ongoing cases and apportioning work for the day. If Carter came out of the building with another couple of men, then the chances are he would actually be working. If Carter came out on his own, then he would be free to go about his personal business which, if Tollman was correct, would mostly be 'Up West' to visit a series of nightclubs with disreputable owners.

Eustace's patience was rewarded when, half an hour later, the detectives came out in dribs and drabs, but Carter was on his own, making his way towards the stop on Millbank where the omnibuses paused on their way to Soho and the night clubs.

Eustace folded up his newspaper and dropped it in the nearest bin, as he strolled across the street to join the queue.

***

The medical team turned up at Mason's again, ferried, this time, by a police vehicle, and, upon Tollman's insistence, they were required to wait for them all day. This had caused Billy to heave a sigh of relief. It was good to know that there was back-up if he needed it.

Billy had his eye on this young lad, Peter, who was supposed to be, according to the gossipy Phyllis in the canteen, the lad that Agnes Whitlock had a relationship with. Billy was doubtful. He looked too young and gormless for a woman of Agnes' age and intelligence. However, there was no accounting for taste, and he would attempt to get friendly with him at some point during the day.

Myrtle Dimmock definitely had her eye on Peter, as she made a brief, and forbidden, appearance in the loading bay. Much to her delight, there was one wolf whistle as she appeared. Tom, the senior labourer scowled and most of the men ignored her.

"Hello Peter," she said loudly, which made the lad blush, but then she swiftly turned her attention to Billy. "I hope you're looking after all these naughty boys, Mr Policeman?" she said coyly, which made Tom curl his lip in disgust and several men wink at Billy.

Fortunately, Billy was prevented from answering by Tom saying gruffly, "Get out of here Myrtle, you know you're not allowed in this shed."

"Oh, pardon me, I'm sure!" she said crossly, and flounced out, but not before giving Billy a sly smile.

"She's got plenty of front," commented Billy, to no one in particular.

"Steer clear of Myrtle Dimmock, lad," warned Tom, "She's trouble that one. I wouldn't put anything past her. Last month she nearly did for one of the other girls for speaking too much to Peter here."

Peter flushed again and said defensively, "I don't even like her! I wish she'd leave me alone!"

"Well you must be like cat nip to women," Billy commented with a laugh, "If you've got two of them fighting over you!"

"It wasn't like that! Agnes was just a friend of my sister's. She asked me to give my sister messages and Myrtle just attacked her. It was wrong!"

Billy nodded and moved away. He decided he must have a word with the lad in the dinner break. He needed to find out why Agnes was friendly with the sister. He also realised, with some distaste, that he would have to get closer to the unpleasant Myrtle. There was always a possibility that she murdered Agnes out of some misplaced jealousy. He noted that Sam was happily chatting to a couple of men and making them smile. He was pleased that his genial friend was fitting in to his new workplace, although it was only temporary. For a while, at least, the shadow of returning to the war seemed to have receded.

***

Myrtle Dimmock had merely made a detour to the loading bay and was now where she should have been, in the makeshift medical room being examined by Caroline. Victoria tried to hide her distaste for this girl who was being sullen, unco-operative and very vocal about her dislike of doctors.

Fortunately, Caroline was highly experienced in dealing with the most difficult patients and simply said, "That is quite enough from you, Miss Dimmock. Kindly keep your mouth shut whilst I examine you, or I shall be forced to put you down on my sheet as 'unfit for work'!"

Obviously, the thought of losing her job was the one thing guaranteed to silence the girl and the rest of the examination passed with a grudging obedience on the part of Myrtle.

Victoria placed a thermometer in Myrtle's mouth, which added to the silence. Caroline began probing around Myrtle's neck, which caused her to squirm. When the thermometer was removed, Victoria passed it to Caroline with a knowing look. Mabel began to swab Myrtle's hand and the girl protested again.

"What's this all about?" she asked in aggrieved tone. She didn't like being pulled about and her eyes flashed when Caroline asked her if she had ever been pregnant.

Myrtle was outraged. "What d'you take me for? Of course I haven't!"

"Is your time of month regular?" Caroline persisted.

"None of your bleedin' business!" Myrtle snapped back and Caroline stood back.

"I'm afraid it is very much my business, Miss Dimmock," she answered grimly. "I think you have a serious health problem."

Myrtle looked frightened. "What d'you mean?" The usually strident voice had dropped to a horrified whisper.

Caroline looked at Mabel and asked, "Any trembling in the hands?"

Mabel nodded. "A little. Not much, at the moment, but it's there."

Caroline softened her tone and looked at the frightened girl. "Mabel, I think you have an overactive thyroid gland, which is making you excitable and irritable, causing your hands to tremble, making you heart race, your eyes red and your monthlies irregular."

"Am I going to die?"

"No. At least you will have a better chance of living if you change jobs. It's not good for you to work with any form of nitro-glycerine. The explosive makes your heart beat quickly and an overactive thyroid does that as well. So, you are putting your heart under tremendous strain working in the cordite shed. I shall recommend to Mr Bradshaw that you are employed in the cotton processing, for your own safety."

"I'll lose five bob a week!" Myrtle was not happy.

"It's better to be alive and in a less demanding job, isn't

it?" Caroline said sharply, giving Mabel a stern look.

"Says you! And I suppose I'll have to find the money for fancy medicine as well, will I?"

Mabel interjected. "I can make you a solution called Lugol's iodine. It is very inexpensive, and you only take a few drops in water every day. Any chemist will sell it. You are in the early stages of having an overactive thyroid gland but, if you don't take action now, it will only get worse."

Myrtle was resentful but Victoria sensed that she was intelligent enough to see that Caroline and Mabel were speaking the truth.

Once Myrtle had left, the team relaxed momentarily. "Nasty piece of work, isn't she?" Victoria observed.

The others nodded and then Mabel said, "An overactive thyroid can make people very irritable and irrational. If she's had it for a while, it could very well have shaped her personality. Isn't she the one that Sissy said was having arguments with Agnes Whitlock?" Victoria confirmed that she was. Mabel continued, "Well then she could also be subject to uncontrollable rages and she could have killed Agnes in such a frame of mind."

"It's possible," agreed Caroline, "but her poor health has made her rather thin and, remember, Agnes was stabbed with such force that she was impaled momentarily to a tree. It takes a lot of strength to do that. Although, I wouldn't rule out that a furious woman could possibly find that strength."

***

When Elsie and Sissy had arrived on the worker's omnibus, early that morning, they found Phyllis looking glum. When queried, she said that Bradshaw had told her to stay late tonight, as they were having a special delivery and a pick-up, so the men would want sandwiches and a brew.

"Oh, we could stay and help you, if you like!" Sissy offered and Phyllis brightened up.

"Do they have these night shifts often then?" asked Elsie.

"No." Phyllis was adamant. "Just now and then. I don't take much notice really. Just give the men some tea and biscuits usually. But this time, Bradshaw says they've got a long trip up to Lincolnshire, so they need sandwiches for the journey."

Sissy and Elsie, therefore, resigned themselves to working a late night shift and devising a way to alert the rest of the team, when Mr Bradshaw came in, flustered and needing a cup of tea. He sat down at one of the tables looking irritated and when Phyllis brought him his tea, he muttered something quietly to her.

She came back to the kitchen and shrugged. "Apparently tonight is off," she said quietly. "It might be tomorrow or the day after."

Bradshaw gulped down his cup of tea and made straight for the loading bay. Scanning amongst the men, he asked Tom where the new man, Sam, was. Tom indicated that Sam was delivering some bales to the oven shed and Bradshaw bustled off. Billy was standing nearby, and he began to feel concern. *I hope he's not going to sack him.* He thought with alarm.

But Sam came back into the loading bay, with a smile

on his face, to retrieve his hat and coat.

"Mr Bradshaw wants me to go on an errand down the docks," he said loudly to Tom and he gave an imperceptible nod to Billy. There was no possibility that Sam could get any more information to his friend before he set off.

**

Victoria had invited the supervisor of the cordite room, Mrs Hawkesworth, to have a cup of tea with her in the canteen, as she wanted, she said, to ask her more about the cordite process. The woman seemed almost grateful to have a break and they sat down at a table, with tea and biscuits served by Elsie, and Victoria prepared to take notes.

"It's a mindless job," said Mrs Hawkesworth frankly. "The women sit there, with a ruler in front of them and they cut the long string of cordite into exact lengths for it to be packed into cartridges or shells. We don't pack the shells here, thank God. You'd need a much bigger factory to do that. No, we put the lengths of cordite, tied into bundles, packed round with straw and then into sealed wooden crates and they are taken to the filling place at the Royal Arsenal."

"Where does the cordite come from?" asked Victoria, looking up from her notes.

"We make it here," was the reply and Mrs Hawkesworth pointed at the explosives shed. "That's where the nitro glycerine is kept. Cordite is a combination of gun cotton, which they make in the main shed here, nitro and petroleum jelly. They put it all in a big machine and it pushes out this long thread, like a sausage machine. Not that I've really seen it, mind," she added hastily. "The women aren't allowed in that shed. Too dangerous."

"Did you work on the cordite processing before you became a supervisor?"

Mrs Hawkesworth nodded. "Bradshaw gave me the job of supervisor, temporarily, because I was prone to fainting. Doctor said it was 'excitement of the heart' or something. Anyway, that was three years ago, and I've only had a couple of fainting fits since so he let me stay in the job."

Victoria sighed. "Yes, the medical team suspect that it's skin contact with the nitro glycerine that affects everyone's hearts, but they will need to do more research."

Mrs Hawkesworth's eyes widened. "Well I never!" Then she looked over at the explosives shed before leaning over confidentially to Victoria. "In the last four years, there have been three men from the explosives shed, who have died. Just dropped down dead, with heart attacks – oh, wait, I think Sydney Adams was a stroke. And what was so strange was that they were all on a Sunday. Mind you, what wasn't so strange was that they all dropped dead in the pub – not in church!" She laughed, then became serious. "Do you think that is caused by the nitro as well?"

"Could be," Victoria was writing furiously now. "Of course there must be a lot of stress in this job."

Mrs Hawkesworth gave a small shake of her head. "I don't think it's that stressful...well, I can only speak for my part of the factory. The women are a decent bunch, for the most part..."

"Except Myrtle Dimmock…" Victoria prompted, causing Mrs Hawkesworth to roll her eyes.

"Oh, don't get me started on that one! There are days when I think she belongs in an asylum, she's that uncontrollable sometimes! She can be the life and soul, having the girls in fits of laughter and the next minute she's in a furious rage. She tried to whip one of the older women with some thick rope last week! It took four of us to drag her off! She can be a demon."

They finished their tea and walked back into the factory. As it was approaching the lunch break, Mrs Hawkesworth agreed that she would not send the next four women for examination until 1 p.m.

"I hope your team of ladies does some good with all this," Mrs Hawkesworth said to Victoria. "East End women often get a raw deal in life, generally…I should know," she said with feeling. "We don't need our workplace making us sick as well. That's just too hard on us."

***

Eustace King was having a roast beef sandwich at a street café in Leicester Square. The whole square was packed with soldiers and women, hell-bent on having a good time but Eustace had chosen the café because it was up a few steps and he had a clear view of Detective Carter, who was eating a substantial lunch at a pricey restaurant on the corner of the square and Leicester Place. Fortunately, because it was such a nice day, Carter was eating outside, with a friend. Unfortunately, Carter's friend was a petty villain known to

Eustace, so he could not get any closer, in order to listen to their conversation. But he did notice that the villain passed the detective a manilla envelope and then he left.

Eustace's lip curled in distaste. He had spent all morning following Carter from one establishment to another. All of the clubs, restaurants and theatres were owned by either the West End kingpin gangsters, the MacAusland brothers, or Alfie Solomons, the head of the up-and-coming Jewish gang called the Bessarabian Tigers. The only reason a lone detective would be visiting such establishments would be to pick up money he was being paid to look the other way. *This Carter is a piece of filth,* reflected Eustace bitterly, *and he's a lousy detective. I've been following him four or five hours now and he hasn't spotted me once.* He could see that Carter was paying the bill and preparing to leave, so Eustace finished his half pint of beer, put his hat back on, and prepared to wear out his shoe leather again.

***

Sam was trying to get through the bustling Victoria Docks but he kept being stopped by men he had once worked with, who were genuinely glad to see him and wanting to know when he was going to come back to the docks to work. He shook many hands and had to keep saying, "It's great to see you...but I've got to do a job for my boss..." However, it was a good feeling to know that he had been missed. He had worked the Victoria Docks for the last ten years and when Bradshaw had asked him to go there, he had had a small flip of his stomach at going back to his old life temporarily. After only six months at the Front, working at the docks seemed a distant memory.

Bradshaw had told him that he had received a telephone call from the captain of the ship bringing a cargo of cotton for Mason's from America. But the captain had said that the congestion was such, in the docks, that he did not know when he would be able to unload. Bradshaw told Sam to go and find out if the captain had been given an unloading berth and when he had been told his cargo would be discharged.

Sam could see the vessel in the distance. It was on one of the holding berths, waiting to be moved on to a berth with hydraulic cranes available. The docks were the busiest he had ever seen them. Experience told him that any ship would have to wait if it was not carrying cargo, like meat, for which the dock had built special cold storage warehouses. Sam decided that rather than walk the mile or so to the holding berth, it would be more productive to find the Harbourmaster and speak to him.

Bradshaw had said "If you have any trouble, just tell them that it is urgent munitions supplies, and the government will come down on them like a ton of bricks, if they hold up shell making." Sam knew that his new boss was right. The recent Shell Scandal, which had been all over the newspapers, highlighting the lack of munitions at the Front, had galvanised everyone into putting the munitions industry first. He set off towards the Custom House to find the Harbourmaster and negotiate the release of Mason's cargo.

CHAPTER FOURTEEN

SECRETS EVERYWHERE

Billy was tucking into a generous portion of cheese and onion pie, like all the workers at Mason's, who were choosing to sit out in the courtyard, in the sun of a summer's day, to eat their lunch. The creation of a proper canteen, with cooked food, was hugely popular, judging by the way that they were all attacking the pie with gusto.

"Proper food and a bit of sunshine, you can't go wrong with that," Tom said to Billy, as they all sat around enjoying their break from the loading bay. "Those ladies in that kitchen want a medal." Billy grinned. He would pass that praise on to his mother and aunty later.

Tom rose to take his plate and cutlery back to the canteen and Billy took the opportunity to shuffle across the bench to sit next to young Peter.

"This Agnes, who was friendly with your sister…" he began, which caused Peter to look alarmed, and Billy registered the look. "Hold on lad…no need to look frightened…I'm on your side, mate." Peter smiled and nodded, so Billy continued, "You know that the police are investigating Agnes' murder, don't you?" Peter looked at him fearfully. "No, lad, don't get worried. We don't suspect you. The trouble is we need to know a bit more about Agnes and your sister might be able to help. Where's the best place to go and talk to her?"

"She works for a packing-case manufacturer in Poplar - Yeatmans…it's in the East India Docks Road. She's there from seven in the morning to seven at night."

Billy made a mental note. "And why was she so friendly with your sister?"

Peter shrugged. "Union business. That's all I know. Fanatics – the pair of them. My mum says my sister's a revolutionary and, if she has her way, everyone's going to join a union whether they like it or not. She used to be a suffragette too, but she's gone quiet on that game at the moment."

"Blimey! Sounds like a right firebrand!" Billy commented, "What's her name, son?"

"Enid...Mrs Enid Oliver. Her husband got killed in January in France. He was twenty two. They'd only been married a year."

Billy patted the lad on the back and tried to ignore the brief feeling of despair at yet another young life culled in the war. Tom had returned, after having a friendly chat with Sissy, so Billy stood up and said, "I reckon I'm going to pay a visit to those lady doctors they've got visiting. I need my gammy hand looking at. Been giving me gyp lately." He rubbed his gloved left hand and winced convincingly.

"Good idea," Tom looked concerned and Billy gave him a watery smile as he strode off in the direction of the temporary 'medical examination' room.

There was no-one waiting outside, as it was still the lunch break, so he knocked and waited for permission to enter. Victoria opened the door, brushing pastry crumbs away from her mouth and Billy grinned. Then he said loudly, "Sorry to bother you, nurse, but I wondered if the doctors could have a look at my bad hand. It's giving me a bit of trouble."

Victoria ushered him in and closed the door. Mabel and Caroline were still finishing their portions of cheese and onion pie. "This is so good!" said Caroline, with her mouth full.

"Yes, it seems to have gone down well with the workforce", Billy agreed. "Any more of this praise and my mum will be taking up a permanent job here!"

Billy then explained that he needed to get a message to Tollman and he asked for a pen and paper, so that he could write down everything he had learned about Peter's sister and her involvement with Agnes. "Tollman needs to go round and interview her. He won't like it, because she's a militant unionist and a former suffragette, but someone needs to find out what she knew about Agnes. So," he paused for a moment to think, "if I can get Bradshaw out of his office, perhaps one of you could ring Mayfair 100 and see if he's there. If he's not, then leave the full information with Lady Maud and ask her to ring the Yard."

Victoria said she would do it. Billy raised his hand, "But, first, I need someone to re-do the bandages on my hand, so that I can walk out of here looking as though I have been attended to."

***

Eustace King had followed Carter around all morning and now it was two o'clock in the afternoon and he realised that he was following him back in the direction of Scotland Yard. However, first, Detective Carter made a stop at a bank near Trafalgar Square. Eustace saw him take several envelopes out of his coat pocket as he entered the bank. *Depositing his ill-gotten gains, no doubt*, he thought, with considerable distaste. He hated bent coppers more than anything else in the world.

Still, it's handy to know the name of the bank and location of the branch, he thought. *It's going to make it a lot easier for Tollman to get the evidence to put this Carter away.*

After a good fifteen minutes, the object of Eustace's surveillance came out and headed off down Whitehall towards the Yard. Eustace duly followed, picking up an early edition of the evening paper on the way. He needed something to read whilst waiting to see if Carter would re-appear once he went into his office.

After about an hour, a group of men came out of the building, of which Carter was one. It was obvious to Eustace that they were off to do some real police work and he could go home and put his feet up for a few hours. He would come back later and see if Carter was going to be out and about in the evening.

***

Billy decided to have a little stroll around the perimeter of the factory grounds. Considering it was producing part of the supply chain for Government purchase, the place had barely any security. It was out in the middle of nowhere, it was not behind high brick walls like the Royal Arsenal at Woolwich, nor was it guarded in any way. It reminded Billy of one of those forts he had seen in photographs of the American West. Except, instead of a stockade made of whole tree trunks, it was just surrounded by a six foot high wooden fence that any schoolboy could climb.

He realised that, when he went behind the canteen building, he was completely out of sight of anyone in the factory. Selecting a couple of the wooden planks, he braced himself against the upper part and gave the bottom of the planks a swift kick with his steel toe-capped boots and, to his satisfaction, the softer wood, which was damp, gave way. A couple more swift kicks and he was able to create a credible hole at the bottom of the fence which looked as though someone had crawled through. He quickly gathered up the pieces of splintered wood and threw them over the top of the fence. He gave a smile of satisfaction and then made his way towards Bradshaw's office to tell him that it looked as though someone might have broken in during the night.

As the alarmed Bradshaw followed Billy out of his office, cursing the name of Winkler, the night security man, for not spotting the problem, Billy gave a swift knock on the window of the medical room, to alert Victoria.

Tollman had, fortuitously, just returned from walking Timmy at the very point that the telephone had rung in Lady Maud's house. Victoria relayed to him the information Billy had discovered and Tollman confirmed that he would immediately go to Poplar and question Enid Oliver.

He was just about to leave, when Eustace also telephoned to report the information from today's surveillance and to confirm that it was permissible to put in some 'overtime', as it were, by shadowing Carter, yet again, this evening. Tollman confirmed that it was.

"He's a bad one, this Carter," said Eustace in a serious tone of voice. "I reckon he picked up eight or nine envelopes of money and deposited them in his bank. He visited practically every disreputable dive in Soho and he lunched with 'Fingers' Marks from the Bessarabian mob."

"Did he now?" Tollman was talking to himself rather than asking Eustace a question. "That's very interesting. Thank you, Eustace. But I'd like to hear about where he goes tonight because I reckon the sort of person he's involved with in this trading with the enemy caper, won't be the sort of person that visits low dives in Soho. I could be wrong – but my instinct tells me otherwise."

Eustace agreed and said he would telephone again in the morning.

Tollman put his head around the door of the parlour to tell Lady Maud that he was going out again. She had her back to him and, unaware of his presence, she was busy talking to Timmy, who had his head on one side as though listening intently. "Now, this is a picture of my late husband, the General…" she was explaining to Timmy, "…who would have thoroughly approved of you. Oh yes. He had a great fondness for dogs…" Tollman closed the door very quietly and raised his eyes towards the heavens. *Are all women daft?* he asked himself as he retrieved his hat and set off on his journey to Poplar.

***

Sam was back at Mason's, having secured a promise

from the Harbourmaster that the *S.S.Maracaibo*, containing the vital supply of cotton, would be unloaded tomorrow. Bradshaw was relieved but Sam was puzzled. He had noted that there were plenty of bales of cotton in the loading bay – certainly enough to keep the production of gun cotton and cordite going for at least two weeks – and he was intrigued as to why Bradshaw was so worried about urgent delivery.

"Go and get yourself a cup of tea before you go back to work," said Bradshaw magnanimously. "And, Sam, there might be a bit of overtime for you tomorrow – after hours, like."

Sam thanked him and made his way over to the canteen. Elsie and Sissy were having a cup of tea themselves, after a long period of cooking and washing up. Phyllis had just left to go and take her turn for a medical examination, so Elsie said, "Hello, Sam, how's it going out there?" and pushed a clean cup towards him, while Sissy took the teapot to be refreshed.

Sam lowered his voice and explained to them that he had been at the docks all morning and that Bradshaw had been 'all of a lather' about the fact that the ship was not going to be unloaded that day. "I don't know why," observed Sam, "There's plenty of cotton bales piled up in the shed."

"Ah, now that's interesting," said Sissy, as she poured the steaming hot tea into his cup. "We got here this morning and Phyllis was a bit down in the mouth because Bradshaw asked her to work late tonight, to give lorry drivers some tea and sandwiches. Then he came in a bit later and called it off. But, before he did that, she said that these night-time pick-ups happened now and then, but it was different this time because the men were going all the way up to Lincolnshire."

Sam nodded and savoured his tea, then he told them that Bradshaw had offered him some overtime tomorrow night, to do a special job. "I reckon it will be this Lincolnshire job, that was put off tonight. We'll see."

***

Tollman stepped off the tram outside Poplar police station in the East India Docks Road. He looked around at its bustling shops, theatre, Turkish Baths and Chinese laundries. The last time he had been to Poplar was in 1897, when the Prince of Wales had opened the new Blackwall Tunnel – that miracle of engineering that went under the river and emerged in Greenwich. Tollman had been part of a detail of detectives making sure that no-one attempted to blow up the Prince and the tunnel.

Two years before that, the Irish Fenians had successfully planted bombs in the House of Commons, Westminster Hall and the Tower of London. From that incident, Special Branch had been created – specifically to deal with the 'Irish problem'. The Fenians had gone quiet after that, but then the Anarchists and the Suffragettes took over. Only the month before the opening of the Blackwall Tunnel, some anarchist group detonated a bomb at Aldersgate Street Station, which had injured sixty people and killed one. Tollman had been drafted in, with some other Met police, to assist the City of London police to remove the injured. It had been carnage and not something he had ever wanted to repeat. The opening of the Blackwall Tunnel had gone without incident but all Tollman remembered was feeling terrified until it was all over and having to have a stiff drink or two afterwards. So, he had never been to Poplar since. Even now, standing in the main thoroughfare, and noting all the hustle and bustle of trade and commerce, he had a cold feeling in the pit of his stomach. It was hard to shake off those dark days.

Proceedings westward, he eventually came to the frontage of Yeatman's – a warehouse-like building, with the front open on to the street. Inside, men were sawing wood on one side and, on the other side there were men nailing together the wood into packing cases. Tollman could see that there was a second floor, accessible by a wooden staircase, and the word OFFICE was painted on the wall, with an arrow pointing up the stairs. He tipped his hat to the curious men and ascended the stairs, where he, indeed, found an office, staffed by no less than five women and, he guessed, a manager, in his own cubby hole. He approached the man, showed him his warrant card and asked if he could speak to Mrs Enid Oliver regarding a police matter. The man wearily got up, put his head around the partition and called "Enid! Someone to see you!" A pale, thin young woman, with a defiant expression on her face, stood up and then strode over.

"Been demonstrating again, Enid?" said the manager sarcastically as he went back to his paperwork.

She looked irritated but when Tollman showed his credentials, she looked alarmed. "It's alright, Mrs Oliver," he said reassuringly, "It's nothing that you have done. I just want to speak to you about a lady called Agnes Whitlock."

A look of relief flitted across Enid's face and she replied,

"I would be glad to…um…"

"Detective Sergeant Tollman", he offered.

Then she turned to the manager and said, "I am due a fifteen minute break – which I am going to make into a thirty minute break, because I didn't have a break at all yesterday afternoon." It was a statement, not a request and Tollman suppressed a smile at the look of irritation on the manager's face, which was then replaced by a look of resignation.

"Whatever you say, Mrs Oliver," he said in a dismissive tone and he resumed dipping his pen into the inkwell and entering figures on a sheet.

Enid Oliver retrieved her coat and hat and said to Tollman quietly, "I have quite a lot to tell you. You can buy me some tea and cake at the café over the road."

Tollman followed the determined young woman with some amusement. She obviously liked to get her own way and, judging by the way the manager had deferred to her, was used to getting it. He guessed that the fanaticism she had once had as a suffragette had been channelled now into union work. *God help any man trying to get the better of this one*, he thought to himself.

Once they were settled in the café, tea and Bakewell tarts on the table, Enid Oliver, without any prompting, began to talk. She had been good friends with Agnes, she explained. They had met at a women's union rally at Caxton Hall and Agnes had explained that she was interested in starting up a union branch in the munitions industry. She had told Enid of the various illnesses that she, herself, had suffered from in her work at different munition factories and Enid had introduced Agnes to some of the leading lights at the National Federation for Women Workers. From that moment on, Agnes had become a fervent discipline of worker's rights. Enid and Agnes often spent evenings together, discussing union business and women's rights. *Sounds like a lot of fun*, thought Tollman, and then immediately felt guilty as a tear rolled down Enid's cheek and she became obviously distressed. He offered his handkerchief and began to feel sympathy for the young widow. From everything she had said, she was obviously great friends with Agnes Whitlock.

"Did she confide in you at all about the place where she was working?" asked Tollman gently.

Enid nodded, took a sip of her tea, and replied, "She said there was something shady going on," she said, leaning in towards Tollman, although there was no-one else in the café at that moment. "She couldn't quite put her finger on it and she said she needed more proof, but she said something about men working in the loading bay after hours and she had caught a glimpse of paperwork from a company in Norway. But she began to be frightened..." she added, "the shop steward they have there, from the Amalgamated Society of Engineers – the union that hates women in the workplace more than any other," she explained, with disgust in her voice, "You know they are negotiating with the government to have all women removed from certain occupations after the war is over? What about all the single women without brothers and fathers, who will have to make a living after the war is over? What about the widows?" She dabbed her eyes with Tollman's handkerchief again and he took that opportunity to bring her back to her assertion that Agnes was fearful.

"You said that Agnes was frightened," he reminded her. "What was she frightened of?"

Enid looked at him and said flatly, "Agnes said that the shop steward, Malcolm Sinclair, had threatened to kill her if she poked her nose in where it was not wanted."

***

Eustace King was back in front of Scotland Yard by eight o'clock in the evening, having first ascertained that Detective Carter was still in the office. He did this by telephoning the Yard and pretending to be a tailor who wished to send round a delivery of a finished three piece suit and wanting to check that the detective was still there. The duty sergeant had obligingly said that the detective was there until eight o 'clock if he wanted to send the parcel around. He chuckled when he put the earpiece back on the hook, imagining Carter being told that a suit would be arriving for him any minute and not knowing what it was all about.

When Carter appeared, Eustace, by now clad in a different coat and hat, followed him at a discreet distance to the address in Pimlico where, Tollman had informed him, Carter lived. He took a stroll round the pleasant square, whilst Carter was inside and, after about twenty minutes, the detective duly emerged, dressed in an evening suit.

"Well ain't we the fancy toff?" muttered Eustace to himself as he hailed a taxicab to follow after the one Carter had entered. Carter's taxicab drew up outside one of the large houses in Berkeley Street and Eustace asked his driver to stop on the corner, so he could observe Carter going into what was, probably, a gentleman's club. The whole area was littered with them. He paid off his driver and strolled along past the houses until he arrived at the relevant place.

The plaque on the door said

THE PUBLIC SCHOOLS CLUB – MEMBERS ONLY.

Eustace King smiled. He just so happened to know an ex-policeman who was now working as an evening porter in The Public Schools Club… and Tollman also knew the man. So, he decided he would arrange a little pub lunch with this fellow, and Tollman, tomorrow.

There was no point in Eustace hanging around, as Carter could be in the club until the small hours, so he made his way to Piccadilly to catch an omnibus to Charing Cross station and then a train back to Clapham Junction for a late supper.

CHAPTER FIFTEEN

A FORTUITOUS DELAY

Commander Todd was frustrated. He and Beech, and over one hundred sailors, had been waiting fruitlessly in an Admiralty barracks at Invergordon for several hours. They had already spent most of the morning travelling from Glasgow to Inverness and then had all changed to yet another train which slowly chugged into the Highlands to arrive at Invergordon. This was the Admiralty base for the Eastern blockade ships covering the North Sea. It was now approaching evening and the light was beginning to fade. Beech looked out of the window at the huge storage tanks of water and oil and the massive coal sheds. It was eerily quiet out on the deep water docks, but it was mayhem in the barracks. The sailors were letting off steam before they took their turn at the grim task of policing the blockade in the treacherous waters of the North Sea and the North Atlantic. From the loud conversations of the men, Beech had gathered that many of them had done a stint on the blockade fleet before and it was not a duty they relished. Terrible weather, vicious currents and small arms battles with renegade ships, trying to run the blockade, seemed to be everyday occurrences and Beech could see that these men were exposing themselves to danger everyday as much as the army was in the trenches.

Todd was pacing around like a caged animal. Beech guessed that the Commander's energy, which he so envied, was hard to contain. Policemen, on the other hand, were so often required to patiently wait for events to unfold and information to be gathered before they could act. It gave him a little comfort to realise that, after all, he might be temperamentally suited to his job, even though he sometimes craved a little more excitement.

"There was supposed to be a ship here from Scapa Flow by now. Due a crew change. Where the hell is it?" Todd was getting fretful. "We're losing valuable time. If we spend much longer here, the ship we're after could have passed through the blockade and be unloading in Norway and we will have missed our chance to follow the cargo." He paced some more and then said, "I'm going to telegraph the Director and tell him we are here and waiting. He might have some information that can be relayed back." Todd strode off in the direction of the Communications Room. Beech sat down gratefully and stretched out his bad leg. The aspirin tablets had worn off a few hours ago but he had no opportunity to privately take some more. Now he was able to swallow another two with some cold tea and he would be more agile when it was time to board the expected ship.

***

The Mayfair 100 team gathered together in Lady Maud's parlour – including Sam – who had been reluctant to enter such an upper class gathering at first, making all sorts of protests about being in work clothes and not knowing anyone.

Sissy had given him an earful, saying, "Work clothes?! Look at me and Elsie! Dressed up in these dreadful khaki sacks! Lady Maud don't care! We're all part of a team, whether you like it or not, Sam Abbott, so get in that front door, and stop shilly shallying. I'm desperate for some grub!" And she had pushed him through the door with considerable force.

Sam had entered but hung back, overwhelmed by the ease with which lower and upper class mingled so easily in the parlour. He had been tongue-tied when Victoria greeted him and even more when Lady Maud, carrying Timmy under one arm, shook his hand vigorously with her free hand. Gradually he had relaxed and, by the time Billy arrived, he was actually chatting to Mabel Summersby who was handing around sandwiches to the hungry 'workers' of Mason's munitions factory.

Tollman finally arrived from Poplar and, once he had had yet another cup of tea and was suitably refreshed, they all began to share information. When Sam had finished telling him about the delay of the ship unloading in London and then Elsie and Sissy reported on the mysterious night job that was scheduled for tomorrow, he leapt up and declared "I have to get over to the Admiralty, now, and tell them this!" He grabbed a few slices of pork pie, wrapped them in a napkin and was about to head out of the door when Billy said, "What happened about Enid Oliver, Mr Tollman?"

Tollman paused at the door and said "Oh, I forgot to say...apparently the shop steward at Mason's...Sinclair? He threatened to kill Agnes Whitlock if she didn't stop poking her nose into things."

Then he was gone, leaving a stunned room to have further conversations about the fact that they now had two suspects for Agnes' murder. The unbalanced Myrtle Dimmock and the nasty Malcolm Sinclair.

***

Tollman found himself amongst a hive of activity in the Admiralty Trade Division. He had been escorted down to an operations room in the basement, after presenting himself at the front entrance.

Captain Webb was seated at a table full of sea charts and a Communications Officer was translating telegraph messages from a clattering unit in the corner. Webb was then calling out names and numbers to other men who were writing on a large blackboard fixed to the wall and moving pins on a giant map on another wall.

Webb stood and shook Tollman's hand. "Welcome to our operations room," he said warmly. "As you can see, we are constantly receiving information about the movement of merchant vessels of interest. We know when and where they loaded their cargoes and roughly where they are at sea. We have identified the ones that are of special interest to us - those are the blue pins on the map – and we relay that information by telegraph on to the HQ of the Northern blockade at Scapa Flow."

It was very impressive and Tollman said so. Then he said that he had vital information about the *S.S.Maracaibo*, which had a cargo of cotton for Mason's.

Webb seemed pleased. "Your information is very timely. I have had a communication from Commander Todd that he and your Inspector Beech are at Invergordon, awaiting a Navy vessel but it has been delayed. Todd is getting worried that they will miss the ship."

"They won't," replied Tollman, and he explained all about the ship being delayed at the Royal Victoria docks and that it wouldn't be unloaded until tomorrow. "But," he added, "our people think that the cargo may be arriving at Mason's tomorrow but then, at night, all or some of it may be loaded on to road transport and sent up to Lincolnshire. We don't know anymore than that. One of our lads has been offered some overtime tomorrow night and the ladies we have working in the canteen have been asked to provide refreshments for the workers and drivers."

Webb took a deep breath. "If they are going to Linconshire, it could be going to a ship docking at Immingham and on to somewhere other than Norway. Or, they could be putting it in a warehouse up in Linconshire and waiting for something else. Either way, we need to know the final destination of that cotton. If it's bound for a warehouse, then we need to know the address. If it's going to a ship, we could do with a copy of the bill of lading – that would add to our evidence paperwork. Do you think your people could do that?"

"Well, it's a big ask, but I'm sure they will do their best," Tollman said firmly.

"Good man. Meanwhile I will communicate with Todd and Beech and tell them to stay put until we give them further instructions. If you can get that information to us as fast as you can tomorrow night, that would be splendid. As you can see, we are here all hours." Webb waved a hand towards the busy room and Tollman nodded in appreciation.

Tollman took his leave and then hailed a taxicab to Belgravia. It wasn't far but, after all the legwork he had put in during the day, he didn't feel like walking another three quarters of a mile. He arrived at the Belgravia house just after Elsie, Sissy and Sam and, unusually for him, he declined the offer of a cup of tea.

"I've drunk that much tea today, Sissy," he said wearily, "You could float a battleship in my stomach."

"Then you just have a drop of whisky and a piece of this fruit cake to soak it up", said Elsie, placing generous portions of both in front of him.

Sam grinned and asked Tollman if he had any orders for them all.

"I certainly do," was the reply, as he waited for the warmth of the whisky to reach his stomach. Then he explained his conversation with the Director of the Admiralty Trade Division. "I said to him it was a big ask, but any information you can get about the destination of this cotton – assuming that is what is being loaded on to road transport tomorrow night – especially any paperwork, would be gratefully received. But," he added firmly, revived by another mouthful of scotch. "I don't want any of you to put yourself in danger, especially as Billy won't be there to protect you."

Sam laughed. "Billy will tell you that I've got a bigger punch than he has, any day! Isn't that right, ladies?"

He looked to Elsie and Sissy for confirmation. They both nodded and smiled.

"Absolutely true, Arthur," Sissy confirmed. "Sam once

knocked Billy right out in a sparring session!"

"He didn't mean to though! Did you Sam?" Elsie added.

"Billy forgot to move!" Sam said, winking at Tollman, who chuckled and stood, fortified with cake and whisky, ready to go home. It had been a long day and, whilst he found being in total charge exhilarating, it was murder on his back and feet, which were now beginning to twinge a little.

"Why don't you stay here tonight, Arthur?" said Elsie with concern. "You look run off your feet. Plenty of bedrooms in this house, you know."

Tollman shook his head. "Thanks, Elsie, but I need to reassure myself that those daughters of mine are not getting up to any mischief and I've, apparently, got an appointment in Clapham tomorrow, that may just throw some light on this case, I hope."

As he walked slowly up the street, in the cool air, Tollman smiled with satisfaction. He truly enjoyed his job, ever since Inspector Beech set up the Mayfair team, and now he was savouring the prospect of, possibly, putting the unpleasant Detective Sergeant Carter behind bars.

***

Beech and Todd had been given beds for the night in the navy barracks at Invergordon. It was just the two of them in officer's quarters, but Beech was grateful that there were proper beds. It would be easier on his leg.

Todd was chafing at the bit because he had received a signal from Webb to say that they had to stay put as the

S.S.Maracaibo had been delayed discharging its cargo in London and it now appeared that the whole cargo marked for Mason's was being transferred to another ship or going to a warehouse, probably up country.

"You see," Todd explained, "What we think they have done before is unloaded the whole cargo at London, Mason's have taken what they needed, marked part of it for the company in Norway or wherever, and loaded it back on the same ship."

Beech was puzzled. "Why wouldn't the cargo just be marked for Norway in the first place – when it was loaded in America?"

Todd smiled grimly. "Profit. Pure and simple. Mason's, or the company that owns Mason's, will have bought the whole cargo from America. They will pay the duties on it, when unloaded. Then they put different labels on whatever part of the cargo they choose, creating a new cargo, which they put back on the same ship, sell at black market price to the middle-man company in Scandinavia, who then sells it on the Germany at an even more inflated price. We suspect that some American and British businessmen are sharing the profits of the over-inflated prices put on the products that Germany is desperate to buy."

Todd then went on to speculate that the cartel operating through Mason's had begun to suspect that the Admiralty was getting wise to them, hence the decision to put the cargo onto, possibly, a British vessel from another port, to throw the Admiralty off the scent.

Beech felt his stomach sink as he privately feared that this change of tactic by the criminal cartel was due to one bent copper in Scotland Yard, but he decided not to divulge this information to Commander Todd for the moment. Instead, he took another two aspirin tablets, washed down with some unpleasant tasting coffee and settled himself down to have a decent night's sleep.

***

Myrtle Dimmock had decided that it was Billy's lucky day. As all the workers had packed into the omnibus on its way back to Stratford at 7p.m, the determined hand of Miss Dimmock had grabbed Billy's jacket and pulled him into the seat beside her. Taken off guard, Billy had smiled and attempted to make pleasant conversation, but Myrtle had been determined to flaunt her new 'conquest' and kept looking back at the other girls and grinning, whilst attempting to fondle Billy's hair. He had found this liberty-taking annoying, but tried to be offhand, whilst privately gritting his teeth. Eventually, he had decided to bite the bullet and ask her if she wanted to go for a drink that night. It would be late though, he explained, as he had a meeting first.

"How about I meet you off the train at Liverpool Street about nine?" he had suggested.

"I can't go drinking with you on my own!" she had replied, with mock virtue. "I'd have to bring along a chaperone."

"Oh yeah?" Billy had reacted with a touch of sarcasm, "Pardon me, your ladyship, I'm sure!"

"You know what I mean," she had said, pouting. "Don't

want to damage my reputation. I'd have to bring my friend with me."

Billy had rolled his eyes. "Go on then. But just one friend, mind. I'm not buying drinks for the whole bleeding cordite shed."

After his meeting at Lady Maud's, he changed into his best Sunday suit and made his way over to Liverpool Street Station. Myrtle was waiting, 'dolled-up' in some mauve creation of a dress and accompanied by a short girl, dressed more conservatively, by the name of Lily. Billy vaguely recalled seeing her on the omnibus, but he rarely paid much notice to the girls at Mason's. A bit rough for his taste, most of them, although Lily seemed fairly quiet – just prone to giggling at everything he said.

They went to a local pub in Bishopsgate and Billy started to ply them both with drinks. Gin and black was Myrtle's preferred tipple, whilst Lily was happy to nurse half a shandy. Conversation started in a general vein, with Billy asking innocuous questions about what the girls did on their days off, whether they liked working at Mason's and stuff about their families. A pleasant hour passed, but Billy found himself pitying their rough upbringing and wondering how girls like that could ever rise above violent and deprived childhoods.

After three gins, talk turned to Mason's and Muriel became quite scathing about her workplace and particularly vitriolic about Arnold Bradshaw, who had actually asked her out once and it had not gone well.

Apparently, he had 'wandering hands and expectations of what a girl would do for a sausage supper' which was way more than Myrtle was prepared to deliver.

Billy tutted and sympathised. It transpired that even Lily had been 'unnecessarily touched' by Bradshaw in the corridor at work.

"Blimey, sounds like old Bradshaw needs a punch on the nose!" Billy remarked, flexing his good hand. Lily giggled and Myrtle, who was on her fourth gin and a little the worse for wear, muttered something about having 'given him what for and he couldn't sit down for a week.'

"Did he have anything to do with that girl who died? Agnes something?" Billy tentatively asked, "I mean that was a funny business wasn't it? Her being murdered up West like that. You don't think old Bradshaw tried it on with her, do you?"

Lily stopped giggling and looked shocked at the thought. Myrtle became venomous. "She was a right bitch," she began. Billy noticed she was slurring her words a bit. She definitely can't hold her liquor, he thought to himself. Myrtle continued her diatribe. "Thought she was better than the rest of us, she did. Tried to worm her way into our good books. Ooh, Myrtle, why don't you come up West with me and do some shopping? Made me sick!"

Lily was becoming agitated by Myrtle's descent into drunkenness. "Myrtle, don't you think….?"

Like a lightning bolt, Myrtle turned on Lily – her supposed best friend- and lunged at her. Lily screamed as Myrtle's hands closed around her throat and Myrtle was shouting "Don't you tell me what to do! Don't you tell me…!"

Billy grabbed Myrtle from behind and attempted to drag her off, but she was possessed with abnormal strength in her rage. Lily was beginning to change colour, unable to breathe, and Billy was forced to punch Myrtle on the side of her head, which he knew would make her black out. And it did. Lily fell to the floor coughing and spluttering, while Myrtle was spark out on the table. The landlord came running over shouting, "Get out of my pub, the lot of you! Bloody ruffians!"

Billy tried to apologise, slung Myrtle over his shoulder and extended a hand to the shocked and sobbing Lily. "Sorry mate…sorry."

"Get 'em out of here!" the landlord continued to rage and, as Billy slowly exited with the two women, he gave a parting shot from the doorway, "And don't show your face in here ever again! Low-life!"

Lily was still sobbing, and Billy decided that he would have to escort the pair of them home, particularly as Myrtle was still unconscious and Lily was frightened. So, he hailed a taxicab outside of Liverpool Street station and almost threw Myrtle in the back, whilst Lily insisted that Billy sit in between her and her unconscious friend.

The driver looked at the three of them with distaste. "I hope she's not going to be sick in my cab," he said pointedly. Billy wearily produced his warrant card and replied, "Don't worry mate. You can charge the cleaning bill to Scotland Yard, if she is."

About one hour later, having delivered a faintly groaning Myrtle into the hands of her outraged landlady and escorted the grateful Lily round the corner to her lodgings, Billy Rigsby was walking briskly towards the station and was thanking his guardian angel that he had had a lucky escape during an unpleasant evening. Myrtle's rage made him shudder.

***

It was past midnight when Mabel Summersby popped into the pharmacy at the Women's Hospital. An idea had formed in her head and she just had to act upon it, otherwise she would not be able to sleep.

The night porter let her in. He was one of the few men allowed to work on the premises and he never went on to the wards. He just sat at the front desk all night and opened up for any emergency admissions.

"It's very late Miss Summersby!" he said jovially, as he unlocked the door. "I thought you were on holiday this week? I've got you down on my list as being away."

"Yes, officially I am. But I'm doing some experiments and I need a couple of items from the pharmacy to complete them. I'm so sorry, I know it's late, but I really needed to strike whilst the iron is hot, so to speak."

The porter nodded and went back to his desk and Mabel continued down to the basement, past the operating theatres and into her pharmacy. All was dark and quiet. The pharmacy wasn't usually open at night – all drugs for night care being dispensed to the doctors and nurses by eight, each night, and locked in the drug cupboards of each ward. Then it would open again at eight, each morning, to deal with the day's drug needs. If anything unusual was needed in an emergency, there was a pharmacist on call who could be brought in to dispense.

It was not uncommon for pharmacists to be called upon

to act as anaesthetists in a surgical emergency, as the profession of dedicated anaesthetist was still a rarity.

Mabel's task was quite simple, she took down some bottles from the shelves and started to mix a solution of potassium iodide with iodine in water. This would be the Lugol's Solution for Myrtle Dimmock. She put a label on and very carefully wrote, in capital letters, the dosage to be taken. Victoria had said that Myrtle could barely read, so Mabel would be sure to explain it thoroughly. Then she went to the storeroom next door and took six pairs of surgical/dispensing gloves and a tub of petroleum jelly. She made sure that she signed for everything she had removed from the hospital. Mabel was nothing if not meticulous. She had an idea which she wished to try out on the women workers in Mason's. It might not work, she reasoned, but then no-one ever made advances in health care without experimenting.

CHAPTER SIXTEEN

MORE INFORMATION COMES TO LIGHT

It had been decided by Tollman and Billy, that they would need to be on hand when the 'extra work' at Mason's was undertaken after hours. Billy wanted to be there to protect his mother and aunty, in case anything went wrong, and Tollman needed to get any paperwork obtained by the team over to the Admiralty as fast as possible. So, it was agreed that Tollman would meet Billy with a car at Stratford, after the Mason's workforce had left for the day, and they would drive back to the factory. Billy would hide outside the fence perimeter, near the canteen, so that either Sissy or Elsie could pass him any documents they managed to obtain. Tollman could then drive off to the Admiralty post-haste with the evidence. All of this had been relayed to Sam very early that morning by telephone, which Elsie and Sissy, over a hurried breakfast, had pronounced as "reassuring."

Tollman, once he had woken from a very deep sleep, caused by exhaustion and the generous whisky from the night before, felt sufficiently refreshed to make his way to the Postmaster General's Office in the City of London. Two days ago, he had used one of the warrants signed by Beech, to ask for all call records made through the Post Office telephone exchange in Wanstead, and also all call records made through the public call office in Wanstead High Street. He could have just walked into the exchange and call office and asked to look at their records but there were so few telephone numbers in the area of Wanstead – probably less than two hundred – that he did not want to risk the telephone operators relaying his interest back to Mason's factory. Despite it being wartime, some operators in small exchanges were known for their lack of discretion, sometimes even listening in to personal telephone calls. So he had had to pursue the more tortuous route of going through the Postmaster General's Office to get call records, which had added at least two day's wait to his investigations.

When he arrived at Aldersgate Street, he was shown into an empty room, save for a table and four chairs, and the records were brought to him, He was told that he was allowed to make notes but that he could not take them away without a court order. So, Tollman began to make notes. He knew Mason's telephone number, of course, WANSTEAD 27, and he began to write down every number dialled from the factory in the last month. It became clear that one number kept cropping up – both in making and receiving calls – MAYFAIR 209. So, then he cross checked with the calls made from the public telephone exchange during the same period and MAYFAIR 209 was shown as being contacted three times from the public facility. This puzzled him. *Why would Bradshaw go out to the public facility to contact this number, when he had a telephone on his desk?* He looked at the times and dates of the calls and noted that they were all around lunchtime on a working day. Odd.

He looked at the clock on the wall and realised that he would be late for this meeting that Eustace King had set up, if he stayed any longer. No time to look through the telephone directories at the moment, so he rang the bell to summon the clerk and tell him that he had finished with the records.

⁂

Mabel was trying out her idea on the women who worked in the cordite room. The supervisor had selected four employees to try to work for the day wearing the surgical gloves.

"It shouldn't be problem," she explained to Mrs Hawkesworth, "because surgeons and pharmacists wear them to carry out quite detailed work and these ladies are only measuring and cutting cordite. It's not that fiddly, is it?"

The women were asked to try the gloves for a day and to only take them off if they went to the toilet or had something to eat.

Mrs Hawkesworth shrugged and said "Why not?"

Mabel, satisfied, then asked if Myrtle Dimmock could be excused for a brief visit to the medical room.

"With pleasure!" was the heartfelt response. The supervisor had already had to deal with Myrtle turning up for work considerably worse for wear and more than usually truculent. Plus, Myrtle's 'best friend' of the moment, Lily, had become tearful at the thought of sitting next to her, so Mrs Hawkesworth had had to ask one of the older women to change places with Lily, who had cast fearful glances at Myrtle all morning. Whatever was going on was a mystery that the supervisor had no desire to unravel.

Myrtle silently followed Mabel to the medical room, where Caroline and Victoria were busy writing up some notes.

"Good God, you look dreadful Miss Dimmock!" said Caroline looking up from her paperwork. "Whatever have you been up to? You look as though you are at death's door."

"One too many drinks in the pub," said Myrtle sullenly. "I've got a splitting headache and a bruise just here," she pointed to her temple. "Must have fallen over but I don't remember nothing."

Caroline examined the bruise and then the girl's eyes, tongue and listened to her chest.

"You know you really shouldn't drink alcohol at all, with your thyroid problem. You are quite thin, and it means that you are very quickly and badly affected by alcohol. I will give you some pain powders, in water and then you must drink at least a pint of water afterwards. Mrs Ellingham will put some salve on that bruise, then Miss Summersby will give you instructions for taking your daily medicine, that she has kindly made up for you, free of charge. Myrtle," Caroline added, "you are also anaemic, which means you don't have enough iron in your blood."

"So, what am I supposed to do about that then?" asked Myrtle defiantly.

Caroline looked at Mabel, who was always up with the latest research on any medical condition. Mabel looked at Myrtle and said, "I'm afraid all I can recommend is eat as much beef, eggs and spinach as you can. And eat less bread."

"Oh, I can do that!" was Myrtle's response, visibly relieved that it didn't involve any more pills and potions.

Mabel gave her the bottle of Lugol's solution and told her exactly how many drops to take in water and how many times a day. She asked Myrtle to repeat it – not once, but twice. When Mabel was sure that Myrtle understood completely, she was allowed to leave and return to work.

Caroline quizzed Mabel, once Myrtle had left, about the diet for anaemia. "Are you sure about that, Mabel? Only the last I read about it – admittedly in medical school – it was felt that iron in food couldn't be separated by the body and absorbed through the stomach. Wouldn't pills be better?"

Mabel shook her head firmly. "I have read recent studies with dogs that suggest otherwise – besides the pills that are on offer are worse than having anaemia. They have arsenic in them, and I won't make them anymore."

Caroline and Victoria looked at each other in alarm and Caroline vowed never to prescribe any medicine again without first consulting Mabel.

***

Malcolm Sinclair made an appearance in the loading bay, which caused a distinct change in atmosphere, Billy observed. The man frequently strutted about as though the factory was his personal fiefdom and the management of it had nothing at all to do with Bradshaw. His eye roved across the men who working, and alighted upon Sam, who was sharing a joke with two other black labourers whilst they lifted a cotton bale from the top of a pile.

"Oy!" Sinclair shouted, "You darkies! Get on with your work and stop slacking."

Sam's face grew angry, whilst the man standing next to him, touched his hand and gave a small shake of the head, as if to say "It's not worth it." Tom, the man who was really in charge of the loading bay, drew himself up to his full height and glared at Sinclair.

"I'm in charge in the loading bay!" said Tom menacingly. "You have no jurisdiction here, Sinclair, get out!"

Sinclair bridled and shouted back, "I'm the only man here who officially speaks for the working man – the unionised working man – and don't you forget it!"

Tom picked up his baling hook and advanced slowly on Sinclair. Billy stood up, in case he had to intervene.

"None of the men here belong to your bloody union, Sinclair…" his voice was low now and he gripped the wooden handle of the baling hook with controlled anger. "So, sling your hook before I sling this one into your scrawny body."

Sinclair looked at Tom with a mixture of fear and contempt. Billy could see the Scotsman was thinking about standing up to the older man, but he was unsure of the outcome, so he just curled his lip in distaste and turned for the door. Then he turned back and said, "You're getting too old for this job, Tom. I just might find myself making a recommendation to Bradshaw that you're not up to it anymore."

Tom gave a hollow laugh. "The moment I no longer work here, Sinclair, is the moment that you have to start looking over your shoulder every minute of the day. Because I will come after you. Rest assured of that." Billy felt a cold shiver run down his back as he looked at all the men's faces. All he could see was a strong dislike of Malcolm Sinclair and he knew that Tom's threat was real.

Sinclair left and the men relaxed. They said nothing but one or two patted Tom on the back, which he shrugged away.

Being basically a fair and tolerant man, he was embarrassed at his anger and did not want the men's support. So, he half-heartedly tried to sound tough as he said, "Come on now – get back to work!" but Billy could see that he was troubled.

Later, during a break, when the men went out, away from the factory, to smoke their cigarettes or pipes, Billy went with them and sought Tom out.

"Do you get much trouble from this Sinclair, then?" he asked the supervisor.

Tom puffed on his pipe thoughtfully and grimaced. "He thinks Mason's is his little empire," he said scornfully. "He's a bully. He throws his weight around and intimidates people into joining his union. Even Bradshaw is scared of him." Tom took a few more puffs on his pipe before emptying it on to the gravel. "There is some secret in this factory that Sinclair is a party to – and Bradshaw – but we are all kept in the dark. I'm sure of that. Odd comings and goings, if you get my drift. Stock disappearing – owners of the place that have never visited – not once. It's odd."

Then Tom nodded at Billy and the men made their way back to the loading bay.

As they went back in, Malcolm Sinclair came out, wearing his hat and jacket and studiously avoiding making any eye contact with the men from the loading bay. Billy watched him walk briskly down the road, in the direction of Wanstead. *Is he leaving for the day?* Billy wondered, as Sinclair seemed to be heading towards the station. He would have followed him but, dressed in his uniform and the fact that there was no-one else about, he would have been much too conspicuous. So he went back into the factory and knocked on Bradshaw's door.

"Yes?" said Bradshaw wearily, as Billy entered.

"This man, Malcolm Sinclair…" Billy began, and noted the look of alarm that appeared on Bradshaw's face. "He seems to come and go as he pleases, and he seems to think he runs this place."

Bradshaw was silent for a moment and then responded, "What is your point?"

Billy found this an odd response. "You seem to forget, sir, that Special Branch is concerned that there may be German spy activity in and around munitions factories and we have been told to watch out for any employees who act suspiciously. Now, this Sinclair, has just been in the loading bay and threatened the supervisor with the sack…" Bradshaw made a noise of disgust but Billy continued, "…and now I see him walking off, down to the town, as large as life. To me, that constitutes suspicious behaviour. Any comment, sir?" Bill had tried his best to be authoritative and it seemed to have worked. Bradshaw invited him to sit down and then he spoke confidentially.

"I suspect. PC Rigsby, that the only person Malcolm Sinclair is spying on is me. He has…a special relationship… with one of the directors of the company…which he flings in my face every time I try to discipline him. This has got worse throughout this year. As you have noted, he feels he can walk out of the factory every time he feels like it – no doubt to go to the public telephone exchange to call this director and report on matters. At the moment, there is nothing I can do about it."

"And who is this director, Mr Bradshaw?" Billy

enquired, taking out his notebook and pencil.

Bradshaw looked agitated and said "I've said too much. Please forget our conversation. Just be aware that the situation with Malcolm Sinclair is not a police matter. Now, if you don't mind, constable, I have work to do."

Billy realised that the conversation was at an end, but he was intrigued now, and he decided that more investigation was definitely required.

***

Commander Todd was restless again. The original ship that he and Beech were supposed to have boarded, had docked, disgorged weary but cheerful sailors ready for a spot of leave, and embarked the new crew that had travelled up from Glasgow. The ship was now refuelling and taking on water. The old crew had rushed to the station, anxious to get their period of leave started – anywhere but Scotland – and the depot was empty, apart from the captain of the navy ship and a couple of his officers, who were enjoying some drink and food on dry land before they set off again.

The captain had explained to Todd why the ship had been delayed. It was, he said, due to the fact that, his ship had arrested a Canadian vessel from Newfoundland, bound for Scandinavia, with a full cargo of steel wire. Then, they had been forced to wait until the Foreign Office sent instructions as to whether the Canadian vessel could proceed or whether the cargo was to be seized and impounded.

"What was the verdict?" asked Todd cynically, knowing

only too well the answer that would be forthcoming.

"Proceed," said the captain, with a rueful smile.

Todd banged on the table in frustration. "That cargo will be in Germany before the week is out!" And he got up and walked away, unable to contain his anger.

The captain looked at Beech and nodded. "That's the fourth vessel that's been allowed by Whitehall to slip through the blockade this week. It's making a mockery of the work we are doing up here. But then, I'm not sure, that that wasn't the plan from the start."

Beech looked concerned. "What do you mean?"

The captain shrugged. "In December, the Admiralty decided – or the government – whoever – to replace all the navy warships on the blockade with armed merchant ships. Like this one…" and he gestured towards the ship berthed outside on the docks. It was painted grey, like a navy vessel but it was not, to the trained eye, a battleship. The captain continued in a scornful tone, "This is one of the largest of the fleet, 19,000 tons. Some of them are as small as 3,000 tons. The crews are not navy, they're merchant seamen, although, I have to say, I couldn't wish for a better crew. They can handle a ship in a force nine gale, of which we get plenty up round the Orkneys, better than any crew I've ever had. But only myself, the executive officer and chief gunner, are navy personnel."

Beech was astonished as he learned that the blockade ships intercepted dozens of vessels a week, risking their lives to impound suspect cargoes, only to have some faceless men in the Foreign Office and the Contraband Committee overriding the navy requests, ordering the release of certain vessels and brooking no appeal or argument.

Todd had come back to the table and added to the tale, explaining to Beech how the decision to arrest vessels was based on his department's statistics on pre-war commodities.

"Take for example, cotton, in the form in which it is used to make gun cotton. Pre-war shipments to Norway, Denmark and Holland – countries we suspect are supplying Germany – pre-war shipments of cotton were around two hundred thousand bales. This year, shipment has increased to almost three and a half million bales. It doesn't take a genius to realise what is happening."

The captain had finished his meal and had decided to return to his ship. He shook Todd and Beech's hands and expressed a fervent wish that the Admiralty Trade Department would be able to put a stop to this illegal trade.

"We have lost over three hundred men in the first half of this year," he said sadly, "and U boat activity is increasing all the time. I don't know how many more men we will lose before the end of the year. Something must be done."

***

Eustace King put three pints of beer on the table and the two other men picked them up gratefully and began to sup.

"Well this is nice," said Tollman with genuine warmth. "All three of us from the old section together again. We should make it regular." He smiled at the others.

The third man, Harry Skinner, nodded contentedly. "It's been too long, Arthur," he agreed. "But I thought you retired?

How come you're back in the force?"

Tollman gave him the story that they were calling all old coppers back into the police to make up for the young men going off to war – plus, he explained, there were old cases to be followed up on and, in this case, a bent copper to be investigated.

Skinner shook his head in annoyance. "Bad business when coppers go off the rails. Tars us all with the same brush. So how can I help?" he asked, after another swallow of beer.

Eustance showed him the picture of Carter, which Skinner instantly recognised, saying "I thought he was slimy git, when I first clapped eyes on him. Not your usual clientele in the Public Schools Club."

"So how does it get in then?" Tollman asked.

"As a guest. He usually comes as a guest of Mr Aubrey Rutledge. He's a *posh* slimy git from the Foreign Office. A bloke with a gambling habit too. Don't know where he gets the money from either. He's only a Senior Officer. Nothing too special."

Upon further questioning, Skinner revealed that Carter and this Aubrey Rutledge frequently played cards with Lord Budlington and Sir Cecil Maydew. Rutledge usually lost money. Carter's luck he couldn't be sure about.

"Very exalted company," commented Eustace sarcastically.

"Nah," was Skinner's dismissive observation. "Minor aristocracy is Budlington, by all accounts, and Maydew's only a 'sir' because he's been in the civil service since Queen Victoria was a nipper. Nothing special."

Skinner also volunteered the fact that Rutledge used the club like his own personal office. He was often there for lunch and he frequently took and made telephone calls, but he couldn't be sure who the calls were from or whom he might be calling because Skinner didn't start work until seven in the evening. "Although," he added, "He did use the member's telephone last night, about eight o'clock, but I don't know who he called. The member's telephone goes straight through to the exchange and they put them through. The staff don't get involved in asking for numbers on that telephone. Do you want me to find out for you? I could ask one of the other lads about the daytime calls." Skinner obviously relished the prospect of being involved in an investigation again.

"No, we'd best not involve anyone else at this stage," advised Tollman. "I'll just use another warrant to investigate that number. What is it?"

"MAYFAIR 209."

Tollman felt a tingle go all the way down to his fingertips. That was the very number he had been writing down in his notebook two hours earlier.

"Oh, and another thing," added Skinner, putting down his empty pint glass, signalling that he was ready for another, "Rutledge receives a lot of telegrams every week and sends quite a few as well. I once heard him, before he closed the telephone booth in the club, say to the operator, "I want to send a telegram…".

This piece of information dictated exactly the place of Tollman's next investigation. The three men fell to talking about old times and Eustace ordered some sausage rolls for lunch. When Skinner paid a visit to the lavatory, Eustace asked Tollman if he wanted him to follow Carter tomorrow. Tollman shook his head.

"No thanks, Eustace. I think we have enough, at the moment. I need to wait for my boss to come back before we can make any more moves. You've been a great help. Send me your bill and I'll get it paid right away."

It's a pleasure," replied Eustace. "Just let me know when DS Carter gets prosecuted and I'll organise a day trip with the lads, to pack out the courtroom."

Tollman smiled. *That would be a great day*, he thought.

Chapter Seventeen

FOREIGN COMMUNICATIONS

Tollman went straight from the pub in Clapham to the Central Telegraph Office, near St. Paul's Cathedral in the City of London. Armed with another of his warrants, he asked the Chief Telegraph Clerk if it was possible to see telegrams sent from a particular telephone number in the West End. The clerk blanched and asked over what period. Tollman decided to be charitable and ask for the last three months. The Chief Clerk said he "would do his best", would "put one of his best ladies on it", but he "couldn't promise anything." Then he gave Tollman a brief lecture about the fact that the CTO sent thousands of telegrams a day and that the police should realise that there is a war on. Tollman took all of this with good grace, despite feeling as though he wanted to arrest the Chief Clerk for obstruction of justice, and agreed to go away and have a cup of tea for an hour whilst the search was made. However, he made the point that he could not wait any longer than that as he had to return to Scotland Yard at five o'clock. Then he went to search for a café in the alleyways of the City of London.

As he stood by an outdoor tea stall, with a cup of tea so hot that he had had to pour some of it into the saucer and drink it, he reflected that the City of London had, so far, been relatively unscathed by the spasmodic Zeppelin air raids. The really big one at the end of May had bombed in a straight line from Stoke Newington, in the north east of London, down through Dalston, Hoxton, Shoreditch, Spitalfields, Whitechapel, Stepney, Stratford and finally Leytonstone. The only bomb that actually had impinged on the City of London itself was the one that had fallen through the Great Eastern Railway's goods yard in Bishopsgate. There had been 41 fires that night, but none in the Square Mile. Given that he was currently involved in investigating a collaboration between British business interests and Germany, he wondered if the Kaiser had also issued orders to not only avoid Buckingham Palace but also the City of London. But then he discounted that theory, reasoning that Zeppelins did not seem to be that accurate. In June, for example, strong winds had caused one Zeppelin to drift off course and drop its bombs on Gravesend in Kent instead of London and he had heard of another one going so badly off course that it ended up dropping its bombs on Hull in Yorkshire. So, Tollman decided to discount any notion he may have had that the City of London had been spared by a conspiracy of unscrupulous businessmen.

After another cup of tea and an urgent visit to the gentleman's public toilet in Paternoster Square, Tollman made his way back to the Central Telegraph Office and found himself having to endure another ticking-off from the Chief Clerk.

"Well, really, Detective Sergeant, if you had told me in the beginning that you were looking for telegrams to overseas locations, it would have made our job so much easier!"

Tollman protested that he had no idea to where or whom the suspect was addressing the telegrams and decided he had had enough of being lectured by a jobsworth, so he said firmly, "It is possible that we are investigating a German spy ring and

I should like to be able to tell my superiors that I have received every possible co-operation from the Telegraph Office."

With that the clerk became both flushed and flustered and handed over the batch of telegrams saying abruptly, "I shall require you to sign a form stating that I have handed over care of these private telegrams to the police." Tollman duly signed, tipped his hat to the man and left. He grabbed the first number 11 omnibus that came along, in order to get back to Scotland Yard and get the motor car that he had requisitioned, so that he could go and pick up Billy in Stratford.

On the bus, as he was seated virtually on his own on the lower deck, he glanced through the telegrams. They were all instructions to companies in Norway or Denmark about ship and cargo movements. Only the Admiralty Trade Department would be able to match them up with their identified suspect cargoes. Also, now, thanks to Harry Skinner, the night porter at The Public Schools Club, he would be able to give Captain Webb the name of the suspect, Aubrey Rutledge.

***

Billy felt on edge because, understandably, he was worried about Sissy and Elsie being on the front line tonight – on their own with Sam – to actually try and learn as much as they could about whatever was going on at Mason's.

His mother had brushed aside his concerns when he managed to speak to them alone after the lunch break.

"Billy," Elsie said firmly, "We were in much more danger when we got involved in the last case. I mean, think about poor Mabel! Kidnapped at gun point! That could have been any one of us. This lot," she added scornfully, "probably don't even know they're involved in anything criminal. They're just the lackeys in all this. The real dangerous criminals are the ones I suspect murdered poor Agnes Whitlock, and who are making all the money out of this enterprise. Don't you worry about us, son."

"No," added Sissy. "We're just a couple of canteen cooks. I mean, who would suspect us of being investigators, eh? Done up in costumes that look like a couple of potato sacks! What would they think we would be capable of? Bashing them over the head with soup ladles?"

Billy had to laugh. They both made his concerns seem so stupid.

"No, you worry about yourself, son," said Elsie. "You're the one who is going to have to eventually arrest the scum responsible for this. You watch out for yourself."

Billy knew they were right and, although he didn't get a chance to speak to Sam, they exchanged looks and nods and he felt reassured that Sam was intelligent and strong enough to deal with whatever might crop up tonight.

So when Billy left on the worker's omnibus at the end of the day, apart from the awkward moment when he was ignored by Myrtle Dimmock, who was obviously embarrassed by her drunken performance the night before, he felt confident that the night's activities would probably be uneventful.

Tollman was waiting for him in the car, near the station, as agreed and, as Billy changed out of his uniform in the back seat, Tollman told him all about the information he had gathered and also the events of his very productive day.

"So, you reckon this Rutledge is the mastermind behind all of this, then?" asked Billy, pulling a jumper over his head.

Tollman made a face and shook his head. "Well…" he said carefully, "I've not met the bloke, of course, but I'm inclined to think that no matter how pompous a civil servant is, they rarely have the front to be a mastermind in a criminal caper. I just have the feeling that there is someone else behind him, that is actually pulling the strings."

"Be nice if we could get Carter for this, though, wouldn't it Mr Tollman?"

"Oh yes, son." Tollman agreed. "That would be a pleasure."

***

Phyllis had some stomach gripes. She had been complaining of them all afternoon and, after a lengthy session in the toilet, which left her a little pale, she announced to Sissy and Elsie that she would have to go home.

"Will you be able to cope?" she asked wanly of the ladies.

"Of course we will!" said Sissy. "You can't be making sandwiches and the like when you've got a gippy tummy, can you? Now you just get yourself off home, take some kaolin and morphine, and put a hot water bottle on your back. You'll be as right as rain tomorrow."

Phyllis agreed and left, clutching her stomach.

Elsie murmured, "I hope that God will forgive us for

putting senokot in her lunch." She felt guilty.

Sissy looked at her and murmured back, "Think of it as a charitable act. We have removed Phyllis from any danger there might be this evening."

About 8 p.m. the back gates, which were at the side of the loading bay, were opened, and the first of several horse and carts pulled into the yard.

"Look alive, Sis!" Elsie remarked, as the first horse clattered in front of the loading bay. "It looks like we're needed!"

Sissy swept up the large pot of tea and started ladling it out into large tin mugs. Elsie followed after her, topping up each mug with the milk. Then Sissy put them all on two big trays with bowls of sugar and spoons and they set off across the yard, offering tea to the drivers and their lads, as they sat patiently waiting to enter the yard. There were eight two-horse carts in total, with more to come, apparently. It was going to be a long night.

Tom and his gang of just five men – of which Sam was one – were unloading as fast as they could and stacking the bales as high as possible in the loading bay. After a while, Bradshaw and Malcolm Sinclair appeared and Bradshaw instructed the labourers to start stacking bales in the yard, in front of the nitro-glycerine shed.

"They can't stay there, Mr Bradshaw," objected Tom, "the men who work in there will need to get in and out tomorrow morning."

"They're not staying there," was Bradshaw's curt reply. "Half of these bales are going somewhere else." Tom looked at Bradshaw quizzically, which earned him the snappy comment, "Get on with it, Tom. Do as you're told!" So, Tom obeyed and nodded at his men to follow orders and stack them in front of the nitro shed.

Elsie and Sissy watched through the window of the canteen as the cotton bales piled up and horses and carts were manoeuvred in and out of the yard.

"There's enough cotton there to keep this factory going for a year," whispered Elsie and Sissy agreed.

Bradshaw approached the canteen and the two women immediately returned to buttering bread for the sandwiches that Phyllis had told them would be needed.

"We are going to have to pile up some bales in front of the canteen windows, ladies," said Bradshaw.

"That's alright Mr Bradshaw," said Elsie cheerfully. "As long as we can get in and out to serve the sandwiches."

"It won't be long," he replied. "There's some motor transport coming later to take half of this lot away." He looked around. "Where's Phyllis?"

"Stomach upset," said Sissy. "She had to go home as she was poorly. Never mind," she added. "We can cope!"

Bradshaw nodded and said, "Very well, ladies. You might want to put the electric light on, as we will be stacking the bales in front of all your windows, temporarily."

Tollman and Billy were sitting in the car, front lights out, and hidden in a thicket off the side of the road. They watched in amazement as the horses and carts kept coming – the cotton bales piled high on the back, covered by tarpaulins.

"Bloody hell," murmured Billy. "That's a lot of cotton!"

"It certainly is, lad, it certainly is," Tollman agreed. "The trouble is, you won't be able to hide by the fence until all this lot has been delivered and then collected, presumably, by motor transport. Because all the traffic is going to go right around the factory. You'll be seen."

"The minute the last road transport leaves, my mum is going to throw a bucket of water over the fence as a signal that all is clear - and I'll leg it over there to get any information they have to give me."

Tollman nodded. He should have known that Billy would organise everything properly.

The men unloading were sweating now, they were having to work so fast, and it was a warm night. Tom gave the order to strip off their shirts and vests and work naked from the waist up. Sissy, watching from the door space between the bales of cotton, decided enough was enough and re-appeared with mugs of tea for the men.

"Here you are, lads," she said cheerfully. "Have a break for a moment and wet your whistles."

The men paused gratefully and downed mugs of tea in almost one go. Bradshaw did not comment but Sinclair decided to complain.

"We haven't got time for these men to idle about," he said loudly, directing his complaint to Bradshaw.

Bradshaw told him to shut up. Tom and Sissy glared at him and the men just shook their heads in disbelief. No-one understood why Malcolm Sinclair was there or why his opinion carried such weight at the factory. Sam began to formulate a plan that might work in everyone's favour but it would depend on how the cotton bales were being collected.

Finally, the first wave of carts had been and gone and they were about to unload the last two carts from the second wave of carts. There was barely an inch of room left in the yard.

"Are there any more carts coming, Mr Bradshaw?" Tom asked, wiping the sweat from his face and torso by using his vest as a towel. "Because there is no more room."

Bradshaw shook his head and said that the road transport would be here soon.

"My men need a rest before hauling these bales again," Tom replied flatly, his voice indicating that he would brook no argument on the matter. Bradshaw nodded and promised more tea and sandwiches. Sinclair made a noise of disgust to express how much he disapproved of this action.

"You are too bloody soft on these men," Sinclair growled at Bradshaw, who merely ignored him.

Sam was watching and waiting for his opportunity. But it was not yet. During the agreed period of rest, Sam offered to go and fetch sandwiches from the ladies and he took the hurried opportunity to give them some instructions.

"When the motor transport arrives, wait until we are well into loading up, then go and suggest to Bradshaw that the drivers come out of their transport and into the canteen, because its easier for you to serve them. Bradshaw will have to come to them with the bill of lading or the documents that they have to present to the ship or the warehouse. If it's a bill of lading, there might be three or four copies. We need the bottom copy. They won't miss it until they get to the ship. If it's a warehouse, we just need the address, so keep a pencil and paper handy.

Once the documents have been signed by the lead driver, I need you to signal me…"

"I'll call out from the doorway, asking if anyone wants some more tea," volunteered Elsie.

Sam nodded in approval. "Then I will create a diversion, so it might get a bit messy in here. You need to grab the documents, if you can. Then hand them back when everything calms down. Understand?" Then he left.

Sissy and Elsie prepared to follow his instructions as best as they could.

Sinclair was obviously on edge and he kept pacing around the yard all the time that the men were having a break and complaining to Bradshaw about the fact that the lorries should have been there by now. Bradshaw shrugged it off, but it was apparent to the casual observer that he was nervous too. It seemed to Sam that wherever this cotton was going, it was on a deadline, which would indicate a ship, rather than a warehouse. A ship that had to load and sail at high tide tomorrow, was Sam's way of thinking, hence the concern about the delay in unloading at the Port of London yesterday and the rush to make an overnight journey tonight.

Within five minutes, the rumble of engines could be heard, and it signalled the appearance of a line of six 3-ton open lorries. Sam vaguely recognised the drivers as being from a firm of hauliers that frequently worked the various docks in London. Their yard was based in the rabbit warren around the docks at Butlers Wharf, near Tower Bridge. Tollman might find it useful to pay them a visit tomorrow. Sam, with his experience as a docker, did a swift mental calculation, and realised that each lorry would be able to take around thirteen bales of cotton but no more, otherwise they would exceed their weight limit. He looked around the yard and, to his practised eye, he thought that they might just manage that number.

The first lorry had reversed, with some difficulty, into the yard. The driver came out of the cab and proceeded to drop down one of the sides, so that the men could begin loading.

Sinclair decided to make his presence known again and said sharply to Tom, "You should be able to get fifteen bales on each lorry."

Sam shook his head and spoke up. "They're only 3 ton lorries. The most you can put on them is thirteen bales, otherwise you'll overload them."

Sinclair looked as though he had been smacked in the face. "Who asked you?" he said indignantly. "You mind your own business!"

Bradshaw came up. "What's going on?"

"Bloody darkie telling me how much should be loaded on this truck…"

Sam was sorely tempted to hit him there and then, but it was not the right time. Fortunately, Bradshaw and Tom both took exception to Sinclair's attitude.

Bradshaw said, "Sam Abbott used to be a docker. He knows what he's talking about. Shut your face, Sinclair and let the men get on with it."

"Yes, go on, get out of our way," added Tom tersely.

Sinclair's face was a picture of evil. He would not forget this in a hurry, and he flashed Sam a look of pure vindictiveness, which was received by Sam with a sneer, which enraged the Scotsman even more. Nevertheless, he stood back, while the men began to load the bales, but he never took his eyes off Sam all the while the work proceeded.

As if on cue, Elsie came over and asked Bradshaw if the drivers could come into the canteen to have some refreshment. Bradshaw agreed and began to go down the line of lorries to tell the drivers at the front that once they had backed their lorry into the yard, they could go and have some refreshments whilst it was being loaded. Those at the back of the line could go now. So, several men got out of their vehicles and trooped gratefully into the canteen for sandwiches and tea. Bradshaw disappeared into the office and Sam hoped that he was going to get paperwork. By the time they were loading the third lorry, Bradshaw reappeared, carrying a clipboard on which were several sheets of paper. He looked at the lorries and decided, to Sam's relief, that the man he wanted was in the canteen, and he set off in that direction.

Sam looked at Sinclair, who was still watching him, and he took some deep breaths. It was time to get ready. He heard Elsie's voice call out "Anyone want any more tea?" and he said to Tom, "I'm just going to get a mouthful of water, my mouth's parched. Is that OK? I won't be a minute." Tom nodded and Sam turned gratefully and locked eyes with Sinclair. As he passed the Scotsman, he gave a grin and, out of sight of anyone else he deliberately raised the middle finger of his left hand in a pointedly rude gesture and swiftly moved on towards the canteen. Sinclair, naturally, responded with an outraged "Oy!" and Sam could hear that he was following hard on his heels into the canteen. As Sam burst in the door, he immediately registered that there were five drivers plus Bradshaw in the room and the paperwork was, thankfully, still attached to the clipboard and was on the middle table. He stepped swiftly to one side as Sinclair came in the door behind him, with a face like thunder.

Sinclair foolishly swung at Sam. Even though he didn't know that Sam was a seasoned boxer, the Scotsman was at least six inches shorter and Sam was, probably, carrying a good forty pounds of extra weight, which was pure muscle.

He heard Sissy say, "Oh my Gawd!" and Bradshaw said, "Bloody hell!" loudly and Sam felt a brief moment of exhilaration. I'm going to enjoy this he thought delightedly, as he realised that he was going to have to play it out a little to give the ladies time to get the paperwork. The first thing he did was give Sinclair a swift, but fairly tame, punch in the guts to wind him. Several of the drivers cheered – not because they knew Sinclair and enjoyed seeing him thumped, but simply because it was a long night and they were bored. Next, Sam grabbed Sinclair under the armpits and literally threw him across the surface of the table where the men were sitting, they all leapt back, whilst paperwork, metal mugs and plates scattered across the floor and Sissy shrieked. Sam noted, with satisfaction, that Elsie scrabbled after the paperwork, grabbed it and retreated into the kitchen. Now Sam needed to play around with Sinclair a little to buy time. By now, the noise had attracted the other labourers, who had crowded in the doorway. Sam picked up the dazed Sinclair, who managed to throw one feeble punch at Sam's chest, before he was swung around and thrown at the men in the doorway, who scattered like ninepins.

Everyone was shouting, mostly words of encouragement at Sam, thankfully, except for Bradshaw who kept bawling, "Stop this! Stop this at once!"

There was a moment's silence as Sinclair was picked up by two of the labourers and he stood there, slightly swaying, but defiant. Sam waited expectantly. He knew the Scotsman was not bright enough to know when to quit. The drivers and labourers held their breath, some with half smiles playing about their lips, as they hoped that Sam would now go in for the kill. Elsie deliberately came into Sam's line of vision and gave a barely discernible nod to signal that she had the paperwork and Sam smiled menacingly.

"I've had enough of you, Sinclair," he said, "always on my back because you don't like the colour of my skin…"

Sinclair looked at Sam venomously and spat on the floor in contempt. "I hate darkies. You should bloody well go back to where you were born and stay out of the way of civilised people."

"Is that right?" asked Sam, with murder in his soul. "Funny that. 'Cos I was born in London. Seems to me like you're the foreigner here, Sinclair," and with that he swung a tremendously powerful right hook into Sinclair's face which landed with a sickening crunch of bone that made everyone in the room flinch and gasp. Sinclair wouldn't be giving his opinion, verbally, for some time, and he smacked into the wall and slid down into a heap. There was a small ripple of applause and the men began to disperse.

Bradshaw was beyond agitated. "What have you done?!" his voice was almost a shriek, "We haven't got time for all this!

Look at the state of him!" He pointed at the prone Sinclair.

Sam turned a contrite face to the manager and said, "I'm sorry, Mr Bradshaw. I suppose you'll be giving me my cards now."

Bradshaw looked confused. "I didn't say that! We can't deal with all this now! Get back to work! These lorries have got to be on their way!"

The driver and labourers – entertainment over – went back to loading. The lead driver, having retrieved the clipboard from Elsie, unclipped the paperwork and stuffed it in his pocket. Sissy and Elsie began handing out sandwiches wrapped in paper to all the drivers. Bradshaw, meanwhile, was standing over Sinclair, looking at him but with absolutely no idea what to do.

"You leave him to us, Mr Bradshaw," said Sissy cheerfully. "I know how to push a broken jaw back into place."

"You do?" Bradshaw was aghast at the thought of such a thing. "How do you know that?"

"I used to lay people out for the local undertaker," she replied, handing out the last packet of sandwiches to a driver who was laughing quietly to himself. "You'd be surprised how many fellas drop dead of a heart attack in the middle of a fist fight," she continued to the dumbfounded Bradshaw. "It's only right to put the jaw back in to place before they bury them… don't you think?"

Bradshaw had absolutely no response to that question and walked out, almost in a state of shock at the turn of events.

Whilst Sissy put her fingers in Sinclair's mouth and began to push the bones into place from the inside, Elsie kept watch at the door of the canteen to see how things were progressing.

"He's lucky," said Sissy to Elsie's back. "It's only broke in two places. Seem like clean breaks. It could have been a lot worse. He could have had a glass jaw and he'd have been drinking his meals through a straw for the rest of his life."

"It could be a lot worse, Sis," agreed Elsie, continuing her surveillance. "He could have been conscious whilst you were putting it all back in place."

***

Tollman and Billy were getting impatient. Billy was worried about his mother and aunt and Tollman realised that he hadn't had anything to eat all day except one small sausage roll and his stomach was growling.

"Taking their time, aren't they?" Tollman grumbled. "If they don't get a move on, they're not going to get up to Immingham, or wherever they're going, by daybreak. They should be on their way by now."

"Hey up!" Billy nudged Tollman. "They're on the move!" They could both hear the rumbling of the vehicles as they began to convoy away from the factory. He got out of the automobile and crouched in the bushes watching for the signal. About two minutes after the last lorry left, Billy saw and heard the bucket of water being lobbed over the fence and he ran towards the lights of the canteen building.

He whistled softly and Elsie said quietly, "Is that you, Billy?"

"Yes, mum, is everything all right?"

"Everything is fine, Billy. I'm going to throw over two

packets of sandwiches for you and Arthur. The paperwork he wants is in one of them."

"Righto!" said Billy, expertly catching the first, and then the second of the packages. "I'll wait for you and Sis at the station, shall I? Escort you home, like?"

"No, you're alright, love," Elsie replied. "Mr Bradshaw's giving us a lift to Stratford because we've got to take Mr Sinclair to hospital."

"Eh?" Billy was concerned. "What's happened?"

Elsie gave a low chuckle. "Sam thumped him, knocked him spark out and broke his jaw in two places."

"Bloody hell!" Billy grinned in the dark and shook his head. "Alright, well I'll meet you at Liverpool Street Station then. Take you for a fish and chip supper."

"Ooh lovely! See you in about an hour."

When Billy scrambled into the automobile, clutching the sandwiches, and relayed the information about the night's escapades, Tollman laughed out loud. "Ah well, at least Sinclair won't be able to do a runner, if he's laying in a hospital bed. I have a feeling he's involved quite deeply in this matter – even, possibly, the murder of Agnes Whitlock."

Tollman retrieved the Bill of Lading and then proceeded to devour the sandwiches. "Cheese and pickle," he murmured gratefully, "my favourite." He took several mouthfuls and then turned on the engine. "Right. I must go as fast as possible to the Admiralty – but I'll drop you off at Liverpool Street on my way."

CHAPTER EIGHTEEN

TAKING TO THE HIGH SEAS

Beech and Todd were woken at two in the morning by the Night Watch Officer bearing a signal from Captain Webb.

"At last!" said Todd, as he scanned the message.

"Any reply, sir?" asked the officer.

"Just say 'understood'", Todd replied, and the officer duly left. "Right, we're in business!" Todd said to Beech. "Your people have obviously worked their magic and we have confirmation that the cotton cargo is being shipped from Immingham tomorrow evening to Esbjerg in Denmark. Consignee is the Universel Import Co., Borgergade 52, Esbjerg. A fishing trawler is leaving Scapa Flow tonight to pick us up in the morning and we will leave on the morning tide, after she has taken on coal. So, I think we can get another four hours sleep, don't you?" and Todd cheerfully lay down again. Within minutes he appeared to be asleep.

Beech was now wide awake. His leg was beginning to ache a little and he decided that he needed more medication, so he quietly picked up his boots and let himself out of the room. He went back to the main common room and put his boots on and sat staring out into the dark night. Despite it being July, Scotland appeared, at the moment, to be cold and windy. He could see the outlines of trees bending in the gusts of wind that occasionally rattled the windows of the navy base. The Night Watch Officer appeared and asked him if he would like some tea and Beech gratefully accepted. Now he could take his pills which would, perhaps dull the pain enough to enable him to get back to sleep.

As he sat there, slowly sipping his tea, he kept turning over in his mind a curious conversation he had had with Commander Todd during their lengthy train journey up from London. Todd had started asking all sorts of questions about Caroline, once Beech had let it slip that she was a childhood friend, and that he had known her since she was eight. It became quite obvious that Todd was attracted to the headstrong doctor and Beech wondered privately if they were the perfect match. Both were possessed of a confidence that Beech envied, both were energetic and positive characters, and both were attractive, impulsive and clever. In fact, the more Beech talked about Caroline and her personality, the more he wondered if perhaps the Commander and the doctor weren't just similar but identical and, if Todd pursued his plan to woo Caroline, the relationship might prove to be a little too combustible.

But also, the more Beech talked about Caroline – relayed anecdotes from their childhood, when she always seemed to come to his rescue, he realised that he had been guilty of undervaluing her for most of his life. Caroline the tomboy, never afraid of anything, always helping out the introverted young Beech. Pushing him, encouraging him, arguing with him, even goading him into action.

Once he had gone to boarding school, they had written to each other every week, until other activities and friends had pushed their closeness into a sort of stasis, which was still in the business of reviving. And, of course, some years ago, he had fallen in love, deeply, with Victoria, who was a gentler, more reserved personality than Caroline. Victoria had shattered his confidence when she had declined his marriage proposal. She had married, instead, a feckless man who had gambled away all his money and then died in France, at the beginning of the war. Victoria had now made it clear that she loved Beech in return but needed time to recover from her disastrous marriage. The situation had sapped what little confidence Beech had left after being injured at the Battle of Mons.

He knew that this was why he had been so determined to accompany Todd on this escapade. He wanted to get back some self-respect and participate in an adventure. Perhaps he had hoped that some of the dashing Commander's verve would rub off on him. Now, sitting here in a bleak naval station in the middle of nowhere, with the wind whirling around the coastline, he was beginning to regret his impulsiveness. He was also desperately hoping that he would not disgrace himself tomorrow by being seasick.

The throbbing in his leg had subsided and he decided to go back to bed and grab what little sleep he could before the race across the sea to Denmark. He wasn't hopeful of any rest, as he lay down on his bunk, but he smiled to himself when he heard Caroline's voice in his head saying, as she had said so many times when he was a boy, "Come on, Peter. Make an effort. You know you can do it."

***

It was decided amongst the Mayfair team that Sam would not turn up at the munitions factory the next day – as if he was ashamed for his actions the night before and expected to get the sack. It was also decided that Billy, upon hearing about it from the men in the loading bay, would go into Bradshaw's office and ask him if he wanted Sam arrested, to see the reaction. When he did, he was gratified to hear that Bradshaw had no intention of punishing Sam, described him as a good worker and dismissed the attack on Sinclair as 'something that was a long time coming'. In fact, he seemed quite cheerful about the whole incident and rather glad to have Malcolm Sinclair out of the way. So Billy volunteered to go and see Sam Abbott to tell him to come back to work, all was forgiven.

Caroline and her medical team also benefitted from Bradshaw's good mood because when they went to his office to explain to him that the women in the cordite room would stop getting headaches if they wore surgical rubber gloves, he seemed quite amenable to the idea, especially as Mabel gave him the name of a wholesaler who could sell him the gloves at a much reduced price.

However, their day rapidly proceeded downhill when Mrs Hawkesworth came running into the office to say that Myrtle Dimmock had collapsed and appeared to be having a fit. The three women rushed into the cordite room and found her now conscious, propped up against a packing case and groaning. One of the other women was cleaning up a small patch of vomit.

"Leave that!" said Mabel and to the disgust of the women, she deftly scooped it up on her handkerchief and made it into a little parcel. "I need to analyse this," she explained to

Caroline and Victoria. "Does anyone know what she had to eat this morning?"

"She ate a piece of cheese on the omnibus this morning," piped up Lily, Myrtle's sometime friend.

Caroline thought she saw signs of jaundice in Myrtle's eyes, when they occasionally flickered open and she had some bruising on her arms. "I had better get her to hospital," she decided and left to use the telephone.

Victoria said she would stay with Myrtle, whilst Mabel asked to see the girl's personal things. Mrs Hawkesworth took her to the back of the room, where there was a series of tall, thin wooden cupboards. She opened Myrtle's cupboard and Mabel began to go through her coat and bag. She found the bottle of Lugol's Iodine and noted, to her dismay, that Myrtle had taken over half a bottle, when she was supposed to only take a few drops a day. Then she found a half bottle of gin, with about an inch left in it. Tucked at the back of the cupboard was a green silk parasol, with an exceptionally long metal ferrule. She pulled it out and held it aloft.

"Is this Myrtle's?" she asked the room. Several women nodded.

"It's her weapon of choice," said one older woman. Another woman agreed. "Many of us have been on the receiving end of that when we've upset Myrtle Dimmock. She pokes you hard in the back of the legs with it when we all get in the omnibus at night," and she pulled up her skirt and rolled down her stocking to show several livid pinpoint bruises.

Myrtle was moaning softly, and kept drifting in and out of consciousness. Victoria could do nothing more than apply a cold flannel to her forehead, which occasioned Myrtle to become aggressive and try to push it away. Fortunately, Caroline came back, with Billy, and announced that the ambulance was on its way from Stratford and Constable Rigsby was going to carry Myrtle outside to wait.

Billy picked up the thin and barely conscious girl, as though she was nothing more than a feather pillow, and the feeling of being in his arms made her come around a little. She smiled and murmured "Hello Billy" before drifting off again.

He carried her through the factory and out in the open air. Victoria wheeled out the examination table from the makeshift medical room and Myrtle was soon lying spark out on top. Caroline began to tap her face to try and get a response. "It will be better if we can keep her conscious and we had better lay her on her side, in case she is sick again." Billy turned Myrtle on to her side and squatted down so that his face was close to hers. Myrtle's eyes flickered open.

"It's alright, love," he said gently, "the lady doctor is going to take you to hospital. You need proper care. Understand?" Myrtle gave a faint nod and smiled. Billy continued. There was something he had remembered from their night out and he needed an answer. "Myrtle…" he touched her arm to make her open her eyes, "You said the other night that Agnes invited you to go 'up west' with her. Did you ever go?" Myrtle looked confused, so Billy repeated his question. She partly frowned and murmured, "Once…we had a row…" then she grimaced in pain and gasped.

"Myrtle, where is the pain?" asked Caroline.

"In my belly…aah", the girl clutched just below her ribs.

Caroline suspected it was her liver, which would account for the jaundiced look of her eyes.

"Don't ask her anymore questions please," Caroline said to Billy and then she spotted the ambulance in the distance, making for the factory. "There is a charity hospital at West Ham, I expect they will take her there. I'm going to go with her. Don't worry, I'll make my own way back."

Billy lifted Myrtle off the table and gently put her into the bed in the ambulance, driven and staffed, he noted, by women. Caroline climbed inside, Billy closed the doors and the ambulance was on its way.

Mabel had disappeared to put the vomit into a jar and Victoria said suddenly, "I heard what she said to you, Billy. Do you think she killed Agnes Whitlock?"

Billy shrugged. "It's possible," he said, "But without a weapon, we'll never know for sure."

"The parasol Mabel found!" Victoria started running back to the factory and Billy followed. In the medical room, he was shown Myrtle's parasol, with the long metal ferrule and Mabel pronounced that she was going to go to the Hospital for Women, after hours, and run some tests.

"If this parasol was used as a weapon, there will be some traces of blood on it somewhere," she said confidently.

"What about Malcolm Sinclair? Mr Tollman said he threatened Agnes. He's in hospital as well. Does he have a storage cupboard?" Victoria was like a dog with a bone. She was determined to uncover some more evidence.

Billy agreed that they should look, so all three of them went to find Sinclair's personal effects. One of the men working the furnace pointed them in the right direction and, once they opened the cupboard, Mabel went through Sinclair's jacket, Victoria started on the contents of the shelf above the jacket hooks and Billy pulled out a toolbox from the floor of the cupboard.

"What about this?" he said triumphantly, brandishing an exceptionally long screwdriver. "Looks like it's about sixteen to eighteen inches long and," he added peering closely at it, "it looks like there are some stains on the handle and some sort of crusty stuff at the base."

"Wonderful," pronounced Mabel, putting the jacket back, as it had yielded nothing.

"Look at this!" Victoria had found a small notebook, which contained page after page of names and times. The last page said simply **GREY DOLPHIN – IMMINGHAM 0900 ESBJERG MIDNIGHT – TRAIN ESBJERG 1000 – KOLDING – TINGLEV – PADBORG – FLENSBURG – SCHLESWIG – RENDSBURG – NEUMUNSTER – HAMBURG.**

"I think that may prove to be very important. I need to get it to Mr Tollman straight away," Billy rose and handed the screwdriver to Mabel and took the notebook from Victoria.

✳✳✳

It was cold and windy, and the ship that had been supposed to arrive at dawn did not, in fact, arrive until ten o'clock, much to Todd's annoyance. When the Admiralty steam trawler, *Maclean*, docked at Invergordon, one of the officers apologised for the delay and handed Todd a radio message. It was from Captain Webb at the Admiralty Trade Division to say that P.C Rigsby had handed in some important information and to telephone Webb immediately. Beech smiled to think that the team in London were making strides and he wondered if they had solved the murder of Agnes Whitlock yet. Todd disappeared to the Communications room to telephone Webb, whilst Beech sat on the dock watching some men skilfully manoeuvring a grab crane that was picking up coal and depositing it into the hold of the ship. Other men were clamping a hose on to a water tank, which stood some yards away from the vessel and were taking on water.

To all intents and purposes, the ship looked like a fishing trawler and carried a full net array but, in reality, it was an Admiralty minesweeper, fitted with a twelve pound gun, machine guns and depth charges, in case of attack by enemy U boats. All the crew were dressed as fishermen and Beech could not tell if they were merchant or naval personnel.

Todd returned and said "Your team are doing a sterling job! I'll tell you about it later," and they picked up their kit bags and boarded the vessel.

The captain welcomed Beech and Todd aboard and told them to go down below, get some food and a hot drink. "The radio operator is down there, tucked in a corner. You might want to send a signal now to tell the Admiralty we have arrived and will depart within the hour," then he added, "we try not to send signals at sea unless it is an emergency."

Todd nodded and the two men descended into the hold. In a small wood panelled cabin, there was the radio operator in one corner and a small galley on the other wall. There was a welcome smell of frying bacon and Beech's stomach growled. While Todd set about sending a message to Captain Webb, Beech gratefully accepted a bacon sandwich and struck up a conversation with the cook.

He discovered that the ship regularly ran minesweeping patrols in the North Sea but they also fished a little so that they could suspend a catch of fish over the deck on the crane, on their way back to port, to make them look like a true fishing trawler. There was a crew of twelve. The captain, driver, two firemen (to stoke the boilers), the cook, radio operator and the other six men were gunners and general crew.

"So far, touch wood," the cook said, tapping his hand on the wooden panelling, "we have been ignored by the U boats. They don't like the nets, which we hang in the water from time to time. Scared of getting fouled up in them. So, they give us a wide berth."

"Will you be minesweeping on this voyage?" asked Beech will a certain amount of trepidation.

The cook shook his head. "No. The captain said it's a straightforward pick up and delivery job. We swept the route all week, so we should have no trouble getting over to Denmark and back."

Todd had joined them and was having a bacon sandwich prepared. His energy and enthusiasm seemed to have returned, now that they were about to get underway, and he asked Beech if he would have any trouble with seasickness. "It's incredibly rough out there on the North Sea today..."

"Huh, when isn't it?" commented the radio operator.

Beech assured him he would be fine. The captain came

down and said "We're casting off now. All messages sent?" Todd answered in the affirmative and the captain disappeared. There was lots of shouting and bawling above decks, the engines started, and the ship lurched out of its moorings and began the voyage.

Once the vessel was out of the harbour and heading into the open sea, the captain re-appeared and summoned Beech and Todd into his small cabin. He pulled out a sea chart from his cupboard and spread it out.

"Right, well obviously we are in a race against time," was the captain's first comment, "We are travelling further than the ship from Immingham – but it is not setting off for Esbjerg until this evening. It will probably dock tomorrow night at around midnight. We will try to maintain a steady 15 knots and, hopefully will get you to Denmark around six o'clock tomorrow evening weather permitting. This ship can only take you as far as here, just off the coast of Hvide Sande, and our launch will take you ashore and leave you. You will have to make your own way to Esbjerg, I'm afraid. We can go into Esbjerg, it's a free port, but we would rather not because then we have to allow an inspection by the harbourmaster. The port is infested with German spies and, as yet, we are not on the list of known Admiralty vessels. The longer the enemy thinks we are just a fishing trawler, the longer we can operate without becoming a U boat target." Beech and Todd nodded, and the captain continued, "I have been told to return to Hvide Sande the night after after dropping you off. We will go up the Norwegian coats to refuel and then return to await your signal. I will give you a Very pistol and two flares. Once we see the two flares, we will respond with a shutter light signal and the lifeboat will come for you. What you do whilst ashore is up to you, gentlemen, but you will have 30 hours after arrival to get back on that beach. I can't wait any longer than that"

The meeting ended and Todd and Beech were left to weather the journey as best they could. One of the seamen offered them his shared cabin for the duration, in case they wanted to sleep, and they gratefully accepted. The previous night had been greatly disturbed for both of them.

Beech realised that he had not really been told the plan of action when he and Todd reached Danish soil and he wanted to know what the Mayfair team had done to earn such glowing praise from the Admiralty.

Todd told him about the information – the Bill of Lading and, now, the notebook - that the team had passed on to the Admiralty. Todd seemed extremely impressed. "They have achieved more in a few days that Agnes, God rest her, managed to achieve in several months. I'm hoping that they will also be able to uncover the names of the men who are responsible for this, and possibly Agnes' murder. We must play our part at this end too."

"So, what is the plan when we reach Denmark?" Beech asked, anxious to be a part of this successful investigation.

"Oh, before I forget," Todd rummaged around in his rucksack and brought out some identity papers for Beech. "Your papers. We are American merchant seamen. Same names just a different nationality. Don't speak much. No-one will know the difference." Then he laughed and continued with a detailed explanation of the plan of action.

"First, we're going to go to the dock and locate the cargo and see if they change any of the markings on the bales. According to the notebook your people found, the cargo is supposed to then be loaded on to a train and shipped across the German border. We need to witness the whole process from dock to Germany and, if we can, pick up any paperwork in the process."

Beech nodded, his uncertainty of the night before having been replaced by a sense of adventure and excitement. He smiled and lay back on the pillow to gain some well-earned rest. As he drifted off to sleep, he conjured up a picture of a ten year old Caroline, smiling and saying, "See? I told you that you could do it, Peter."

✳✳✳

Caroline returned to Mason's factory in the middle of the afternoon and she was very despondent.

"Myrtle has suspected cirrhosis of the liver, probably caused by heavy alcohol consumption, dietary problems and who knows what else."

Mabel was annoyed with herself because she had not made sure that Myrtle Dimmock fully understood that just a few drops of the iodine solution was all that was needed each day. "She took half a bottle of it and, possibly, the toxic shock of that tipped her liver into crisis. Is there anything they can do for her?" she asked, knowing that it was unlikely.

Caroline shook her head and explained that, in fact, the hospital was going to organise Myrtle's removal to a hospice run by the Sisters of Charity in Hackney.

"Myrtle asked us to get her things from her lodging room and take them to her. I'm not sure I can face answering any more of her questions because I feel I have failed her."

"Me too," said Mabel quietly.

Victoria agreed to do it. "I'll go round to her lodgings now and collect her stuff. I doubt that she will have much and I'll take it straight round to the hospice, if you give me the address." Caroline nodded and began to write it down. Mabel said she would go and see Bradshaw, now, and get Myrtle's home address.

"Don't blame yourself, Caro," Victoria said quietly. "You tried your best for the girl."

"It wasn't enough, was it?" Caroline refused to be consoled. "I know that Myrtle Dimmock could very well be a murderer, but I do wonder whether some of these women are lost to society because they are in such poor health due to their upbringing, in poverty and ignorance. They have no decent food or living spaces, then they come and do a man's job in industry, spend their money on drink to cheer themselves up and the deterioration in their health just continues."

"The problem is," Victoria countered, "that you – I mean caring doctors like you, Caroline – can't undo, in adult women, what poverty and ignorance has created in their childhood. Only a change in society and the law can do that. Don't blame yourself."

Caroline smiled ruefully. Victoria was always practical, clear thinking and rarely swayed by her emotions, which was why she was so suited to the legal profession. She saw life in terms of rights, regulations and social effort and, Caroline reflected, she was probably right.

CHAPTER NINETEEN

CLOSING IN ON THE CULPRITS

In the evening, after work, the team all went their separate ways. Victoria to Myrtle Dimmock's lodgings and thereafter to the hospice; Mabel to the Women's Hospital to run some tests; and Caroline went back to Mayfair to have a rest. Billy and Tollman, meanwhile, having delivered the notebook to the Admiralty Trade Department, decided to go and visit Malcolm Sinclair in hospital to see if they could get some more information out of him.

"He won't be able to actually talk," Billy advised, having had some experience of boxers with broken jaws. "Best take a writing pad and a pencil."

So, the two policemen turned up at the West Ham and Eastern General Hospital in Stratford, armed with writing implements, and found themselves sitting either side of Sinclair, whose face was bandaged up like a mummy. There was a slit for his mouth and the nose, cheeks and eyes were visible. Billy winced when he saw the bruising that extended from Sinclair's cheek, just above the bandages, to his hairline. Sam had certainly given him one hell of a punch, that was for sure.

Tollman explained to Sinclair that they needed to ask him some questions and they had brought a writing pad and pencil for him to communicate. Sinclair immediately grabbed them and scribbled furiously: *I want that darkie, Abbott, arrested.* Obviously, having his jaw broken by Sam had not taught the unpleasant Sinclair a lesson.

"All in good time, Mr Sinclair," Tollman responded. "At the moment, we would like to speak to you about two matters. Firstly, the murder of Agnes Whitlock and secondly, your involvement with the owners of Mason's, whom, we have reason to believe are involved in acts of treason. I would just like to remind you," Tollman added, "that both of these crimes carry the death sentence."

Sinclair's eyes registered panic and Tollman noted the emotion with some pleasure. "So, let's start, first of all, with the murder of Agnes Whitlock."

Sinclair scribbled furiously on the pad: *Nothing to do with me.*

"Ah," said Tollman, "but we have a witness who says that you threatened Miss Whitlock with actual bodily harm if she didn't stop making enquiries about the company's activities." Sinclair made no move to write anything, so Tollman took this as confirmation that the threat was made. "Also," Tollman continued, "PC Rigsby here found a very long screwdriver in your toolbox which has, what appears to be, blood on it. The screwdriver has been taken away for forensic testing."

Sinclair attempted a sneering smile, but it hurt so much that he groaned instead. He scribbled again: *Hurt myself with long reach screwdriver trying to get behind the furnace.* Then he pulled up his pyjama sleeve to reveal a long gash on his left forearm that almost went from wrist to elbow. Tollman nodded and realised that this called an end to that line of enquiry, so he would have to change tack. Although the team were still waiting on the final evidence from Mr Beech and Commander Todd regarding possible trading with the enemy, Tollman reasoned that Sinclair was in no position to let the mysterious owners of Mason's know that the police were on to them, so he decided to take a chance.

"The Metropolitan Police and Naval Intelligence are now aware of the illegal activities of Mason's regarding selling cotton to Germany. We have addresses, copies of Bills of Lading and other information." Tollman was looking straight into Sinclair's eyes and he could see the mounting fear in the man's face. Tollman decided to raise the pressure. "We know that you regularly telephone the owners of Mason's from the public telephone exchange in Wanstead High Street – we have the records from the telephone company – and we know that you telephone MAYFAIR 209, the Public Schools Club." Tollman could see that Sinclair had flushed and a damp layer of sweat was forming on his face. He pretended to consult his notes and added, "And we know that you speak to a Mr Aubrey Rutledge." He could see that Sinclair by now was almost paralysed by fear. "We would like you to write down the name or names of the other men who are involved with Mr Rutledge." Sinclair tried to shake his head, but it caused such pain in his jaw that he sank back onto his pillow, groaning.

Tollman waited for the pain to subside, then he put the pencil back in Sinclair's hand. "I would remind you that being an accessory to treason will carry the death penalty."

Sinclair scribbled furiously: *Don't know anyone else. Only Rutledge. Ask Bradshaw. Not me. Just report to Rutledge. Don't know anything about treason.*

Tollman sighed and looked at Billy in defeat. It appeared that they had come to a dead end.

Tollman picked up the pad and pencil and said. "It won't end here, Sinclair. We may not be able to arrest you at the moment but, be assured, we will be back." And Billy and Tollman went, leaving Malcolm Sinclair not only in terrible pain with his broken jaw but also gripped with fear that he was about to be dragged into the sordid business of doing trade with the enemy in wartime.

***

Victoria had spent a good half hour packing up Myrtle Dimmock's meagre belongings in a small suitcase. She had three skirts, three blouses and some underwear and stockings. There were a few scrappy bits of jewellery, mostly 'glass and brass' – as Lady Maud would have described the trinkets. There was a hatbox which contained two hats – one straw and a 'best' one with ostrich feathers. Victoria wondered if Myrtle would ever get a chance to wear them again, but she would take them anyway. There were no books or periodicals because, of course, Myrtle had never learnt to read. There were no ornaments and precious little in the way of cosmetics, apart from a bar of soap. Like Agnes Whitlock's room, this was not a home, it was a spartan reminder of having no family or life to speak of.

Victoria found it depressing, especially when she explained to the landlady that Myrtle wouldn't be back. Despite the fact that she had been told that Myrtle was very ill, the woman said "Myrtle Dimmock won't be missed in this house,

I can assure you," adding that "she was always trouble – getting drunk – having arguments with people, never paying her rent on time." It seemed that no-one, except Caroline, Mabel and Victoria felt compassion for the girl.

When Victoria arrived at the hospice by taxicab and walked on to the ward, Myrtle looked awful. Her skin, as well as eyes, had a yellow tinge and she was listless and nauseated. Victoria wondered how much longer she would linger. Her general health seemed to have accelerated downwards since this morning.

Myrtle was not very responsive, although she managed a weak smile when Victoria opened her suitcase and she asked for her 'string of pearls' – a necklace of paste beads made to look like pearls. Victoria fastened it around Myrtle's neck and the girl's hand fluttered up to caress her 'pearls' and she smiled. They were obviously very important to her.

"Where did you get that lovely necklace, Myrtle?" Victoria asked softly.

"Southend," was the reply, "Girl's day out at the seaside. I won them in a fairground. Best day of my life." Victoria felt like weeping at the girl's obvious joy at the one day-trip memory.

"Can I ask you something, Myrtle?" Again, Victoria was trying to be very gentle and not upset the fragile girl. Myrtle nodded and Victoria continued, "You told Billy Rigsby that you went 'up west' with Agnes and you had a row with her. What was the row about?"

Myrtle frowned and Victoria feared that she would be unco-operative but she was just in pain. At that moment, one of the Sisters of Charity came to the bed and said, "Myrtle, I'm going to give you some medicine for the pain," and gave the girl what Victoria assumed were two teaspoonfuls of liquid morphine. The nun was also carrying a bowl of water, with herbs in, and she wrung out a cloth and gently wiped over the girl's face, which made Myrtle sigh with pleasure.

The nun smiled at Victoria who said softly, "I won't be long, sister."

"Stay as long as you wish, my dear. We have no rules on visiting hours here. But I warn you that she will be asleep in about ten minutes." With that the nun glided quietly away to minister to another soul.

"Myrtle," Victoria reminded her, "you were going to tell me about the row you had with Agnes."

The morphine was beginning to take effect. Mabel was in less pain but drowsy and her mouth was dry, so Victoria poured her an invalid cup of water and helped her drink it.

"I hate water," said Myrtle with a feeble smile, "sooner have a gin but they won't let me have any in here."

"Agnes?" Victoria hated to persist, but she could see that Myrtle was drifting off.

"We had a row because first of all she wanted to take me to a place where they would teach me to read and then I realised she was on the game and I didn't want anything to do with it. I may be a bad girl, Miss, but I'm not that bad."

Victoria was confused for a moment and then she realised that Myrtle meant that Agnes was a prostitute, which was a surprise.

"How do you know she was…on the game…Myrtle?"

Myrtle smiled. "We came out of this church in Piccadilly, which was where she wanted me to have the reading lessons. I was in a mood 'cos I thought we was going to have a good time and I stormed out. She wanted me to stay there for an hour being treated like a child, but I wasn't having any. But that was Agnes, always preaching. Then she said I should go home because she had important business to attend to. I said what and she said she was meeting a bloke in Berkeley Square and it was private. That's when I knew she was on the game. So, I called her all the names under the sun and took off for the nearest pub to have a few drinks before I went home. The next day she never showed up at work, so I supposed her client had done for her. I wasn't going to tell anyone. I didn't want to be mixed up in no assault or murder or collared by the peelers 'cos they thought I was on the game too."

Myrtle was, by now, having trouble keeping her eyes open and was slurring her words. "Thanks for bringing my things, Miss," she said, touching Victoria's hand gently. "I know I don't look much cop at the moment, but do you think Billy would come and see me?" Her eyes were glistening a little with supressed tears.

"I'm sure he will." Victoria answered. "I will ask him myself, the first chance I get." Myrtle smiled and nodded and gently drifted off to sleep. Victoria looked at the girl for a little while, overwhelmed with a feeling of pity and anger. *What chance did she ever have in life?* She wondered. *Poverty, no education, no family and rudderless in a swiftly changing world. And yet, she had enough pride to consider herself above prostitution.* Ever practical, Victoria wondered how she could help.

She stood up and gathered her own bag and prepared to leave. The nun stopped her on the way out and said, "Bless you my dear for coming to visit Myrtle. If you know of any relatives perhaps you could tell them that the doctors don't think she will last for much longer. We will keep her pain free, but we don't expect her to last out the week, sadly." Victoria nodded and looked back at the yellow-tinged girl, still clutching her 'pearls' in her morphine-induced stupor and she hoped she was dreaming of 'the best day of her life' in Southend.

***

It was a sombre group that met up at Lady Maud's house in the late evening. Maud had organised a light supper of soup and bread, cheese on toast and some rice pudding but appetites were dulled by the day's events.

Lady Maud lamented the fact that not only were the assembled humans not eating but Timmy had gone off his food too, although he had perked up at the sight of Billy. However, as the team picked their way through their food, Timmy neither cared nor sought after titbits and just kept his eyes fixed on the door.

"I think he's pining for my mum and aunty," Billy observed. "Don't worry Lady Maud. I'll have him in my room to sleep tonight and there is only a couple more days before he'll be back in his familiar surroundings in Belgravia."

Billy then explained that Sissy and Elsie had gone straight home from work because they were worn out from the previous late night but they had reminded Billy to ask Lady

Maud if she could organise a proper pair of cooks to take over the canteen function at Mason's. Maud was pleased to announce that she had been to see Lady Londonderry and it was all arranged. Another pair of cooks would be there to take over feeding the workers within a week.

Mabel had arrived, halfway through supper, and gratefully ate some cheese on toast whilst reporting to Tollman that she had found nothing on the parasol but confirmed that it was blood on the screwdriver.

Once supper was finished, Lady Maud retired for the night and the others had a brief meeting. Tollman reported that they had got nowhere with their interview of Malcolm Sinclair, who was obviously guilty but swore he could name no-one other than Aubrey Rutledge in connection with the ownership of Mason's.

Victoria then relayed her sad visit to Myrtle in the hospice and everyone fell silent. Billy promised that he would visit Myrtle as soon as he could the next day. Caroline had been very quiet all through supper and she still said nothing. Mabel added the information that she had analysed Myrtle's vomit and it contained blood – a sure sign that her liver was diseased. Victoria then spoke about Myrtle's assertion that Agnes was 'on the game' and Tollman visibly brightened.

Caroline finally spoke, and it was with a degree of irritation, "I can't believe that Agnes Whitlock was a prostitute! Everyone describes her as an intense and committed radical. Surely someone who believed in women' and worker's rights wouldn't prostitute herself?"

Tollman shook his head. "She didn't. Myrtle made an

assumption because Agnes said she 'had an appointment with a man'. I'm willing to bet that Agnes had found out about Rutledge and had arranged to speak with him in Berkeley Square. After all, his gentleman's club is barely 100 yards from the square. I think she was probably hoping that while Myrtle was having a reading lesson, she could meet up with Rutledge and get him to admit involvement. But it didn't quite work out like that."

Tollman decided that tomorrow was going to be the day that they arrested Bradshaw and held him for questioning but, ideally, they needed to arrest Rutledge at the same time, without alerting anyone else who may be involved in this conspiracy. Arthur Tollman was thinking, in particular, of Detective Carter. When the time came, he wanted to catch Carter off-guard and savour the moment.

He decided that the best thing to do would be to consult the Commissioner, in the morning. They were getting too close to the conclusion of this case for Tollman to bear all the responsibility. So, he gave Billy instructions not to go to Mason's in the morning, but to meet him at Scotland Yard at eight a.m. Sir Edward Henry was known to start work early and Tollman wanted to get in first, before the day began.

He was nervous, as he knocked on the Commissioner's door the next morning. Although Sir Edward Henry was a calm, reasonable man and totally supported the work of the team, Tollman always felt that the man could see into everybody's soul. He was impressed by the deeply analytical nature of the Commissioner. Beech had said once that the Commissioner never interrupted people. He just waited until they had said everything they had to say and then he would either support or demolish their idea calmly, never with any rancour or even particular enthusiasm. Tollman had never seen or heard of the Commissioner getting angry or aggressive. This was an individual who had appeared in court to appeal for leniency for the man who had attempted to assassinate him in 1912. There were rumours that the Commissioner still suffered from the pain of the assassin's bullet wound in his stomach.

When summoned, Tollman took a deep breath and entered. The Commissioner offered him a seat, which in itself was a kindness, as Tollman knew many a senior officer that, upon principle, would make a subordinate stand in their presence – even if they were making a report that lasted up to an hour.

"So, Detective Sergeant Tollman, how are you finding the responsibility of this investigation? Not too onerous, I trust?"

Tollman replied that he was coping, thanks to the efforts of the team, but he would be pleased to see Inspector Beech back at the helm.

Sir Edward smiled and asked Tollman to make his report. Starting from the beginning of the week – had it really only been a week?! – Tollman told the Commissioner the full story, so far, of the investigation and what had been uncovered by the team. Sir Edward listened intently, made a few notes, raised an eyebrow here and there, smiled and shook his head at the fight incident in the canteen at Mason's.

"Extraordinary work, Tollman," he said with genuine admiration, when the report was finished. "Extraordinary. I know that Captain Webb is pleased, as he telephoned me yesterday to commend your team. So…" he paused and looked up, "…what would you like to do now?"

Tollman replied that he would like to arrest Bradshaw and Rutledge at the same time, so that neither could warn the other – and he would also like to arrest Detective Carter. Sir Edward mulled it over for a moment and made a measured reply.

"There are two things to consider," he began. "First, much as I am sure it will disappoint you, we need to put the business of Detective Carter to one side for the moment." Sir Edward noted Tollman's expression of dismay and continued. "Let me explain why. You have no concrete evidence of Carter's involvement with this treason case. You do have some possible evidence of Carter's general corruption, however, and this may be useful to us at a later date, when we can use his special contacts, without his knowledge, to reel in some big fish in the criminal underworld. We won't let Carter escape eventual retribution, I can assure you. In fact, we cannot afford to. It would not do for London criminals to think that they can buy the protection of the Metropolitan Police with such ease. I guarantee you that Carter will face a prison sentence. But, for the moment, I want us to concentrate on the acts of treason."

"Yes sir." Tollman was disappointed but he could see the Commissioner's point.

Sir Edward continued. "The second matter to consider is that we should allow the Admiralty Trade Division to arrest and interrogate Aubrey Rutledge. He is a civil servant working in support of the navy and, technically, is subject to Admiralty law. They will be just as rigorous, if not more so, than the police and, if it is found that Rutledge and any persons associated with Rutledge, are guilty, beyond any doubt, of treason, the Admiralty can conduct a private trial and insist on the death penalty, without recourse to the criminal courts and public scrutiny."

Tollman indicated that he understood and derived some grim satisfaction from the fact that Rutledge would disappear into some hellhole of interrogation by the Royal Navy Police.

"What about Mr Bradshaw?" Tollman was concerned that the manager of Mason's should be arrested at the same time.

"I will suggest to Captain Webb that you arrest Mr Bradshaw, at his place of work, at 11.30 a.m. this morning and the RNP will arrest Mr Rutledge at exactly the same time as he leaves his office to go to his club for lunch. It will all be, I am assured by Webb, extremely discreet. You, however, are bound by no such niceties and may burst into Bradshaw's office and handcuff him on the spot. I would suggest that we offer Bradshaw a deal of the lesser offence of Misprision of Treason - thereby removing the death penalty, in exchange for as much information as he can supply us with, which you will then share with Captain Webb and myself. Neither of the men will be charged until Chief Inspector Beech and Commander Todd return with, we hope, yet more concrete evidence of the crime. Any questions?"

"No, sir. It's all perfectly clear." Tollman was satisfied.

"Good man, Tollman. You may call me at any time."

Tollman left the room and went to find Billy, who was

sitting in a waiting area by the front desk.

"Come on lad," Tollman said briskly. "We need to get a car. We have an arrest to make. I'll tell you about it on the way."

CHAPTER TWENTY

THE RACE TO TIE UP LOOSE ENDS

"What's Misprision of Treason?" asked a confused Billy, as he drove the police automobile skilfully around Parliament Square.

"Well," explained Tollman, "it's when someone knows about or learns about a conspiracy to commit treason, but they don't report it. It's like being an accessory to a crime, but not quite…if that makes sense."

Billy observed that, in his opinion, Bradshaw knew quite well what was going on and should be prosecuted like his boss – or bosses. Tollman agreed but pointed out that offering life imprisonment instead of hanging or a firing squad was a powerful way to get maximum co-operation out of a suspect.

"In my experience," Tollman observed drily, "many of those who endure life imprisonment wish, after a few years, they'd taken the death penalty. There are certain crimes that even convicts take exception to, and I suspect that treason is one of them. The average scum-of-the-earth hardened criminal can be surprisingly patriotic."

Billy grinned and agreed.

When they reached Mason's factory, Tollman insisted that they sit in the vehicle until exactly 11.30 a.m., as per the wishes of Captain Webb, then they purposefully marched straight ahead to the office, passing a puzzled Sam and a curious medical team, who had their door open, ready to accept the next batch of female workers for medical examination.

They knocked, did not wait for a response, entered and Tollman displayed the arrest warrant. Then he said loudly, "Arnold Hubert Bradshaw, I am arresting you under several sections of the Defence of The Realm Act and the laws of Treason, in that you, Arnold Hubert Bradshaw, have materially aided the enemies of this realm, pursued actions against the public safety and defence of this realm and endangered the successful prosecution of this war. Constable Rigsby... handcuff this man."

Bradshaw, who had stood open-mouthed in shock, throughout the reading of the warrant, promptly fell to the floor in a dead faint, as soon as Billy produced the handcuffs from his pocket.

"Bugger," said Tollman with feeling, then he called for Caroline. As she appeared, he said, "Doctor, could you possibly examine Mr Bradshaw, please, and give a verdict on whether he is fit enough to be removed to a police station or whether we have to take him to hospital? I would be grateful."

Caroline rushed in, brandishing her stethosocope and asked Billy to turn Bradshaw over so that she could remove his stiff collar and unbutton his waistcoat. After much listening to his chest, she said, "I'm very sorry, Detective Sargeant, but I do believe that Mr Bradshaw may have had a heart attack. His heartbeat is very irregular, and I can't guarantee that it won't stop any moment."

Tollman sighed. "Right, then would you be so kind as to call for an ambulance, doctor?"

Caroline picked up the handset on Bradshaw's desk and agitated the cradle to get a response from the exchange. Then she asked to be put through to the hospital.

"Dropping like flies in this place, aren't they?" Mrs Hawkesworth observed from the doorway. "That's the third one hospitalised this week!" She turned back to the medical room line, where she had been queuing and said to the other women, "I think we'd all better look for another job!"

The ambulance arrived and Billy co-opted Sam to help him carry Bradshaw out of the factory. The workers all looked on in silence. Tollman turned at the doorway and addressed them all.

"Mr Bradshaw won't be back, one way or another. Neither will Mr Sinclair. So, I am going to telephone the Ministry of Munitions and get them to send someone down here to take over. Meanwhile, I suggest you all get on with your jobs as normal. Who's the most senior here?" Everyone looked at each other and Mrs Hawkesworth said, "Probably Tom in the loading bay."

"Right, well get him out of there and in the office. Tell him he's got to run the show until someone else arrives." Mrs Hawkesworth nodded, Tollman made a telephone call and then left to ride in the ambulance with Bradshaw, whilst Billy followed in the police vehicle.

The two policemen were forced to sit in the corridor whilst Bradshaw was examined. Tollman was fretting about the delay.

"I should have known that Bradshaw had a dicky heart," he said, without expecting any answer from Billy. "Overweight, nervous types like that, always have heart problems. I should have known and not sprung the arrest on him like that."

The doctor appeared and said that he did not believe that Mr Bradshaw had technically had a heart attack. He believed that the patient had possessed an irregular heartbeat for some time as he, apparently, was prone to fainting fits in times of excitement. Therefore, the police were welcome to interview him, but they must not overexcite him or the hospital would not be responsible for the consequences. Tollman said that he understood, so he and Billy entered the room. Bradshaw was pale and sweaty, but a little bit of colour came into his cheeks at the sight of the police.

Tollman held up a hand and said calmly, "Let's not get overexcited, Mr Bradshaw. We don't want you to have another turn..."

Bradshaw interrupted, "Look, if I hadn't passed out, I was going to tell you that I have kept a record of everything... all the stuff you want to know about...and I was going to take it to the police very soon."

Tollman was surprised. He had been expecting Bradshaw to deny everything, not confess straight away to knowing about the illicit dealings at Mason's. "If you were privy to this trading with the enemy, why did you wait so long to report it?"

"Sinclair was constantly watching me. His job was to spy on me. He got extra money from the directors to keep me in line. I was expecting to be sacked anyway, because I found the locked drawer to my desk had been opened and the book in which I keep all the details of the German trade, had been opened – one of the pages was folded down and it shouldn't have been. I thought it was Sinclair but then Agnes Whitlock disappeared. I expected to be sacked but I wasn't, so I realised that it must have been Agnes who had found the book. Then you turned up and said she was dead, and I began to fear that I would be next – the men who own Mason's are obviously capable of anything. I've been in a state for a couple of weeks now."

"Where is this book now, Mr Bradshaw?" Tollman was anxious to progress the matter.

"In my lodgings. In the wardrobe. The keys are in my jacket pocket. 42 Hillman Street, the top flat. If my landlady asks, just tell her I'm in hospital and you are getting me some things." Bradshaw was getting a bit breathless by now. "Detective Sergeant…am I still going to be charged with treason?"

"Well, it's not for me to say, Mr Bradshaw. But I shall personally put in a good word for you with the Commissioner, once I've read this book. I wouldn't worry too much about it. You just have a rest and we'll see what we can do."

Bradshaw's rooms were just off Wanstead High Street and 'the book' turned out to be quite a substantial file of Mason's dealings with America, Norway, Denmark and Germany. When added to the stash of telegrams Tollman had obtained, plus the Bill of Lading for the Immingham consignment and Sinclair's notebook – there was more than enough evidence to prosecute everyone concerned.

Tollman sat on the bed and started to painstakingly go through the documents and notes, looking for the one that Bradshaw had described. The page 'that was folded down and shouldn't have been'. And there it was. A letter, from a month ago, on The Public Schools Club headed paper, written by Rutledge to Bradshaw, saying "Lord Budlington and I wish to know when the *SS Granforth* will discharge its cargo this week, as we may have to make other arrangements for onward shipping." And it was signed by Aubrey Rutledge.

"So, it was the lord," Tollman muttered to himself. "I might have known it."

"Eh?" Billy hadn't quite heard him.

Tollman explained what he had found and then announced his intention to take the paperwork to the Admiralty but then he would make a quick detour to see his old friend Harry Skinner at his home.

"If it turns out that this Lord Budlington is the murderer of Agnes Whitlock, then I need to ask the Commissioner's permission to arrest him. So, while I'm doing that, you might as well go back to Mason's and see what's happening there."

"Actually," Billy asked tentatively, "would it be alright if I went to see Myrtle Dimmock first? Only I don't know that she has too much time left, according to Mrs E. and I may not get the chance again."

Tollman nodded. "Of course, lad. It's going to take me a while to follow this trail. I'll telephone you at Mason's later on today and tell you what's happening."

***

The sun was shining, by the time Billy got to Hackney, and he visited a market, near the omnibus stop, to buy Myrtle a bunch of flowers, from the nearest flower stall, to cheer her up.

"'Allo darlin'" said a middle-aged woman on the next stall, "Ain't you a sight for sore eyes, handsome?" She winked at him and gave him a paper bag of ripe plums. Billy laughed and thanked her. Myrtle would probably like those as well.

When he walked into the cool ward of the hospice, some of the patients looked alarmed and a nun came quickly over. But then a voice from halfway down the ward called "Billy!" – it was Myrtle, but he hardly recognised her.

The nun smiled and said, "She was hoping you would come." Meanwhile Myrtle was telling anyone who would listen that Billy was her 'boyfriend' and 'I said he would come, didn't I?'

Billy felt a sense of panic rising as he approached the bed. He had expected her to look ill but not as bad as she did. She was yellow – dark brown shadows under her eyes and her cheeks were sunken. He made a supreme effort and said cheerily "Hello Duchess!" and kissed her hand. Myrtle smiled, like a wizened old lady and stroked his hand, whilst looking around at the other women in the ward to make sure that they were looking at Billy. He felt as though his heart was breaking. He had never liked Myrtle Dimmock but now his sense of pity was so strong, he actually couldn't remember how he once felt about her. He gave her the flowers and she showed them to the woman in the next bed with immense pride. Billy surmised that no-one had ever given the girl flowers before. The nun came and put the flowers in a vase and stood them on the table next to the bed. All the time Myrtle looked at them as though they were the most wonderful thing she had ever seen.

"How ya doin, Duchess?" he said quietly, when the nun

had gone, and she just shook her head.

"Not good, Billy," she said. "On my way out, I reckon."

Billy tried to protest but she just said, "Shush. I ain't stupid." Then she became serious. "Billy, I want to know if you can help me?"

"I'll do my best, Duchess. What do you want me to do?"

Myrtle looked hard at him and her eyes filled with tears. Billy took her hand and held it. "What is it?" he asked, desperate to help.

"I know I've not been good…" her voice trailed off and the tears trickled down her cheeks.

"Don't…" Billy couldn't bear to see her like this. "Tell me what I can do?"

"I don't want to be buried in a pauper's grave," she sobbed quietly.

"Eh?"

"Like my mum. We were too poor to afford a funeral and a plot, so she went in the pit with all the scum from the streets. She didn't deserve that. My mum was a good soul. I don't want to be like that. Laying in a pit with strangers. I want my own plot and a little headstone, so that people will know that Myrtle Dimmock was a real person."

Billy was biting the inside of his cheek to stop himself from crying. He nodded his head and breathed in hard through his nostrils. "You are going to have a swanky funeral, when your time comes," he said. "Mason's is going to pay for the whole thing – Bradshaw told me this morning," he was lying but the idea had formed in his head and he told himself it was possible. Despair for Myrtle was turning gradually into resolve.

"Yeah?" Myrtle was open-mouthed and smiling happily. "God's honour?"

"God's honour," Billy insisted, then he elaborated, "Mrs Hawkesworth told me that the ladies in the factory are going to have a whip round for your headstone."

"You're telling a fib!" she said, with a look of delight on her face.

"No. Straight up." Billy's creativity was getting bolder. "I wasn't going to tell you 'cos I though it was a bit morbid, discussing your funeral and all. So, I'm glad you brought it up and I can put your mind at rest."

Then he produced the bag of plums from his pocket. "Bought something else for you, as well. Some nice juicy plums."

Myrtle was overwhelmed by his kindness, but she said quietly, "I ain't got no appetite, Billy."

Not to be defeated, Billy took a penknife out of his pocket and said, "They're lovely and juicy. How about I cut one in half for you and you can just suck the juice, eh?" Myrtle nodded and Billy cut a plum, took the stone out, and help it up to her lips. Soon, she was giggling happily as he squeezed the plum and kept wiping the juice that escaped down her chin with his handkerchief.

Billy laughed and his presence seemed to liven up every dying woman in the room. Inside his head, Billy Rigsby just kept seeing Myrtle, as a little girl, watching her mother's makeshift pauper's coffin being tipped into a municipal grave and he knew, that even if he paid for it himself, Myrtle Dimmock was not going to have the same fate.

***

Tollman had been forced to wait for half an hour at the Admiralty Trade Division, before they could locate Captain Webb, who was, apparently, 'in an important meeting'. Tollman knew damn well that Webb was busy interrogating the civil servant, Rutledge, but he impressed upon one of Webb's aides that it was 'vitally important' that he saw him.

Eventually, Webb appeared, looking somewhat harassed, "This is not a good time to interrupt, Tollman," he said abruptly, "our interrogation is proving difficult."

"Perhaps this will help," Tollman held up Bradshaw's file and opened it at the document that mentioned Lord Budlington. Webb's eyes lit up but then he looked confused as Tollman snapped the file shut. "This Lord Budlington is my collar," he said firmly. "If, as I suspect, he is the murderer of Agnes Whitlock, it's a police matter – not the Admiralty. You can have him after we have charged him with murder."

"Treason is far more serious than murder, Tollman," Webb countered.

Tollman shook his head. "Nothing is more serious than murder – especially when it is committed by a member of the aristocracy against a member of the lower classes. We can't have all these lords thinking that the lower orders can be disposed of at will. No. If you charge him for treason, he'll disappear into the Tower of London, or wherever they are putting enemies of the realm nowadays, the government will slap a D notice on it and we'll never hear of it again."

Webb looked at Tollman's face and could see that the

policeman was deadly serious, so he nodded in agreement.

"I'll make a deal with you," Webb offered, "If you have the evidence that Budlington is the murderer, then you and your men can arrest him. But…if I get further evidence from my interrogation of Rutledge and evidence from Commander Todd and Inspector Beech in Denmark, then we need to take custody of Budlington and mete out the appropriate justice – do you understand? The Admiralty will demand it. But you can have first crack, in case we cannot turn up the evidence we need. At least then we will know that one of us has been able to put the noose around his neck."

Tollman had no option to agree. In time of war, the Admiralty would always possess more clout than the Metropolitan Police.

✳✳✳

When Billy got back to Mason's, he found himself facing the affable Captain Wallace, who had arrived from the Ministry of Munitions to sort out the problems in the factory.

"Got into a right state here, hasn't it?" Wallace said with a broad grin, as he shook Billy's hand. "So, what's the current state of play regarding the manager, Bradshaw, then?"

Billy explained that, as far as he was aware, Mr Bradshaw would not be returning for two reasons – his heart problem and the fact that he was looking at a prison sentence, possibly reduced on account of his co-operation with the authorities. He also told Wallace that one director of the company would be facing severe punishment for treason but there could be a second director in the frame too.

"Blimey," was Wallace's response. "Right, well, lucky for Mason's, there have been several government initiatives this month which may just solve everyone's problems. Let's go and talk to Tom in the office."

Tom was sitting comfortably, going through some order sheets, when Billy and Wallace entered. It seemed to Billy that Tom looked as though he belonged in the manager's office as he seemed to be taking all of the extra responsibility in his stride. Wallace relayed Billy's information to Tom, who shook his head in disbelief.

"I knew that Bradshaw was incompetent, and that Sinclair was a nasty piece of work, but I had no idea the whole company was corrupt," Tom sounded shocked. "So, I suppose the whole place will be shutting down now, then?" Tom looked miserable. "That means over a hundred people will lose their jobs."

"Good Lord no!" Wallace was cheerfully emphatic. Then he proceeded to explain to Tom and Billy about the provisions in the Defence of the Realm Act which allowed for the government to create their own munitions factories, or take over ownership of any factories, in order to avoid munitions shortages. "I think I can persuade the Ministry that Mason's comes under the provisions of the Act. The paperwork will take a bit of time. Government, even in wartime, rarely move quickly but I'm sure you can keep things ticking over here in the meantime, Tom. You seem to have a pretty good grasp of things, and the men seem to look up to you."

Tom seemed pleased to be, at last, recognised for being

an able man who had the advantage of having worked in most of the areas of Mason's, apart from the cordite cutting room, but he was concerned about who would take over the management of the loading bay. "Sam Abbott would be ideal, as he's got lots of experience on the docks and most of the men seem to admire him now – ever since he put Sinclair in hospital," he explained, but Billy cut him short and explained that Sam was on leave from the army, although he wasn't too keen to go back because the black soldiers weren't actually being allowed to fight.

Captain Wallace smiled. "It seems to be my day for solving problems!" he said cheerily and explained about a new government directive that had just come in this month, called Release from the Colours. "Mr Lloyd George and Lord Kitchener, between them, have decided that any man skilled in the munitions trade, can be released from the armed services back into munitions in order to carry out important war work. In fact," he said as he produced a piece of paper with a flourish, "I just happen to have one of the new forms on my person today. How very fortuitous!"

Billy grinned and asked if he could go and tell Sam, personally, of this new option. He sped off and asked Sam to come to the canteen with him for a minute. Gathering together Sissy, Elsie and Sam, Billy gleefully explained the new government option of release from the army to work in munitions. Sam could hardly believe his luck. Billy's mum and aunt were beside themselves.

"Oh, thank Gawd!" said Sissy, giving Sam a big kiss on the cheek. "One less friend we won't have to worry about!"

Elsie hugged him fiercely and wiped away a stray tear, whilst Phyllis looked on in amazement.

"So, you know him then?" was her confused question to the women. Sissy laughed and told her not to worry about it.

Billy suddenly realised that Sam actually hadn't been asked by anyone if he wanted the job, so he expressed concern that they had all been assuming he would be happy.

For a moment, Sam looked troubled, and everyone else looked troubled, until he burst into a big laugh and said "You should see your faces! Of course I want the job! I like it here. I like the blokes and now that Sinclair's gone, I'm gonna like it even more!"

Billy told him to go to the office and get the forms signed as quickly as possible, which Sam duly did.

Once Sam had left, Billy slumped in a chair and told his mum, aunt and Phyllis about visiting Myrtle. By the time he finished, all the women were in tears and Billy was struggling to keep his own tears at bay.

Phyllis said, "I never liked Myrtle, but no-one deserves what she's going through." She disappeared into the kitchen and returned with a metal bowl. "I'm going to sort this out," she said in a determined voice, and off she marched. Billy, Elsie and Sissy watched her through the window as she went over to the loading bay and started talking to the men. Some of them curled their lips and turned away, but she persisted – either by tears or bullying – until the men began to put their hands in their pockets and put coins in the pot. She came running back to the canteen with a triumphant smile on her face, emptied the pot on to one of the tables and started to count it.

"Twelve pennies!" she crowed, "and that's just from the handful of men in the loading bay! Keep an eye on that money," she ordered, "I'm off to get donations from the rest of the factory. We are going to get that girl the best headstone we can."

***

Harry Skinner was just having his substantial afternoon tea, before leaving for his night duty at The Public Schools Club, when Arthur Tollman knocked at the door.

Mrs Skinner answered and ushered Tollman into the kitchen.

"Can I get you a bite to eat, Mr Tollman?" she asked, poised to fill up the frying pan again.

Tollman was tempted but he declined. "I wouldn't mind a cup of tea though, if you've one going, Mrs Skinner" and he smiled gratefully as she poured steaming hot tea into a china cup and placed it before him.

"Harry," Tollman began, "I know that women aren't allowed in that club of yours but, think carefully now, has a woman ever dropped by, in the last couple of weeks – to, say, leave a message for Mr Rutledge?"

Tollman held his breath, whilst Skinner thought.

"There was one," Skinner said, slowly, "Dressed really nice. But she didn't leave a message for Rutledge, she gave me a message for Lord Budlington…she waited while I delivered it…he said to tell her "understood". That was all, just "understood". I told her, she left, he went out about ten minutes later and didn't return that evening."

Tollman breathed normally again, reached into his inside pocket and produced the picture of Agnes' corpse. "Is that her?"

Skinner scanned the picture and nodded. "Looks very like. She took the note out of a silver bag, made of sort of chain mail."

"That's the one we have down at the Yard." Tollman said with satisfaction. Then he continued, "Are you still willing to help us out, Harry?"

Harry Skinner grinned. "Name it, Arthur. I'm game."

Tollman took another swig of his excellent cup of tea and began to outline the plan.

Chapter Twenty One

CLOSING THE NET

At 8 p.m. Harry Skinner, stationed at the front desk of The Public Schools Club, took delivery of a telegram, which he placed on a silver salver and delivered to Lord Budlington, who was playing billiards with another man in the Games Room.

Skinner waited whilst Budlington read the communication and then he bowed slightly when Budlington said tersely, "no reply."

Skinner then went back to his desk, picked up the telephone and asked to be connected to Scotland Yard. Tollman took the call and Skinner simply said, "Message delivered." Tollman smiled grimly, nodded at Billy, who then went down to the garages to collect a car and mobilise four policemen in another car. Tollman knocked on the Commissioner's door and said, "It's time, sir."

So, at 9 p.m. two police cars were sitting in the shadows at the north end of Berkeley Square, with a perfect view of the end of Berkeley Street and Lord Budlington's house on the east side of Berkeley Square. The telegram that had been delivered by Harry Skinner to his Lordship had said BEEN DETAINED IN WHITEHALL. HAVE IMPORTANT NEWS. WILL TELEPHONE YOU AT HOME TONIGHT AT 10 P.M. RUTLEDGE. So, the police were waiting, patiently, for their suspect to walk home, any moment, across the square.

Tollman had three warrants in his pocket. The first was to enable the police to search Lord Budlington's residence; the second was to arrest him for the murder of Agnes Whitlock, and the third was to arrest him for aiding the enemy in time of war. All three warrants had been approved by the Commissioner and signed by a judge and Tollman was looking forward to using them. What had been surprising was Sir Edward Henry wanting to come along and participate in the arrest. Most unusual for a Commissioner to be involved. Tollman assumed that it was because the case was a matter of national security. However, Sir Edward made it quite clear that he would only enter the premises once the search warrant had yielded the results that sealed the arrest for murder. Then they would proceed with the next charge of treason.

"Mr Tollman," Billy alerted him to the appearance of the suspect striding across the square, the metal tip of his walking stick flashing in the lamplight.

"Right, sir," Tollman said to Sir Edward. "We'll give him five minutes and then we will move in. I've sent a man around to the mews at the back, in case his Lordship decides to leg it through the servant's tunnel." Sir Edward nodded in satisfaction. Tollman added, as he got out of the car, "I will send a man out for you, when we have arrested him for Agnes' murder."

The policemen gathered at the front door of the house and Tollman banged the heavy knocker ferociously. After a small delay, it was opened by a butler, who looked alarmed as the police barged past him and Tollman waved a warrant under his nose.

"This is a warrant to search the premises of one, Lord Budlington," said Tollman loudly. "And, I'm starting with these," He gathered up an armful of walking sticks and umbrellas in a stand, by the door. "Now, take me to your master."

The astonished butler scurried ahead of Tollman and Billy and into a study, where a surprised and annoyed Lord Budlington was sitting at a desk, presumably waiting for his telephone to ring. Before he could open his mouth, Tollman dumped all the walking sticks and umbrellas on to a Chesterfield sofa and waved the search warrant in the air.

"Lord Budlington, I am Detective Sergeant Tollman, and I have a warrant to search these premises." Then he instructed Billy to stand guard over Budlington, whilst he began inspecting all the walking implements he had liberated from the hallway.

"I'm expecting an important telephone call," Budlington said in an aggrieved tone of voice.

"Ah yes," said Tollman, not looking up from his inspection, "from Mr Rutledge." He looked up then and saw a look of concern appear on Budlington's face. "Yes, I'm afraid, my lord, that Mr Rutledge will not be calling after all. He has been detained by the Royal Naval Police and is, at present, singing his little heart out to the Admiralty Trade Division about your nefarious dealings at Mason's."

Budlington decided to feign ignorance. "Whatever Rutledge has been doing, it is nothing to do with me! Rutledge is insane, you know. I deeply regret ever investing in his company. I was persuaded to do it against my better judgement..."

Tollman suddenly said loudly and triumphantly, "Yes!"

and he pulled a vicious-looking rapier out from inside a walking stick. He examined it closely and said, "Tut, tut, my lord, you really should clean up after yourself. If I'm not mistaken, there is clear evidence of dried blood on this weapon." Then he turned to Billy and said "Constable Rigsby, handcuff this man."

Whilst Billy applied the handcuffs and Budlington protested, Tollman produced the arrest warrant and began to read out the charge relating to Agnes Whitlock's murder.

"Who?" Budlington was confused. "There must be some mistake! I do not know any such woman!"

Tollman slapped Agnes' photograph on the desk and Budlington's shoulders dropped in resignation. "Oh, her," he said dismissively.

"Yes, her," said Tollman. "The woman whose name you couldn't be bothered to remember, even though you murdered her in cold blood with your gentleman's toy here." He brandished the rapier. "We know that she delivered a message to you at your club, the night that she died. We know that she asked you to meet her in Berkeley Square. And we know that she found out that you and Rutledge were selling cotton to the Germans."

"It's all a lie!" Budlington was becoming truculent. "You have no way of proving any of this."

"Oh, but we do," Tollman decided to be creative with the truth, "Rutledge has told us everything and we have other witnesses."

Budlington laughed. "Nice try. You have nothing. No proof." He was so scathing and so sure of himself, that Tollman realised, with a sinking feeling, that Rutledge probably knew nothing about Agnes Whitlock being murdered. Budlington had never told anyone. Their case was going to founder unless Budlington confessed.

Tollman called in one of the policemen and told him quietly to go and get the Commissioner. Then he turned back to Budlington.

"No matter," he tried to be nonchalant. "You'll hang or be shot – one way or another. Aiding the enemy in time of war carries the death penalty too."

Budlington snorted in derision. "As I told you, nothing to do with me. Do you seriously think that a jury is going to believe anything said by an insane man, who has, undoubtedly been brutalised by navy interrogators…"

Sir Edward Henry's voice cut through Budlington's rant, as he entered the room and said firmly, "Jury? Come now Budlington…you can't have forgotten that your trial for high treason will be heard in the House of Lords, presided over by the Lord High Steward. Think of the shame…and the resulting publicity. Detective Sergeant, read out the warrant."

Tollman duly read out the charge and Budlington's eyes glittered with spite. He looked straight at Sir Edward throughout and then said, "I expect that someone as common as you, Henry, takes great delight in bringing a peer of the realm down. I understand your father was a shopkeeper and you were born in Stepney." His sneering laugh was brought to an abrupt end when Billy, who was standing behind the handcuffed suspect, took exception to the high-handed insult to Sir Edward Henry, and said loudly, "Oy!" as he smashed

Budlington's face forward into his desk. Tollman and Sir Edward winced, then Billy grabbed the back of Budlington's hair and pulled him upright again. His nose was broken, and bleeding, and he grimaced in pain.

"I'll have you thrown in prison for this, you animal!" he spluttered at Billy, as blood ran into his mouth.

"Oh yes?" answered Billy sarcastically. "Will that be before or after you are shot for treason?"

Sir Edward Henry suppressed a small smile and said solemnly, "If you must know, Budlington, my father was a doctor and I was born in Shadwell." Tollman's eyebrows shot up in astonishment. Areas didn't come any rougher than down by the docks in Shadwell. Sir Edward gained a whole new level of respect at that moment.

Budlington laughed through his pain. "I've never liked you, Henry. Never approved of nasty little middle class people taking over positions of power in this country. People who have come up the ranks through the Empire and throw their weight about in the Civil Service and the House of Commons…"

"And yet you chose to betray your country in partnership with a civil servant? How very noble you hereditary peers are!" Sir Edward was scathing in his judgement. "I doubt whether your fellow peers – many of whom have lost sons in the trenches – will be quite so appreciative of your sentiments about the middle classes who are, along with the working classes – bearing the brunt of this war, in both casualties and organisation. Take him away, Tollman, and lock him up. The sight of a member of the nobility, who is a traitor, is more than any decent person can be expected to bear."

Billy roughly dragged Lord Budlington to his feet and propelled him out of the door. Sir Edward stopped Tollman, as he followed, and murmured, "Try and restrain Constable Rigsby from breaking any more of the prisoner's appendages. It won't do to serve him up for justice bandaged from head to foot." Tollman nodded and smiled.

As they loaded Budlington into the police car, Tollman was still worried about the lack of concrete evidence they had. He wanted to ensure that the man would receive the maximum penalty for both crimes. He just hoped that the navy or Mr Beech could come up with some more evidence in the next couple of days.

✳✳✳

Beech had decided that Hvide Sande was possibly the most beautiful place he had ever seen. Miles and miles of pure, almost white, sand, with gently sloping dunes behind the beach. Todd and Beech had been dropped by a small launch, as near to the beach as possible – made easier by the fact that there was an incoming tide. Todd and Beech dropped over the side into the water, which was waist deep, holding their canvas rucksacks over their heads, and waded to shore. Then they watched the launch turn slowly and make its way back to the ship.

Everything was quiet. The captain had explained that Hvide Sande was, primarily, a fishing port, and that all the working fishing vessels would have returned to harbour long before the British minesweeper arrived. As Beech and Todd climbed up the incline of the beach towards the dunes, Beech could see clusters of gaily painted wooden houses around the harbour area, and then the ingress of the sea, which made an inland lake, beyond that. Men were mending nets and working on boats in the harbour. It was picturesque and calm. There was no urgency or sense of war. Beech felt a sense of lightness and smiled.

Todd, as usual, seemed impervious to any tranquillity and bristled with his usual restless energy. "We need to walk to the northern end of the town and catch an omnibus to Ringkobing, to then get a train to Esbjerg." He looked at his watch. "We have one hour to get to the bus, so that we can get the last train from Ringkobing, which should get us into Esbjerg before midnight," and he strode towards north with Beech following behind as quickly as his stiff leg would allow.

Men looked up curiously from their repairs, as the two strangers passed, but quickly went back to their work, assuming them to be 'foreigners' and therefore passing through. The groups of women that they passed, wearing embroidered waistcoats and skirts, shawls and capes, seemed to all be engaged in some sort of craft work – knitting or weaving, hands and fingers in constant movement, no time to pay much attention to passing strangers. Once again, Beech marvelled at a community with no darkness at its core, no dread of the war. The tranquillity of normal life.

Todd kept up a relentless pace and, finally, they arrived at what seemed to be a small omnibus depot. There was a hut which contained a ticket office, a couple of benches in a waiting area and a drinking fountain. Beech gratefully sank on to one of the benches and rummaged around in his rucksack for his tin of aspirin pills. His leg was beginning to throb, and he needed to take pain relief before it got any worse. He put the pills in his mouth and went to the drinking fountain. Todd, meanwhile, was scanning the timetable on the wall, to make sure that there was, indeed, an omnibus on the way.

The ticket clerk appeared, smiled and said something in Danish. Todd apologised in English for not speaking the language and the clerk just looked bemused and shrugged. Todd then repeated the apology in German and immediately the clerk understood, and they began a conversation. Beech felt unnerved by this discussion in German and sat down again to wait whilst Todd bought two tickets.

"It's all good," Todd came back to report. "The omnibus will be here in about half an hour and we will arrive at Rongkobing in good time to get the last train."

"Your German seemed very fluent. I have retained very little of the language from my schooldays, unfortunately," Beech commented.

"Thank you. My French is not bad either, but I have no command of Danish at all," Todd replied with good humour. "But, because they are next door neighbours, many Danish are able to converse comfortably in German, thankfully."

"Well, I'm sorry that I shall have to leave all the conversation to you," Beech responded with a rueful smile and inwardly cursed the fact that he was beginning to feel useless on this mission.

Once they were on the omnibus, in the company of just one other man, Beech looked out again at the endless sands and sea on the horizon. A place to come back to, one day, he thought to himself, Victoria would like it here. Then the gentle motion of the vehicle caused his eyelids to droop and, eventually, he succumbed to sleep as the light faded outside the window.

He awoke with a start, as Todd shook him and said, "We're here". A befuddled Beech grabbed his rucksack from the overhead webbing and stumbled off the omnibus with his companion. They were five feet away from Ringkobing station and the train was getting up steam, so there was no time to lose. Todd darted through to the ticket window and purchased the tickets, then they proceeded to board the train.

Surprisingly, after the emptiness of the omnibus, the train was full, it appeared, of families, with their luggage, which a harassed ticket inspector was trying to organise so that no suitcases and hatboxes were blocking the aisle. Todd and Beech were able to find two seats together in a corner and stowed their rucksacks underneath. The babble and disagreements between passengers and inspector grew to a crescendo until the harsh train whistle blew, signalling departure, and everyone was suddenly panicked into stowing luggage wherever they could. Beech noted that almost all the conversations were in German and it made him uncomfortable.

Todd was busy writing a note, which he then passed to Beech. It read:

If anyone asks, remember, we are two American merchant seamen on leave but going back to join our cargo ship at Esbjerg. Denmark is neutral, of course, so no problem.

Beech read the note, nodded, and then put it in his rucksack. As he sat back, he noted that the man in the seat opposite was watching them. As Beech caught his eye, the man smiled, extended his hand, and said,

"Guten Abend. Ich bin Herr Scholz und das sind meine Frau und meine beiden Töchter." He indicated his wife, seated beside him, and his two daughters, seated across the aisle. They all smiled and nodded.

Todd grasped the man's hand first and said briskly, "Guten Abend. William Todd." Beech then took over the man's hand and said, "Peter Beech."

The German families' faces clouded momentarily and the man said, in perfect English, "You are British?"

Several pairs of eyes swivelled towards them as they both said "American".

"Ah! Amerikanische!" This seemed to delight the German, his family and the nearby passengers as they nodded at each other amiably.

" I have a cousin in America," Herr Scholz said grandly. " He lives in Milwaukee. Do you know it?"

Beech and Todd shook their heads.

The German family now seemed to want to concentrate on their evening meal, as various waxed paper packages were unwrapped.

Beech knew that he would have problems sleeping, as he had succumbed on the omnibus, so he contented himself with closing his eyes and conjuring up images of the white sands at Hvilde Sande and imagined that he was resting against one of the dunes and enjoying a gentle sea breeze against his face.

***

The Metropolitan Police had a little arrangement with the military, when they wanted to incarcerate someone of particular interest but not want the British press to hear about it from any loose-lipped policeman working at Scotland Yard. There were some particularly unpleasant cells in the basement of the Central London Recruiting Depot – a building that had once belonged to the Met – in a road known as Great Scotland Yard.

The police were allowed to borrow the cells, when they were not in use, for 'special' interrogations. Sir Edward Henry had made just such an arrangement for Lord Budlington.

Thankfully, the front of the building, which, in this time of war, was usually packed with young men wanting to volunteer to serve in the army, was quiet at night, and Tollman and Rigsby were able to bundle the errant lord from the car to the cells with only one stray cat on the cobbles bearing witness.

Budlington had gone from loud protests, to worried silence, as he realised that he could not intimidate the police and his situation had become a stark reality. Billy removed the handcuffs and pushed the prisoner forcefully into the cell.

As the door clanged shut and was locked, Tollman said diffidently, "An army medic will be down shortly to see to that busted nose." He hoped that he was giving the impression that he really didn't care.

An orderly appeared with mugs of tea for Tollman and Rigsby. Pointedly, there was nothing for the prisoner. The two policemen drew a table and a couple of chairs into the middle of the room. Billy took off his helmet and jacket and rolled up his sleeves. Budlington looked nervous. Tollman took off his hat and raincoat and took a long drink of his tea.

The army medic came in, took one look at the prisoner and grinned. "Bit of a mess isn't it?" he said, looking up at Billy, who towered above him. "Accidentally walked into a wall, did he?"

Billy nodded. "Something like that." Then he unlocked the cell door and they both went inside - the medic to patch the prisoner up and Billy to protect the medic.

Whilst Budlington was being cleaned and bandaged and was groaning a great deal, a navy courier arrived with a box of papers and notes. He handed them over to Tollman, who signed for them and the courier said that the Detective Sergeant was to send a message to Captain Webb when he had finished with the evidence.

Once the medic had gone and Budlington was alone in his cell once more, Tollman opened the box and began to read the notes, silently. Billy supped his tea and never took his eyes off Budlington, which caused the prisoner to resort to staring at the floor to escape Billy's surveillance.

"Right!" said Tollman loudly, causing Budlington to jump involuntarily. "It appears that your friend, Mr Rutledge, has grassed you up good and proper, my lord. According to our friends at the Admiralty Trade Division, he has named names, dates, bank account numbers – all incriminating you. A search of his flat has produced copies of Bills of Lading from America, issued by a company that you partly own, receipts from import/export companies in Norway and Denmark and much more."

Budlington was contemptuous. "It is not against the law

to own an American company. Cotton is on the free to trade list, along with oil and rubber. The British Parliament decreed it so. Germany is free to import free list goods but, you will not find any evidence of my American company trading with Germany. In case you hadn't realised, detective, there is no law that prevents any American company from doing trade with the neutral countries in Scandinavia."

"Ah, but we know all about your little fiddles, Lord Budlington." Tollman continued. "Apparently, the navy also found documents that show that you also own considerable shares in the Universel Import Company, which has offices in Norway and Sweden."

Budlington seemed a little rattled at this news but persisted with his show of bravado. "Again, I will say to you, that there is no law against me owning companies in neutral countries. What are you going to charge me with? Capitalism?" he laughed mirthlessly, but it made his broken nose hurt, so he stopped.

Tollman knew that until they had confirmation from Mr Beech and Commander Todd that they had proof of trading with the enemy, they had nothing that would sway a court to give a guilty verdict on the charge of treason. So, he turned his line of questioning to the murder of Agnes Whitlock.

"We have a witness that identified Agnes Whitlock as the woman who came to give you a message at your club on the night she was murdered." Tollman decided to lie. "We also have a witness that saw you meet Agnes Whitlock in Berkeley Square some ten to fifteen minutes later." Billy looked at Tollman and then down at the floor. He did not want his face to betray the fact that he knew Tollman didn't have such proof.

There was a silence. Tollman continued. "We have your sword stick, which is now being analysed for blood and traces of tree bark – because we know that you speared her so hard with your sword, that it impaled her to the tree behind, and you had to pull it out with great force. Pieces of tree bark were found in the wound – pulled through when you yanked your sword out of her body. The senior pathologist who performed the autopsy will match your sword to the wound on the victim."

"I never knew the woman…" Budlington's voice trailed off quietly and the nervousness in his voice betrayed his guilt. Tollman smiled in triumph. In the next presentation of evidence, he would get a confession of guilt from Budlington, he was sure.

"No," Tollman agreed, "You didn't know Agnes Whitlock, but she knew you. She worked for Mason's and she had been investigating your company and its operations for months."

"But why?" Budlington was incredulous. "What business was it of hers? Who was she?"

"She worked for the Admiralty Trade Division, Lord Budlington. She effectively worked for the government. Agnes Whitlock was an undercover investigator for the Admiralty."

Budlington's face was a picture of shock. His entire life was in ruins because of a resourceful woman and he just simply could not believe it.

"Now, Lord Budlington," said Tollman, with an air of finality, opening his notebook and taking a pencil from his jacket pocket. "Let's start at the beginning, shall we?"

***

The majority of the German families stayed on the train when it reached Esbjerg because the train was carrying on over the border. Esbjerg was obviously a refuelling station, as the train was now taking on coal and water. Some of the passengers got off the train to stretch their legs.

Beech and Todd could see the dock gates in the distance and the funnels of the ships at berth beyond that. There were lights and activity. Obviously, Esbjerg was a very busy port. Beech stopped walking suddenly, at the sight of what was obviously a German U boat crew coming out of a bar. Todd grabbed his arm and urged him on.

"It's not an unusual sight in neutral ports," said Todd quietly. "Especially ports so close to Germany. They duck under the blockade, through the minefields, and come into Esbjerg for a break." Beech nodded but then was further alarmed by Todd's next statement. "Do not look around, Beech, but a man has been following us ever since we got off the train. Just keep walking straight ahead."

When they reached the dock gates, the gatekeeper asked them for their papers and Todd asked him, in German, if the *Grey Dolphin* had docked yet. The gatekeeper pointed in the distance to the holding berths, for ships awaiting inspection and transfer for unloading. Todd gave him a story about his brother being on the ship and he wanted to meet up with him. The gatekeeper said that he estimated that the vessel would be inspected at about six in the morning and then moved to a berth near the railway line for unloading. Todd thanked him and then took Beech to one side. "Let's go in a bar and get some food and drink," he suggested, "then we can see if our friend from the train comes in too."

The bar was busy and noisy. Todd ordered two beers and some local dish, which turned out to be sausage, mash and pickles. Beech tucked in greedily. It was some time since they had both eaten and hot food and a cold beer was most welcome. They both faced the door, and, after a while, it became obvious that the man from the train was not following them. It had just been a coincidence. Beech said nothing throughout the meal, for fear of being overheard speaking English. Finally, food eaten and beer drunk, Todd said "Lass uns gehen," and Beech knew enough German to know that it meant "Let's go." The serious work was about to start.

CHAPTER TWENTY TWO

U BOAT LISTS

The dock area of Esbjerg appeared to never sleep but in the quiet back streets, higher up in the town, there was very little sign of life. Unfortunately, Borgergade, the street in which the Universel Import Co. had its offices, was quite close to the docks and, as such, was not so quiet. There were a few modest hotels, catering to crew on shore leave or passing through, a few bars and offices of shipping businesses. None of the buildings were more than three stories high, which was a relief to both of them, in case they had needed to scale the outside of the building to gain entry. Fortunately, they scouted around the back and found a rear entrance in a dark alley, which was recessed and not overlooked. Todd tried to use a penknife to open the lock, but Beech tapped him on the shoulder and whispered, "Let me," and produced his own penknife which had many tools. Holding up a hoof pick, he then proceeded, in a few seconds to tumble the lock and open the door. Todd gave him an impressed thumbs up as they crept into the building.

They slowly and quietly ascended the stairs. There was no sign of life. This was a commercial building only. There appeared to be no residences. On the second floor they found the office they wanted, and Beech again performed his trick with the hoof pick. Once inside, Todd closed all the curtains and then they both took torches out of their rucksacks..

"I'm going to look through some of the files and see what I can find," Todd said quietly, "why don't you look through the desk. We are looking for anything incriminating. Any communications with Mason's directors in Britain or any communications with the Germans." Beech nodded and stealthily opened the drawers of the desk, whilst Todd began to open filing cabinets.

Beech found an accounts book in the main drawer of the desk and began to look through it, on the off chance he might see something of interest. The accounts were fairly sparse, so it was easy for him to pick up the recurring income and expenditure items. Every month there were entries which said

Direktorens Vederlag:

Budlington

Rutledge

Dastrup

Beech continued to scan the book. He noted that every month there was an expenditure:

Telegrammer:

Wilmhelshaven

London

"Todd!" Beech hissed, "Look at this!" Todd came over and Beech pointed out the regular entries each month. "I think this one is monthly payments to the company directors and this one is regular payments for their telegram account."

"Good God!", Todd almost forgot to keep his voice to a whisper. "Wilhelmshaven is the headquarters of the German High Seas Fleet and, more importantly, the U boat division." He turned over the pages for the first six months of 1915, and began to read the entries, Todd was aghast. "Look at the number of telegrams they have sent to both places!"

"We need to find copies of those telegrams," said Beech. "I'll look for them, whilst you photograph the accounts book." He began to rifle through cabinets, whilst Todd produced his Vest Pocket Kodak camera, put the accounts book on the floor, suspended his flashlight, by its strap, from the drawer handle and began to photograph the evidence.

Beech was midway through the second cabinet when he found a box file full of telegram copies. With typical Nordic efficiency, the sender had written down the full message, addresses of despatch and delivery and time sent before, presumably, dictating the message over the telephone. But there were also many telegrams sent from Rutledge in London.

"Todd! There are too many telegrams here to photograph! What do you want to do?"

Todd, having finished his own task, came over and read a handful of the messages. "These are all ship movements – either from London, giving details of ships leaving the Port of London for Norway or Sweden – or from this office to the Germans, which seem to..." He broke off and sounded confused. "I don't quite understand. The telegrams from Esbjerg to Wilhelmshaven just seem to repeat the information from London...Oh God!" He had pieced it together. "This office is sending names of ships to the U Boat command – the ships they *don't* want to be torpedoed! You remember the captain who brought us to Denmark said that, so far, his ship 'was not on any list of minesweepers' and he wanted to keep it that way? Obviously, the U boats have two lists – one of ships to target and one of ships to leave alone."

There was a moment's silence whilst they both digested

the level of collusion with the enemy orchestrated by the directors of Mason's.

Todd made a decision. "We need to write down a list of all the ship's names and the dates of sailing from London for the last three months, so the Admiralty can match them up with ships that were inexplicably given permission by the Foreign Office to pass through the blockade. Then, perhaps, we can remove a few of the older telegrams, that won't be missed, as further proof. If you can do that, Beech, I will continue searching for some bank statements or – proof of payments in the form of cleared cheques – to show these payments to the British directors. Your people at Scotland Yard should then be able to pinpoint the payments and conversions to sterling in the bank accounts in England."

Beech agreed and sat down at the desk with the box of telegrams and began to make a list. Todd continued his search through the cabinets.

After two hours, sufficient evidence had been found, listed, photographed and removed for both men to feel they had done their best. Everything was put away carefully, so that there was no sign of any disturbance and they crept out of the building, locking everything behind them.

"Where now?" asked Beech as they came out into the crisp night air.

"The station," Todd answered firmly. "We'll have a nap in the waiting room and wait for the train carrying Mason's cotton to appear in the morning. Then we'll board it. If we can get sight of the railway freight manifest and witness the cotton crossing the border, then we will have done as much as we can." So Todd strode off towards the station.

As they stretched out on the hard wooden benches in the rather grand Esbjerg railway station, Beech finally felt that he had been an equal partner in their endeavours that night, which made him feel good. However, his leg was hurting like the blazes and, despite having swallowed some more tablets on their walk from Borgergade, they were having little effect. Sleep, this time, would come very slowly.

***

There were tears and confusion in London in the morning, for several reasons.

Billy had received a message at the Central London Recruiting Depot, at around one o'clock in the morning, from the hospice, to say that Myrtle was in a very bad way. The message had been relayed through Lady Maud, then Scotland Yard, then through the army clerk on the front desk, so it was already a good hour old before it got to him. Tollman told him to go and take the police car that was still parked outside in the street, because there would be no trains at this time of night. Gratefully, Billy set off.

Lord Budlington's confession, regarding the murder of Agnes Whitlock, had been wrung out of him in a war of attrition waged by Tollman, who just talked, reasoned, verbally bullied and cajoled the truth out of the prisoner. Budlington had cried – often – as he realised there was no way out and his privileged life was in tatters. Billy had marvelled at how a man of Tollman's age never flagged and kept up a relentless barrage of probing questions, wearing down the defiance of the prisoner, until he was a weeping mass of self-pity. Tollman had then given a strange smile of triumph and scorn for the worthless, greedy man in the cell.

When Billy had arrived at the hospice, one of the nuns had told him that Myrtle was unconscious and unlikely to revive. "But do talk to her," she had said. "We believe that the last sense the dying lose is their hearing. Talk to her naturally, try not to be upset. Comfort her and encourage her to pass over peacefully."

They had moved Myrtle into a side room, so she was all on her own. She looked terribly ill but peaceful. Somehow, to Billy, she seemed to have shrivelled in the bed to about the size of a child. It was his imagination, he knew. He sat and took her hand and he fancied that he saw a twitch of her lips into something that passed for a smile. He began to talk, quietly, to this girl that he really hadn't liked but now pitied. Her breath was raspy and irregular. He told her about Phyllis collecting from the other workers for her headstone and he made up a story about Mrs Hawkesworth going and picking one that had angels carved on it. Myrtle let out a kind of sigh, which Billy took for pleasure. He told her that Mason's was going to pay for her funeral, for sure, and a wake, and the women in the cordite room were going to put some lovely flowers on her grave. He was going through the names of flowers that he knew, as though he was making a bouquet for her, when he realised that Myrtle was no longer breathing. At that moment, the sister came in, put her hand on Myrtle's neck, to check for a pulse, and then made the sign of the cross.

"That was quick and peaceful. Thank you, constable. She must have been waiting for you." Then she took Myrtle's hand out of his and crossed both the girl's hands across her chest and brought the sheet up over her head. "Now come and have a cup of tea, Mr Rigsby and we have another side room where you can have a rest on the bed until you feel ready to leave."

Billy took a last look at the small form of Myrtle Dimmock, draped with a sheet, and allowed himself to be led off to the warm kitchen and some consoling words from the kind sister.

***

Phyllis was in tears for most of the morning, because it was Elsie and Sissy's last day, and she was going to miss the companionship. Nothing that the women could say would console her.

"I'm sure the new women will be just as friendly," said Elsie hopefully.

Phyllis shook her head.

"We've written out all our recipes for you," said Sissy, trying to be positive.

Phyllis just burst into fresh tears. Then Sissy had one of her bright ideas. "Why don't you go for a complete change and apply for Myrtle's old job?" she suggested, and Phyllis looked up in surprise.

"Do you think I could?" The thought definitely seemed to cheer her up and she half-smiled.

"Don't see why not," countered Elsie. "By all accounts it's a dead simple job and you'd get more money. Go and see Tom now and ask him!"

Phyllis dried her eyes and allowed the women to tidy her hair and set off across the yard to the office. Fifteen minutes later, she was back with a smile on her face.

"He said yes! As long as I finish the week off and handover to the new cooks, I can start in the cordite room on Monday!"

However, that was the last piece of good news in Mason's for the rest of the day. When Billy arrived at the factory, he brought nothing but sadness and worry. The news of Myrtle's death caused a ripple of grief throughout the entire workforce – mostly prompted, Billy suspected, by guilt at the fact that no-one had really liked her. Lily, however, her sometime friend, was inconsolable, and all the women in the cordite room were afraid that Myrtle's death had been caused by the cordite and there were rumblings of concern. Mrs Hawkesworth came down to tell Captain Wallace, who was still supervising Tom, as the new manager, that the women were close to "chucking it all in" unless someone reassured them that Myrtle Dimmock's death had not been as a result of her work.

Captain Wallace then called in the medical team and Caroline gave him a report concerning the health hazards of cordite and nitro-glycerine, in particular, which, basically, recommended the wearing of rubber gloves at all times, and, at the very least, the men in the nitro shed should wear cotton masks and have regular breaks away from the shed. Captain

Wallace then asked them to speak to the entire workforce and, as it was a nice, warm day, he assembled them all outside in the yard and handed over to Caroline.

She explained that Myrtle had died from cirrhosis of the liver, caused by heavy drinking of alcohol, but that she had also had various other health problems, which had been aggravated by exposure to nitro glycerine. She allowed the general murmur of concern to die down and then she explained the simple procedure of wearing rubber gloves that would stop them absorbing the nitro through their skin and the fact that the men working with the nitro should have extra protective measures.

She was halfway through her speech of reassurance, when Billy appeared to tell Captain Wallace that Detective Sergeant Tollman was on the telephone, wanting a word.

Caroline had just finished her speech when Wallace re-appeared and said he had another announcement to make. He waited for silence and then he said, "The police have just telephoned to confirm that the directors of this company – a Mr Rutledge and Lord Budlington – have been arrested, as have Mr Bradshaw and Mr Sinclair."

There was a collective explosion of shock from the workforce. "Is this to do with Myrtle?" shouted one woman. "What have they done?" shouted one of the men.

Wallace held his hands up for silence. "I'm sorry to say that the directors of Mason's have been charged with the very serious crime of trading with the enemy in time of war. Bradshaw and Sinclair have been charged as accessories. But, further to that, I have to report, regretfully, one of the directors has been charged with the murder of Agnes Whitlock."

There was a stunned silence from the workforce. Some women started quietly weeping. Poor Agnes was another woman, like Myrtle, who was not liked, but the women still felt sorrow at her brutal death.

One man said quietly, "Does that mean the factory is going to close?" All eyes looked towards Captain Wallace and when he said, "No, absolutely not," there was a collective sigh of relief. Wallace continued, "Munitions are too important to the war effort and the Ministry of Munitions has decided that it will take over and run any company that has problems. In a few weeks, you will all be government employees. It will be business as usual."

✳✳✳

Beech had woken, around about dawn, in the most incredible pain. Laying on a hard wooden bench had taken its toll on his body. He dragged himself into a sitting position and started rubbing all his limbs to ease the pain and stiffness. Todd was already awake and standing outside the waiting room looking down the line towards the docks. Beech downed some aspirin tablets and slowly stood up. The pain shot like a dagger through his wounded leg and he caught his breath. There was nothing he could do except grit his teeth and accept the pain and he slowly walked towards Todd, every step causing an agony that he had not felt since his days in the field hospital in France.

Todd, oblivious to the tension in Beech's face, said cheerily, "I think the coaches are coming with the loaded cotton. They'll probably link them up to the passenger section on the next platform. We'll wait for them to do that before we get on the train. We might be able to see if any of the freight labels have changed."

Beech nodded and managed a weak smile. The pain was easing a little, although he now had a sharp pain in his stomach. He reasoned that it was probably hunger. "It will be good to get something to eat," he said, and Todd agreed.

They watched as the freight section of the train came slowly along the tracks from the docks and they walked across to the next platform. Beech was sweating a little from the effort of trying to give the appearance that he was not in pain and he leaned against a wall to give himself some support.

The goods wagons arrived, being pushed into position by a small engine, which was then uncoupled, and the other end of the six wagons was coupled up to the passenger section.

"You get on the train and find us some seats," suggested Todd, "and I'll duck through to the other side, climb up and see if can see any labelling under the tarpaulins." Beech nodded, grateful that it wasn't being suggested that they both climb up. He waited until Todd had disappeared from view, then he slowly limped across to the train and hauled himself up the steps into the passenger wagon. To his relief, the seats were padded, and he stowed both their rucksacks underneath before thankfully sinking into a window seat and stretching out his bad leg. The pain had eased a little. It was no longer a fierce stabbing, which almost took his breath away, but it had dulled down into a continuous ache, which made him feel nauseous.

Todd reappeared, with the smile of a schoolboy who

successfully been scrumping apples. "Look," he murmured, opening his hand and revealing a cardboard label that he had obviously ripped from one of the bales. It read:

CONSIGNOR:

Universel Import Co.

Borgergade

Esbjerg

CONSIGNEE:

Deutsche Waffen und Munitionsfabriken AG

L12

Hamburg

Beech looked quizzical. "Who is the consignee?" he asked.

Todd smiled triumphantly. "The German Weapons and Munitions Manufacturing Company, Warehouse 12. Now all we have to do is sit back and watch it go over the border and our job is done. Shall we find the buffet car?"

Beech nodded gratefully and hauled himself up. The train had begun to move, so he was glad of the excuse to be able to legitimately stumble down the aisle, clutching on to the seats for support.

***

Late afternoon, when the ladies of the Mayfair 100 team assembled in Lady Maud's parlour, everyone was subdued, except for an ecstatic Timmy who kept bounding for joy around Elsie and Sissy, and Tollman, who felt that he had acquitted himself well during the week.

Caroline and Mabel were frustrated and saddened by

their inability to correctly diagnose and save Myrtle Dimmock, although Mabel had reasoned that if they had been aware of her liver condition, there wouldn't have been much that they could have done about it. Caroline did not find that thought any consolation whatsoever. She even said that she felt the medical team had not contributed anything much towards the investigation at all, which caused Tollman to become irritable and state that the actions of *everyone* in the team had contributed to the final outcome.

Victoria felt compelled to agree with Tollman and pointed out that, in any event, they had made a great difference to the health and wellbeing of the workers at Masons, "And," she added, "Let's not forget that the initial investigation that we undertook to find the identity of Agnes Whitlock, was the foundation of the whole case."

"Absolutely," agreed Lady Maud. "Although I have only played a very small part in this case, I have to agree with Victoria. The initial legwork was done by us ladies."

Everyone agreed but Caroline said nothing. She was determined to feel grumpy and no-one was going to persuade her to snap out of it.

"So, is it all over now, Mr Tollman?" asked Lady Maud.

"Bar the shouting, Lady Maud." Tollman seemed satisfied. "We have Lord Budlington's signed confession regarding the murder, which guarantees him the death penalty. The navy seem to think they have enough on Rutledge and Budlington to warrant the death penalty as well. Personally, I'm not so sure. I think it depends what Mr Beech and Commander Todd can lay their hands on. The navy are going to need some very watertight evidence – no pun intended – to put a peer of the realm in front of a firing squad."

"Dear me," Maud expressed genuine astonishment, "they can't hang him *and* shoot him, surely?!"

Tollman smiled. "I expect the treason charge will take precedence, as it's wartime. But I don't expect we'll read about it in the paper. The government don't like to admit such activities happen. Bad for the country's morale, I suppose." He then explained that Bradshaw and Sinclair had effectively been charged as accessories to the treason charge and had both been moved to prison hospitals. Tollman added that he expected that Bradshaw might get a modest prison sentence, as he had gathered information with the intent of informing the authorities. Sinclair would be looking at a possible life term.

Timmy had finally wheedled his way on to Elsie's lap and had snuggled down. Both Elsie and Sissy expressed thanks to Lady Maud for taking care of him.

"Anytime, ladies," she said with a smile, whilst privately hoping the occasion would never crop up again. She had found it most disconcerting to find herself subject to a small dog's every whim. Timmy had managed to both enchant and intimidate her at the same time. For a woman used to running committees and engaging in conversation with members of parliament, it had been a humbling experience.

Chapter Twenty Three

UNEXPECTED DEVELOPMENTS

The train from Esbjerg to Hamburg had taken its time to amble through the Danish countryside, so it was quite late in the afternoon when Beech and Todd left the train at Padborg – the last stop before the German border. Todd had harboured some fanciful idea that they should stay on the train and jump off just before the border but Beech had dissuaded him from such foolishness, mainly because he knew that he would not be able to jump from a moving train in his present condition, the pain in his leg and his stomach having returned with a vengeance.

"It is enough to witness the cargo leaving Padborg for the four mile journey into Germany. You have the label. There is no station between Padborg and Flensburg for them to offload the cargo. We have done enough, Todd."

The terseness of his comment caused Todd to sulk for a while. *I have frustrated his action-packed adventure*, thought Beech, with a sense of despair that his body had let him down and caused him to snap at his companion.

As they watched the train slowly ease out of the station and begin the short journey into Germany, Beech began to shiver.

"It's cold," he said, which caused Todd to look at him anxiously.

"Are you unwell?"

Beech shook his head firmly. "No. We've been sitting

on the train for a long time, that's all. I need to get my circulation moving again," and he began to rub his arms and legs, being careful not to press too hard on his wounded leg, which had become hot and a little swollen.

"Good idea," said Todd, doing the same and then running on the spot for a little. "Unfortunately, the train we need to catch back to Esbjerg will be here in just a few moments and we will be sitting again. Still, we can get some hot coffee and pastries, eh?"

Beech nodded and managed a watery smile. Food seemed to make the pain in his stomach go away, although he was not very hungry.

✳✳✳

Tollman and Billy were spending the day at the Yard doing paperwork for all the arrests that had been made. This was the part where Tollman really wished that Beech was there to assist him with the legal procedurals. Although Tollman knew criminal law inside out, it was the correct choice of words and phrases that paralysed him with indecision. Billy was no help, as he was relatively new to policework. Suddenly he had a brainwave.

"Billy, let's take all this paperwork round to Mayfair. We need Mrs E's help." Victoria, with all her legal training, and a study full of legal books, would be able to help him choose the right terminology for this very important paperwork.

So, they packed everything up in Tollman's briefcase and proceeded to leave for the Mayfair house.

On the way out of the building, they unfortunately bumped into Detective Carter, who never wasted an opportunity to bait Tollman.

"Solved the case of the attempted assassination of Queen Victoria yet?" he said sarcastically and then looked at Billy. "Why have you always got the ape in tow, Tollman? Is he your bodyguard or something?"

Billy always had to restrain the urge to thump Carter and Tollman merely said, "I would be very careful, if I were you Carter. Eventually, you are going to need all the friends you can get."

Carter laughed. "What's that supposed to mean, Tollman? I've got plenty of friends!"

"I'm sure," replied Tollman over his shoulder, as he headed for the door, "Just not in the Metropolitan Police."

At the house in Mayfair, Victoria was only too delighted to assist with the police paperwork and soon the three of them were engaged in productive activity, with Tollman explaining what needed to be done, Victoria forming the right phrases and Billy retrieving law books from various shelves as directed.

They continued for most of the day, uninterrupted, as Caroline had gone back to work at the hospital and Lady Maud was making the most of her new-found freedom from the demands of Timmy, to visit friends and generally bustle about London.

Eventually, paperwork completed to Tollman's satisfaction, the three of them sat enjoying afternoon tea and cakes. Tollman thanked Victoria warmly for her assistance and said, "Mr Beech will be very pleased that we have progressed everything so well in his absence."

Victoria smiled. "Yes, although I'm sure he will be far too full of his great adventure to care about our paperwork!"

***

It had been another long and boring journey on the train back to Esbjerg but Todd was beginning to be concerned about Beech. Both of them had managed to sleep on the train but Todd had been woken by Beech's agitated behaviour, moving his head from side to side and muttering, as though he was having a bad dream. At one point, Beech shouted out and aroused the interest of the other passengers. Todd clapped his hand over Beech's mouth to silence him and realised that his face was hot and damp with sweat. He managed to rouse Beech, who seemed disorientated.

"You're not well," he said quietly, "but we'll be in Esbjerg soon and I'll try and get us some private transport to Hvide Sande."

Beech nodded gratefully. "Tablets in my rucksack. I need some water."

Todd bounded to the dining car and obtained a carafe of water and a glass, then he rummaged in Beech's rucksack for the tin of tablets. Beech took two and drank the water gratefully. By the time they reached Esbjerg, he seemed to be more alert and capable.

Todd helped him to stand and manoeuvred him off the train, but then he realised that Beech could only limp painfully for very short distances and required support.

"Put your arm around my shoulder," Todd instructed, moving to the side of Beech's good leg, and he put his arm around Beech's waist to support him as best he could. Together they slowly hobbled out of the station and Todd sat Beech down on a wall. "I'm going to find some transport, don't move."

Beech nodded and then said, "Thank you, sergeant." In his mind, he was laying in a trench, wounded, and a soldier was patching him up and ordering assistance. "Stretcher bearers," he murmured, as the heavy guns continued to pound in his head. Then he was falling, it seemed for a long time, until there was a pain that shot through his head and darkness.

When Todd returned, with a horse, cart, and driver, he found Beech laying on the pavement unconscious. The driver helped him lift the sick man into the back of the cart and they set off – Todd praying that they would reach Hvide Sande before midnight and that Beech would not die on the way.

It was nearly eleven when Todd and Beech were dropped off on the road behind the dunes and the driver, for extra money, agreed to help carry the semi-conscious man on to the sands. He didn't ask why two foreign men – he assumed German – needed to be on a beach at such a late hour. Most Danish people knew better than to ask questions. He just left them to their own devices, turned his cart around and made for the nearest inn and some stabling for the night. He had enough money in his pocket now to pay extra for a very late meal and a bed. He looked up briefly as he saw the first of two flares light up the night sky, but then concentrated once more on navigating his horse and cart down the road to the town and he ignored the second flare completely.

By the time the launch arrived, from the waiting ship, Beech was able to stumble, with assistance, through the gentle waves, up to thigh height, and be pushed into the launch. In fact, the cold seawater had roused him and provided relief to his hot and painful leg.

On board the ship, they managed to get Beech down into a bunk and the captain came down to have a look at him. He commented that the leg looked infected.

"I have morphine onboard and I can give him a shot of that to ease the pain. Meanwhile, you'd better keep applying cold flannels and see if you can bring that fever down. I'll ask the Admiralty for permission to divert to Leith, so we can get him into a hospital in Edinburgh. How long has he been like this?"

Todd shook his head. "I don't know, to be honest. I suspect he's not been feeling well for a couple of days, but he's been hiding it. He got wounded at Mons."

The captain gave a grunt of respect and disappeared to get the morphine. Todd filled a bowl with bold water, found a couple of flannels and began the long business of applying cold, damp flannels to Beech's face.

***

It was breakfast time and Tollman had just arrived at Lady Maud's house to pick up Billy, when Victoria told him there was a telephone call from the Yard.

It was a sombre Sir Edward Henry. "Detective Sergeant

Tollman, you need to get down to the Central London Recruiting Depot as soon as possible. It appears Lord Budlington has committed suicide."

Tollman just said "Christ," then, "On my way now, sir." He put the telephone receiver back on its cradle and bawled, "Billy! We have to go now!"

Billy came hurtling out of the dining room, a piece of toast in his mouth and grabbed his jacket and helmet. Tollman hailed a taxicab and they clambered inside.

"What's to do?" Billy asked. Tollman placed his fingers on his lips and then indicated his head towards the cab driver. Billy then understood that it was a matter that could not be discussed in public.

When they reached Great Scotland Yard, Tollman's face was like thunder and he shot out of the taxicab like a bullet out of a gun, leaving Billy to settle the bill.

"Where's my guvnor?" asked Billy as he entered the depot. The army clerk just pointed down to the basement and Billy ran down the steps, two at a time. As he turned the corner into the holding cell area, he stopped dead at the sight of Lord Budlington slumped in the corner of the cell, half his head blown away and a revolver on the floor by his right hand.

"Bloody hell!" he said loudly.

Tollman replied, without taking his eyes off the dead body, "Bloody hell indeed." The two squaddies guarding the body registered nothing on their faces but just stared straight ahead.

The Senior Officer was not in the depot, so Tollman sent one of the squaddies to summon the Adjutant. When he arrived, he had no idea of anything, was basically an administrator and feigned ignorance of how this suicide could actually have taken place.

Tollman got shirty and raised his voice. "The army was supposed to keep him safe in this cell for two nights...just two nights!" He was quivering with rage. "When I left here, the night before last, the prisoner had been thoroughly searched and did not have so much as a boiled sweet in his pockets or about his person. So how...HOW...did he manage to get hold of a revolver?"

The Adjutant bridled and said that if Tollman cared to look closely, he would see that it was not an army issue revolver.

"If that is the case," Tollman continued to express his rage by being extremely articulate and sarcastic, "who gave him that 'non-army issue' revolver? If it wasn't one of your men, what visitors have been allowed in here?

The Adjutant explained that he, personally, had not been on duty last night but he would go and get the visitors book and see.

Tollman fumed inwardly, put his gloves on, and opened the cell door to get a better look at the body. "Don't touch anything Billy. Go and telephone the Yard and get the fingerprint bloke down here." He took out his handkerchief, dropped it over the gun, picked it up and passed it to Billy, who carefully took the wrapped gun and put it in his jacket pocket, then went upstairs to contact the Yard.

The Adjutant reappeared and said that there was nothing in the visitor's book and handed it over to Tollman, who scanned the page of yesterday's visitors and discovered that the last person was signed in at 4.30 in the afternoon. This seemed to him a little unlikely, so he bent the spine of the book and discovered that a page had been removed, with great precision. He then pulled on a page further on in the book and it came out in his fingers with very little resistance, showing that it should have been stitched to the companion page that was removed.

"I want to know who was on duty on the front desk last night," he said firmly.

The Adjutant took the book back, scanned the page and pointed to a scribble of a name in the left hand margin.

"A Corporal McKenzie," he said. "According to the book, he signed on at 0800 yesterday evening and he should have done a twelve hour shift. But I can't see his sign-out signature anywhere. He's supposed to sign out when he leaves."

"That's because the page has been removed," Tollman pointed out, acidly."Do you know this Corporal Mackenzie personally?"

The Adjutant raised his eyebrows and explained that he couldn't possibly know all the personnel at the depot, as they were sent, on a rota basis, from Wellington Barracks.

Tollman looked at him in disbelief. "So, basically, in time of war, any idiot – possibly even a German spy – could put on an army uniform and present themselves in this facility as part of the workforce and you wouldn't challenge him?" As there was no answer, Tollman assumed it was true.

After the fingerprint officer arrived from Scotland Yard, a police surgeon had been summoned to do an examination of the corpse and then the body wagon arrived to take the corpse away, Tollman said quietly to Billy, with an air of resignation, "I just have to find out one more thing," and asked Billy to follow him.

They walked down the road to the Admiralty Trade Division, by which time Tollman appeared to have resurrected some of the anger he had felt earlier on. By the time they were ushered into the presence of Captain Webb, Tollman went on the attack.

"Was it you?" he said menacingly.

Webb looked confused by both the question and Tollman's tone. "Was what me?" he answered icily.

"Lord Budlington's apparent suicide. A mysterious revolver appeared in his cell and he used it."

A grim smile appeared on Webb's face, which took Tollman aback. This was not the reaction that he had expected.

"Ah," Webb said, "I would imagine that the deed was perpetrated by the same people who insisted that I release Rutledge."

"What!" both Billy and Tollman were shocked.

Webb continued. "Yes, gentlemen. An official appeared this morning with paperwork signed by the Attorney General's office to say that, basically, we did not have enough proof that the directors of Mason's were aiding the enemy." Webb looked at some papers on his desk and quoted, "Cotton is on the free-to-trade with Germany list, and we have no proof that Rutledge and Budlington in any way endorsed the onward sale of cotton to Germany by an associate company in Denmark. And..." he added sarcastically, "apparently, Mr Rutledge is urgently needed in some god-forsaken outpost in India. My only consolation is that he will probably suffer a lot more by being cast to the ends of the Empire, without even running water, than he ever would in a British prison."

"So, what you are saying is that Budlington was murdered, by the government?" Tollman was shocked.

Webb shrugged. "It's possible. But, frankly, I think it's far more likely that someone convinced him that, even if he escaped the death penalty, the shame would be visited on his family for generations. I think they encouraged him to kill himself and left him the means to accomplish the task. All done for the good of the war effort, of course. Much better for morale if we don't know that people are profiteering from trading with the enemy." He sounded bitter.

Billy felt moved to comment. "So, Commander Todd and Mr Beech have gone all the way to Denmark for nothing, then?"

Captain Webb shook his head. "Not if I have anything to do with it. I've already spoken to your commissioner and we have some plans. We don't intend to let any of the information gathered go to waste, I can assure you."

***

At six o'clock in the evening, Caroline had just returned home from the hospital when the telephone rang. As she was, literally passing the handset, she answered and a woman's voice said, "Is Dr Allardyce there please? It's very urgent! Telephone call from Edinburgh."

Caroline identified herself and, after a click, a man said, "Caroline – it's Commander Todd. Peter Beech wanted me to ring you. He's very ill. We think his leg is badly infected. We were going to put him in hospital in Edinburgh, but he refused. He's worried that they will amputate his leg and he will only be treated by you…"

"Where are you?" Caroline asked urgently, her heart beating in her throat so hard, she found it difficult to speak.

"Just about to board a fast mail train from Edinburgh. It should arrive in London Kings Cross at about two in the morning."

"I'll be at the station with an ambulance. What medication has he had?"

"He's just had an injection of morphine and he's been taking these aspirin tablets for the last week. He has a fever."

"If you can get hold of any ice, put it on his leg and keep bathing him with cold water to bring down the fever."

"Will do. I have to go now." Then the telephone went dead. A woman's voice said, "The party has disconnected. Do you wish to reconnect?"

"No. No thankyou."

Caroline burst into the parlour, where everyone had assembled, having been summoned by Tollman and said urgently, "Peter's seriously ill!" Everyone stopped speaking and looked at her. Victoria went pale.

"What's happened?" Tollman was the first to speak.

"His leg. Commander Todd says it has become infected. They're giving him morphine."

Victoria found her voice and asked, "Is he in hospital?"

Caroline shook her head. "The damn fool won't let them take him to hospital. Todd says Peter is afraid they'll amputate. He will only be treated by me and they are on a fast train to London now."

Tears appeared in Victoria's eyes and Maud moved to comfort her daughter.

"How can we help?" asked Tollman, ever practical.

"Only Mabel and Billy can help. I need Mabel to be on anaesthetic and I need Billy for his strength."

"Let me be there!" Victoria asked plaintively and Caroline replied tersely, "No, I'm sorry, Victoria. The less people the better. I'm going to take Peter to the operating rooms at the Hospital for Women, which is totally against the rules. The less of a crowd we are, the better. Maud, can we bring him back here to recuperate?" she added.

"Of course, my dear, there's no need to ask," Maud replied.

Caroline immediately regretted speaking to Victoria so sharply and took her hand, promising that, if Peter pulled through, she would be able to take care of him, day and night, here in the house. Then, she gathered up her things again, to telephone Mabel, to meet her at the hospital to assemble what equipment they needed. After that she went back into the parlour to instruct Billy to meet them at King's Cross at one thirty in the morning. Billy hailed a taxicab for her and when it pulled away, Caroline found herself silently praying that Peter Beech would survive the train journey so that she could give it her best shot at saving his leg.

CHAPTER TWENTY FOUR

WAS IT ALL WORTH IT?

Beech was shaking with fever when Caroline touched him, and his clothes were damp with sweat. Todd informed her that he had vomited blood on three occasions in the last two hours. The mail train had been on time and Billy and Todd had stretchered him out to the waiting ambulance. Mabel was inside and, on Caroline's instruction, she had prepared, in the hospital, a bag of saline to be administered intravenously. Beech also needed to be turned on his side, in case he vomited again. At that time of night, there were few impediments to making a relatively short journey from Kings Cross station and, as the ambulance drew up at the hospital and discharged its occupants, the night porter looked surprised.

"This man is a very, very important policeman who needs urgent emergency treatment," said Caroline in her best 'I will brook no interference' tone of voice. "I am just going to perform emergency surgery on him downstairs and then he will be removed to another facility, so there is no need to wake the night matron."

The porter had noted the presence of the uniformed Billy Rigsby, so he had no reason to doubt what Dr Allardyce was saying, and he motioned them through, darting ahead to open the doors of the lift down to the basement.

It was dark and Mabel ran ahead, switching lights on. She and Caroline had prepared Operating Theatre 2 with everything they might possibly need, but the fact that the unconscious Beech had leaked a small amount of blood from the side of his mouth on to the stretcher, they decided against using a Hewitt Airway and chloroform-ether mixture.

"I don't think it's a good idea to put something down his throat when he may continue vomiting," said Mabel, as she and Caroline began scrubbing their arms, hands and nails.

"Why do you think he is bringing up blood?" Caroline asked.

"What medication has he been taking?" asked Mabel.

"Apparently aspirin tablets, by the handful…constantly"

"I'm afraid there is your answer," was Mabel's response. "I've read several papers that show excessive aspirin intake can cause stomach bleeds, and also thin the blood."

"Damn!" Caroline realised that Beech was going to lose an excessive amount of blood when she operated.

Mabel assisted her into her surgical gloves and tied her gown on, and Caroline did the same for Mabel. Then she had an idea and stuck her head out into the corridor, where Todd and Billy were sitting, waiting.

"Are either of you blood type O?"

"I am," said Billy.

"Right. We will need you at the end of the operation to give Peter some of your blood. Is that alright?"

Billy nodded and Caroline went back into the theatre. Beech was on his side, unconscious, head on a pad that was soaking up the little bit of bloody salive that was trickling out of his mouth.

"Best way to proceed, Mabel?" Caroline asked. "The patient is unconscious, internal bleeding and possible clotting problems due to thin blood. I need to completely irrigate the wound, which is probably causing him terrible pain anyway. We can't use an anaesthetic that may cause his breathing to be depressed or block his gullet...any suggestions would be appreciated."

"An injection of cocaine, distributed around his leg," advised Mabel firmly. "It will numb it and it's a vasoconstrictor, so it should decrease the bleeding a bit. But work fast. I'll try and monitor his blood pressure."

Caroline nodded. When Mabel left to go down the corridor to the pharmacy and prepare a syringe of cocaine, Caroline bent over Beech and pressed her lips to his cheek. "I love you with all my heart, Peter Beech and I'll be damned if I am going to let you die or lose your leg. Just keep strong and keep that heart beating for me. Please, please don't die." Then she straightened up hastily and brushed away a tear as Mabel backed through the swing doors with a syringe in her hand.

Caroline worked quickly, with Mabel's extra hands assisting. She injected the cocaine around the livid and hard scar on Beech's leg.

"Wait three minutes," counselled Mabel, whilst she herself listened to Beech's heartbeat with a stethoscope, which was rapid, due to the fever. Caroline swabbed the leg with iodine and, after what seemed like a lifetime, Mabel said, "Heartbeat is slowing, go ahead." Caroline's scalpel deftly slashed open the scar and she was met by an avalanche of pus cascading out of the incision and on to the operating table, Mabel was immediately on hand with cotton soaked in saltwater and the pair of them began to clean out the wound.

Caroline could see that the army medics had done a hasty job in France. They had obviously caught the main muscle of the thigh into the closing stitches, which had led to the muscle distorting and tearing in a few places and would have caused Beech pain, every time he flexed the leg. That and the lack of proper circulation, over time, had probably led to the infection.

They finished clearing out the wound and Mabel returned to monitoring Beech's heart. She had also placed a leather strap between his teeth in case an involuntary action caused him to clench his jaws and bite his tongue. Caroline's nimble fingers were now separating the scar tissue from the muscle and trying to find and cut away any dead tissue in the hope of avoiding gangrene.

Mabel said softly, "You need to close up soon, and we need to transfuse. His heartbeat is getting a little weak."

"I'm going to irrigate with a weak saline solution, Mabel, then I will stitch – but it's going to need several layers. Do you think you could set up the transfusion with Billy while I'm working?"

Mabel hustled Billy in through the door and he involuntarily grimaced at the sight of Beech's leg. It was split open from knee to thigh, Caroline was speedily, but carefully stitching, wiping away blood, and there were buckets of pus-covered cotton under the table. Billy had to strip everything off above the waist and Mabel scrubbed his arm in preparation for Caroline inserting a needle. Meanwhile, she set up the collection bottle and rubber tubing. Caroline had now finished closing the wound and she put a long pad of clean cotton around Beech's thigh, so that he could be turned on to his back and raised up a little. Mabel wheeled over another table for Billy to lie upon and the complex procedure started where the two women collected a pint of blood from Billy, then Mabel filtered the blood into another bottle, which was then introduced into Beech's veins.

Finally, the two women pronounced that they had done as much as they could, and it was now in the hands of Providence. They dressed Beech's leg properly and wrapped him in a blanket. Billy got dressed, Commander Todd was summoned to assist with the transfer of Beech back to the ambulance and then to Mayfair.

Todd looked at the operating theatre with a degree of shock, as he entered. It was like a battle zone. Caroline and Mabel's aprons and gloves were covered in blood and pus. The floor was bloody. A trolley was full of discarded bloody instruments. There were even bloody hand marks on the door.

"This must be what a medical tent looks like at the Front," he said, with awe in his voice.

"If you could just take Peter to Mayfair and put him in my bed at the house," said Caroline, weariness in every syllable she uttered, "Mabel will order the ambulance to come round. I will clear up here and we'll be along in a while. Tell Victoria to keep Peter warm but to sponge his face now and then with cold water. I'll fix up another saline bag to his arm when I get back to the house, so take a drip stand with you," she pointed at the metal stand in the corner.

"I'll come back for you both," said Billy firmly, his voice brooking no argument. "Don't move until I get back."

Caroline nodded gratefully and Mabel escorted the men

and the patient out of the building. When she came back, Caroline was scrubbing the floor and weeping softly. Mabel, never usually one for demonstrative gestures, nevertheless knelt on the floor and wrapped her arms around her friend and gently rocked her until the crying stopped.

***

Over the next week, the house in Mayfair was hushed as everyone waited and prayed that Beech would recover. For the first two nights Caroline slept in a chair by his bed, in case there was any crisis, until Mabel and Victoria insisted that she slept in Victoria's bed at night, whilst Victoria napped during the day and kept watch over Beech at night.

"I'm not working during the day and you are, Caro," Victoria said stubbornly, "besides, if there is a problem, I can always wake you." So, Caroline gave into her exhaustion and finally slept in a proper bed.

On the third night, she was shaken awake by a beaming Victoria who said that Beech was awake and wanted to see her. She rushed into the bedroom in her nightdress to find Beech smiling weakly, with his hand on his bad leg.

"I knew you'd save it, old girl," he said feebly, and Caroline laughed whilst brushing away a tear. "Hurts like the blazes though."

"It will, for a while. I couldn't have done it without Mabel and Billy," she said. "You must be sure to thank them – and Commander Todd, who had heroically managed to keep you alive all the way from Denmark to London."

"Ah yes," Beech looked a bit sheepish, "I rather ruined his splendid adventure, didn't I? Made a fool of myself, thinking I could gallivant around everywhere like a healthy chap can,"

"Don't be silly, Peter," said Victoria. "Commander Todd is terribly in awe of you. He came round yesterday to see how you were and said what a very brave man you are, and he admires you very much."

Beech looked at Victoria with a frown, embarrassed that people should have been talking about him whilst he was unconscious, then he sank back on his pillows.

"Now you must get some proper rest and lots of nourishment." Caroline ordered. "Mrs Beddowes has instructions to feed you up, starting with nourishing soups and stews. You know that you damaged your stomach taking far too many aspirin pills?"

Beech closed his eyes. "It seems I got everything wrong," he said ruefully, as he slipped back into sleep.

***

Tollman had been in a bad mood for several days. The fact that all the work the team had done on the two investigations had been a wasted effort, and he wasn't even going to get the pleasure of arresting Detective Carter, had seriously affected his disposition. Even his daughters began to complain that he was grumpier than usual. He certainly couldn't face going to the Mayfair house to explain to Beech how everything had gone haywire, thanks to unknown persons in the government. He gave strict instructions that everyone else should avoid the subject of the investigations when Beech finally awoke. Victoria, who spent the most time at Beech's bedside, was ordered to say, if asked by Beech, that 'Tollman is dealing with all the complex paperwork and will give him a full report in due course.' Frankly, he felt that Beech would have to be a hell of a lot stronger to face the news that it had all come to nothing.

In fact, such was Tollman's frustration that he could not tie up all the loose ends, he felt compelled to request an interview with Sir Edward Henry.

When he entered the room, he was ready to state his grievances forcefully but was instantly disarmed by Sir Edward saying, "Ah, Detective Sergeant, you have no doubt come to tell me how unfair this whole situation is!"

"Y..yes, sir," said Tollman, hesitantly, suddenly unsure of his next step.

Sir Edward smiled sympathetically. "Sit down, Tollman and let me reassure you that Captain Webb and I have taken personally the maneouvering by person or persons unknown in either the government or the civil service. Such actions were despicable."

"Yes, sir," Tollman said forcefully, but before he could expand on his opinion, Sir Edward continued.

"All, I can say to you at this moment is that Captain Webb and I have a plan, in which we have enlisted the help of Lady Maud, and, if it works, we will at least vindicate some of the splendid work that your team has done. I'm afraid I can't tell you anymore at the moment. It won't, of course, enable you to prosecute the murderer of Agnes Whitlock but I think we can say that justice was served by his own hand on that one."

Tollman decided that, although he didn't know what the plan entailed, he felt relieved that the team's work had been recognised and that the Commissioner intended to try and find some sort of resolution. So, he thanked Sir Edward and got up to leave.

"Oh Tollman," Sir Edward murmured, "I haven't forgotten about Detective Carter. Just be patient and we shall select our time for action. But be rest assured, he will be held to account."

Tollman closed the door behind him and smiled. All was right with the world again.

***

Billy, Elsie and Sissy were together in Wanstead once more, attending the funeral of Myrtle Dimmock. All the Mason's workforce was there. They had been allowed two hours off to pay their respects to Myrtle and take tea and sandwiches in the church hall. Mason's had paid for it and the workers had purchased a headstone, which would be installed once the soil had settled on the grave. Mrs Hawkesworth had laid a big bouquet of lilies on the coffin, which had been set aside by the gravediggers to be put on the soil later.

It had been a simple but moving service and Billy smiled to himself, imagining Myrtle sitting on a cloud looking down on everything and being ecstatic that she had been spared a pauper's grave. By coincidence, Agnes Whitlock was also being interred today, as well. Tollman had decided to attend that service, as he felt that he had let down the murdered woman by not bringing her killer to court. Billy imagined that, as the navy were paying for Agnes' funeral, it would probably be a rather grand affair. Tollman had said that he was going to escort Agnes' friend, Enid Oliver, to the ceremony because he knew that Agnes would have wanted her there.

At Myrtle's wake, in the church hall, everyone chatted away happily. Although none of the conversation was about the dear departed – because, sadly, no-one really had a good word to say about Myrtle Dimmock - there was an air of satisfaction that they had 'done right' by one of their own, no matter how difficult she was.

Sam broke away from his workmates and came over to Billy and his family. Some of the assembly nudged each other at the sight of Elsie and Sissy hugging and kissing Sam, but then they went back to their tea and treats and forgot about it.

"I hope you won't take it amiss, ladies," Sam said tentatively, "but I'm going to move out of your place into some lodgings in Stratford. It will be easier for work. I hope you understand."

"Of course we do, love," said Sissy.

"But you'll come round now and then for a Sunday roast, I hope?" added Elsie.

Sam laughed. "Of course I will! But only if I can bring round three mates to help me eat it! You ladies are gonna kill someone with your food portions – you know that, don't' you?"

Billy laughed and shook Sam's hand. Sam said how much he had enjoyed working with them all on the 'special project', and they could always rely on his discretion and call on him if they needed him.

Billy said definitely, and added, "Especially if I want someone's jaw broken."

"About that…" said Sam seriously.

"I'm only joking!" said Billy, thinking Sam was about to apologise.

"No, no. It's about the boxing." Billy looked at Sam with interest and Sam continued, "I'm thinking about coming back to boxing – proper like. It's time I did more than sparring. Now I've got a proper full-time regular job, I wondered if, on Sundays, you would be my trainer? Help me have a crack at a few professional bouts?"

Billy beamed. "Straight up? Me? Train you?"

Sam nodded and Billy hugged him fiercely, which caused a lot of raised eyebrows amongst the Mason's work force.

"It would be a pleasure, mate!" Billy put his arm around Sam's shoulders and turned to Elsie and Sissy. "Mum, Aunty – you are looking at the next heavyweight champion of Britain and his trainer!"

"I don't doubt it, lads! I don't doubt it!" Sissy said and Elsie agreed.

***

Beech improved gradually throughout the week and Caroline decided to remove the bandage and inspect the wounded leg. Thankfully, she pronounced it clean and looking much less inflamed and Beech almost laughed with relief. But then she ruined the moment by saying "Peter, you stink. It's about time you had a bath!" Which made him flush with embarrassment. Only Caroline could speak to him like that, he reflected.

"I can help you," offered Victoria and Beech immediately refused.

"Ask Rigsby if he wouldn't mind helping me bathe." He was adamant that no woman was going to bathe him as though he was a small child. Besides, he said, it wouldn't be decent.

Caroline sighed and pronounced him to be a prude but said she would ask Billy.

Billy, of course, was only too happy to help. Lady Maud had borrowed a wheelchair from one of her charities and, in the evening, Billy wheeled Beech down the hall to the bathroom. As they traversed the landing, Beech looked down and saw Sir Edward Henry arriving with his wife and he could hear a hubbub of people in the dining room.

"What's going on?" he asked Billy.

"Oh, some important dinner party," Billy explained. "We don't know much about it, except Tollman said that the Commissioner arranged it with Lady Maud. Captain Webb and his wife are there and some very important people. The Commissioner said it's to do with the case we were working on and he'll tell us about it later."

Beech was intrigued. Despite his questions over the last week, everyone had been rather evasive and, frankly, he had been too ill and tired to press them for more detail. Now, he was feeling better, he was brimming over with questions and frustrated that he could not be attending the dinner party himself.

The hot bath had been drawn and, because he was under instructions from Caroline not to put any weight on his leg for several weeks, Billy had to lift him into the bath. As Beech sank into the hot water, which made his leg sting and throb, initially, he reflected how long it was since he had had a bath and he wrinkled his nose at the smell of stale sweat coming from his own armpits. Beech began to attack his body with soap and a flannel, and to ask questions about how the team had succeeded, whilst he had been away.

Tollman had, that morning, given Billy permission to tell Beech everything that had transpired in his absence – if he asked about it - but to stop at the arrests and not divulge, for the moment, the disappointment of the interventions that had stopped any prosecutions. Sir Edward reserved the right to give Beech the final details.

So Billy, in his own inimitable manner, told Beech the highs and lows of the complicated week at Mason's – from his mum and aunt's success at setting up a proper canteen, to Myrtle's death, Sinclair's jaw being broken, Bradshaw's heart attack, Mason's being taken over by the Ministry of Munitions and Sam being offered a Release from the Colours job.

Beech was so entranced by the complexity of all that had happened, interleaved with Billy's usual sense of humour, that he barely noticed that the bath water had gone quite cold.

✳✳✳

Several hours later, Beech, between fresh sheets, in clean pyjamas and smelling sweet, was visited by the Commissioner, who had escaped from the gathering downstairs.

"I hear that you are much improved, Beech," said Sir Edward, as he sat down in a chair by the bed.

"Yes, sir, thanks to Dr Allardyce, Miss Summersby, Constable Rigsby and Commander Todd. I owe so many people a deep gratitude for saving my life."

Sir Edward waved away any concerns with the observation that, as far as he was aware, they had all been more than happy to make the effort.

"You have a fine team, Beech. They have exceeded my expectations on this case, or rather cases. And they have all felt keenly, the disappointment of being unable to bring the cases to a satisfactory conclusion."

"Sir?" This was not the story that Beech had been told by Billy and he was concerned.

Sir Edward then went through the whole sorry saga of Lord Budlington's assisted suicide and Mr Rutledge's removal to a far-flung part of the Empire.

Beech felt total despair welling up inside him. All he could think of was the ordeal of going to Denmark and the fact that all that would be wasted. He said so to the Commissioner, who shook his head firmly.

"Not at all, Beech. The paperwork that your team uncovered and the extremely valuable documents that you and Todd brought back, have been put to very good use tonight and will bear fruit for many weeks to come."

Sir Edward then explained that the dinner party tonight

had consisted of some very important men and their wives. Apart from himself and Captain Webb, the guests were the French Ambassador; Lord Harmsworth, the owner of the Times and the Daily Mail; Rear-Admiral Consett, and the Liberal MP Sir Henry Dalziel.

"Whilst our wives were playing an after-dinner game of cards, we have been enlisting the help of these powerful men. Captain Webb's division has provided each of them with a complete dossier and report on the Budlington/Rutledge affair, although all names have been removed. All the papers that you, Todd and your team, discovered, have been photographed painstakingly and included in the dossiers. It has impressed all four men so much that they are going to start a concerted campaign to get cotton, oil and rubber removed from the free-to-trade list. The French will be putting strong diplomatic pressure on the government to stop the Germans obtaining supplies of these goods from neutral countries; Lord Harmsworth is going to start a campaign in all his newspapers; Consett is going to produce definitive statistics that show the amount of unacceptable trade that has been going on, and, finally, Sir Henry Dalziel is going to put his career in jeopardy by tabling questions in the House. We are confident that, within a matter of weeks, we can put enough pressure on the government to change the legislation."

Beech looked at Sir Henry with renewed admiration. For him to become involved in such a plot was a great risk. For his part in this pressure group, he risked losing his job. Selfishly, Beech found himself worrying about what would happen to his team, without the protection of the Chief Commissioner.

Sir Henry rose and patted Beech on the shoulder, advised him not to worry and to just concentrate on getting his health back. Then he left, but Beech heard him exchange pleasantries with somone in the corridor. Caroline appeared, looking radiant in an evening gown and jacket.

"I'm just checking on you," she said cheerfully, "and I've brought you a visitor." Commander Todd stuck his head around the corner and said brightly, "How are you, old chap? Gave us all a fright last week, you know!" Then he stepped into the door frame, looking smart in his evening suit.

Beech made an effort to be breezy and said, "I want to apologise for being such a burden, Todd. Thank you so much for getting me home."

Todd shrugged. "Having seen the aftermath of this lady operating on you, I can understand why you wanted to get back here. Caroline would put any army medic to shame! Her and her trusty assistant, Mabel. What a pair!"

Beech laughed but the comment had brought to the fore of his mind a strange dream he kept having, where he was about to be operated on and Caroline was kissing his face and saying, "I love you with all my heart, Peter Beech…"

"You both look extremely glamorous," he said, with false jollity, "Where are you off to?"

Caroline linked her arm through Todd's and said, "A late supper at the Ritz!"

Todd looked at his watch and reminded Caroline that they must be going, so she unlinked her arm, bent over Beech and gave him a kiss on the forehead.

"Mm. You smell much better after your bath!"

Todd laughed out loud. "Isn't she priceless?" he said to Beech with a wink.

"Priceless – and my very important doctor, so I hope you look after her, Todd."

"I will!" said the retreating Todd over his shoulder, whilst propelling Caroline out of the room by her waist.

Beech sat in the gathering gloom, looking at the glow from the streetlamps outside the window, and fancied he heard Caroline and Todd laughing and chattering as they left through the front door. Deep down inside himself, he felt a disturbing emotion and he had no idea how to deal with it. The sight of Caroline with Commander Todd had made him jealous.

THE END

If you like history and nostalgia,
then Iris Books has more publications
that may interest you.
Look at the following pages.
All our books can be purchased from
our website and via Amazon in printed
and Kindle format.

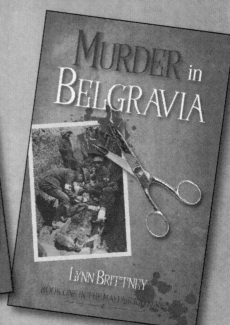

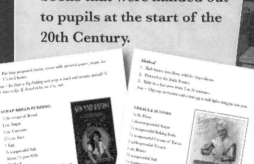

Made in the USA
Columbia, SC
03 May 2024

35250142R00180